Poor Souls

POOR SOULS

Joseph Connolly

faber and faber
LONDON · BOSTON

First published in 1995
by Faber and Faber Limited
3 Queen Square, London, WC1N 3AU

Phototypeset in Palatino by Intype, London
Printed and bound in Great Britain by
Mackays of Chatham PLC, Chatham, Kent

A CIP catalogue record for this book is available from the
British Library

ISBN 0-571-17395-0

2 4 6 8 10 9 7 5 3 1

This book is dedicated to Giles Gordon in return for his dedication to this book.

Chapter One

AT THE MOMENT he said he would break her neck, he knew their love was dying. Of course, Barry had said it loads of times before – meant it once or twice – but this time, God help him, his two hard thumbs were pressing deep and bruising into Susan's throat. Her rather long fingers typed a wooden semaphore of token submission, while a gasp that hinted at anxiety was heard to fight to the front of her mouth. Susan's now shot eyes rolled away – when suddenly she lost interest in all of this and kicked Barry hard in the stomach. There was no time for even a gutted grunt; he just fell back into a table of drink, which disintegrated. Susan would later admit to having rubbed her neck in a mechanical way, but her real attention now was devoted to the teasing of a ringlet, while asking herself frankly whether this was what she *really* wanted.

It had been a long day, and yet another charade was nearly done. If only she didn't *act* with everybody; if only everyone wouldn't require a different *act*. Was this – all this (and she asked herself sincerely) – *enough*? It was a question too deep and, candidly, too fucking important to be answered in any way that might be thought glib, and certainly not now as Barry tinkered brokenly amid the tinsel of drink things.

'You hurt me,' he said.

Which was just, Susan reflected, the sort of thing he would say. He would ask her whether she was all right only at times when, clearly, she was not.

1

'You were choking me.'

More of a sigh than anything. He hadn't been, and they knew. It had to be said, though, for completion's sake.

'I wasn't. Not really.'

'*I* should know,' she returned. 'Anyway.'

This, he thought, was the trouble. Even hate couldn't breathe and was dying; even anger suffocated. Neither had the energy to even go through it. There was a stain of spreading whisky on the carpet, but she had never liked the carpet.

'I'll hoover,' he said.

She could have told him that cold water and salt were needed, then drying, and each little shard picked out of the pile.

'Fine,' she said. 'There's something sticking in you.'

'What is it?'

'I think Dartington.'

There had to be more, she knew, because there had been once. Maybe it was just a question of adapting.

She stood up, the vinyl cushions wheezing relief.

'Is there any drink left?'

'Of course there's some drink left,' he snapped, and then said more softly: 'I still love you, you know, Susan.'

She pulled her mouth into taut and humourless acknowledgement of an old one.

'Yes,' she said, which could mean anything.

He hit the back of his trousers, and a drizzle of glass fell out.

'Anyway,' he said.

Susan snapped shut a table lighter and sucked harshly on a very long cigarette. She let the smoke hiss out, because preoccupied women do.

'I'd better get changed,' she sighed.

'Do you still want to go?'

'I don't want to stay here.'

And she left the room – rather well, he thought – while the

2

cigarette was still very long. He slumped into a swivel chair – cyclamen bouclé, rather good once, bit old now – and then he held his head. The despair never came, though; he didn't feel bad at all. It seemed to him that halfway through the eighties, no one was meant to feel bad about anything – you had to simply go on wanting more: the gospel according to Thatcher.

He supposed he'd better change, then. Or should he bother? After all, they did say it wasn't *dinner* dinner, it was just going to be a, you know. No, he'd better change; Gavin would be wearing that bloody smoking jacket for sure, and making a big thing of the candles. What should he wear, then? Whatever was not too unpressed.

The carpet was an awful mess, but he just couldn't bring himself to do anything about it, which was odd, and a shame, as he had always been rather fond of it.

'Barry!'

She was calling him.

'Hallo?'

'It's late.'

'Coming.'

Maybe he'd just go as he was. It wasn't even as if he wanted to go at all; they were *her* friends. He hated them, really, Gavin and Moira. They were so bloody absurd.

'Barry!!'

'OK. Coming.'

No, he'd better change.

The bedroom was always a harsh place, coming from 'the room'. They called it 'the room' because Susan hated 'lounge'. The lights were never right in the bedroom: they had never been properly concealed. There wasn't one regular lamp in the place, just fluorescent tubes running the length of the pelmet and under shelves and over a perfectly dreadful built-in dressing-table, with a circular mirror too high to see in. Cowboys, Barry had said. Susan had told him he had got what he paid for. The lighting was fine in 'the room', though, since they had discovered British Home Stores. No honestly, Susan would say, it's really *good*. Of course, she would add, there's an awful lot of tat too. They talked about the British Home Stores lighting department at parties, as if it brought them together, and also as a counter to others singing the praises of St Michael apples and knickers and pies. Susan was usually the first to check it, covering her nose with her hand, saying they were sounding *very* Posy Simmonds, and they had better shut up now. This usually worked, as most people would laugh for reasons of their own, someone showing off and saying Grauniad. And anyway, Susan asked frankly, who had the *time* these days for papers?

'You're not wearing that bloody awful suit again?'

'This "bloody awful suit", as you put it, happens to be my best. And I wouldn't have to wear it so often if you could find the odd moment in the day to iron something else.'

'You don't "iron" suits.'

'Well *you* don't anyway – that's for sure!'

It wasn't the crabbiness that either found upsetting, it was just the dangerous adjacence to, well, comedy.

'Anyway just get a move on. We've got to be there soon.'

'What time are we expected at this ghastly thing? I don't even like them.'

'She said seven-thirty for eight.'

'Seven-thirty for eight! Yes, I believe she probably *did*! God, it's barely *believable*, the pretentiousness of those people! Like a bloody Buck House garden party – seven-*thirty* for *eight*! Why can't people just tell you what time you're wanted, and what time you can get the hell out?!'

'Just get changed, will you? Save your turgid rhetoric for when Moira gets drunk after pudding.'

Susan disliked 'dessert'. Even saying it.

'I rather like that dress,' Barry said.

4

Susan looked down, as if she couldn't remember.

'I've had it for ages.'

'I know. I've always rather liked it.'

'Yes. Saves you buying another.'

'Oh now come on Susan now! You've got dozens of dresses.'

'Oh yes. Dozens.'

'Necklace is new, though, isn't it?'

'Necklace?'

'Necklace?' Barry mimicked. 'Necklace? Honestly, you sound like a B-picture. I was merely passing a comment on your *necklace*, for God's sake. Surely I can do that, can't I?'

'It's old. I've had it for ages.'

'I don't remember it.'

'You bought it.'

'*I* did?'

'Ages ago.'

Barry tied his tie.

'I don't remember.'

'No, well,' said Susan, 'you wouldn't.'

It had been an elaborate ploy, Barry considered. Safe to say it was old – it was true he was not observant – and then the big, brave lie: *he* had bought it. But he had seen the little pink box and the tissue in the bin; the necklace was very new.

This in itself, reflected Barry flicking off the lights, was not disturbing. What was clear, though, was that he had been meant to see the wrappings, he was meant to know she was lying, meant to appear to believe her, and meant to wonder.

And as they left the flat, he thought he would oblige. It would keep her happy till they got to Gavin and bleeding Moira's. Or else she'd hate him again for not rising to it all: one or the other. Barry got it wrong quite often now, but it hardly seemed to matter. Pleasing the woman had become such a bother, and the time just never seemed to be there.

*

5

Gavin and Moira had a nice house. Everyone said so. Some even believed it. It was just that one felt one *had* to say so. They both smirked self-confidence at you, and smug, catlike, pride of possession, Barry always felt. And Gavin held Moira's shoulder a lot and asked her stupid questions that weren't questions at all, really – merely requests for confirmation of his latest fatuous generalisation, which she invariably delivered in a cooing, brainless sort of a voice, bloody Moira. Sometimes – and this really got to Barry – Moira would pat Gavin's hand while he was holding her shoulder. All in all, they got on Barry's tits – he was sorry, but they did, and it had to be said.

'Never anywhere to park in this bloody road.'

'There's a space over there.'

'That's miles away from the house. All right, I'll shove it in there. Oh God, I hate this.'

'Look, if you're going to be like this all evening, why don't you leave now? Just drop me and go.'

'I'll be all right.'

'You don't have to come.'

'I said I'll be all right. Now just shut up and let me park this blood thing. God, I wish you'd learned to drive.'

Susan made a noise. She was painting her mouth, which involved the forming of her lips into an 'O', but did not prevent her talking.

'What did you say?'

'I said,' she repeated, blot-kissing her own mouth, 'you always say that when you're parking.'

'Yes, well. It's the lock on this thing. Like a tank.'

'Oh do shut up, Barry.'

'I won't bloody shut up. *You* shut up.'

'Are you going to keep this up *all* evening?'

'Why? Is this evening different from any other evening?'

'Oh shut up, for God's sake.'

Barry jangled keys.

'Let's go if we're going.'

There was a highly lacquered slice of wood saying 'The Cedars' in Gothic, and it was nailed to an oak tree to the left of the storm porch. The mat in the porch said Welcome, the door-chime said Push and Moira said How Lovely. When Susan and Barry were inside – very cosy, much maroon in evidence – Moira said they must be freezing and could she take their coats. Barry was directed to the drawing-room so that the two men could be together, and Moira took Susan to the breakfast-room which adjoined the kitchen via double doors which Gavin and Moira had often thought of taking away. Susan was asked if she wanted to powder her nose and requested a gin. Gavin had his rump to the fire when Barry walked in, and was wearing, of course, his damn bloody smoking jacket. He was delighted to see Barry, called him old man, and proffered a snort.

The whisky was welcoming, and Barry told Gavin how the world was treating him; Gavin, for his part, could not complain.

'Always sorry to drag you out to the back of beyond,' expanded Gavin. 'I know you're not the night-driving man.'

'It's the damned lock on that thing.'

'Little Panda, isn't it?'

Barry took in some Scotch, and nodded while ballooning his cheeks. 'Poor man's Range Rover,' he said.

'Nifty, though. Economical, I dare say.'

'She's a little mover, all right,' agreed Barry, once again furious that he always so soon began talking like Gavin.

'Where are the little girls?'

'Oh, plotting dark deeds, I expect,' said Barry, who *never* comprehended just how banal he could be when talking to Gavin.

7

'Well, I think Moira will do us proud. Are you an escargot man, old man?'

'I've had them. Acquired taste. Interesting.'

'Basque recipe, apparently. Kill any decent wine stone dead, I said, but she says it's not plastered with all that garlic muck, so it shouldn't be too bad.'

'Sounds interesting.'

'And a decent Pomerol. 'Seventy. Think you'll approve. Château-bottled, all that.'

'Great.'

Gavin moved to a gold trolley covered with bottles and hated Barry for never making the effort. If Gavin didn't trouble to steer the conversation, there would be total and utter silence. And if only he'd dress a bit, of an evening. Gavin was so sick of that bloody suit of his. Still, he concluded, walking back over with a brand-new smile, noblesse oblige and all that.

It was, Barry supposed, a pleasant enough room if you like that sort of thing. It was two knocked into one, which seemed a mandatory 'improvement' these days, along with double-glazing the brandy balloons and, Barry had once remarked with bitterness, lagging the Yorkshire terrier's bloody tartan coat. There was a sort of Second Empire flock paper contained within panels, and dripping crystal wall-lights seemed plentiful. The mantel was decent – debased neo-classical, but not without dignity – but the twinkling glass coals didn't help. There were two huge sofas, green and pinky orange, and writhing with, Barry thought, peacocks and jungle and nuts, upon which the scatter cushions were placed precisely. A brass and glass sofa table was covered with bits of brass and glass, and a clutch of new Bilston enamel boxes – garish – saying things like 'Easter 1979' and 'I love you'. Turner, Constable and Monet were well remembered, and a ship's clock-cum-barometer told Barry that it was 20.16 and Fair. Not for the first time, Barry reflected that affluence had been good to Gavin and Moira, but looking around more critically now – his eye had just been caught by a tantalus on a galleried salver, together with six toning silver coasters – he was forced to revise his earlier, and rather generous evaluation: it was an exceedingly ugly and aggressive room, and he was not at all surprised at how proud of it Gavin was, nor how at home he appeared. Still, the drinks kept coming. Good old mine host.

'Working hard?'

Barry shrugged. 'You know. Same. Up and down.'

'How is the world of publishing these days?'

'Oh, much the same. Not very exciting. Recession did bite. Bit better now.'

'It's the same the world over,' offered Gavin, to which Barry said that he expected so, because you *never* asked Gavin about *his* line of work because he'd never stop bloody telling you. He was in, Barry thought, 'casings' – whatever in Christ's name *they* might be – and he earned a sodding fortune: that's all Barry knew, and it was far more than he cared to.

Moira and Susan came in then, and Gavin said 'Ah!' very loudly and raised an arm in salutation, as if he had seen neither of them for several years.

'So sorry to have been rude,' simpered Moira, putting a hand to her head in mock exhaustion and momentarily sagging at the knees. 'Everything seems to be taking ages tonight.'

'Don't you worry, my love,' assured Gavin, talking more loudly now that there were four people in the room. 'Sit yourself down, and let me get you something. Some of our very best Tio Pepe?'

'I can't stop, actually, Gavin. I just came to say hello.'

'Hello,' said Barry, thinking why the hell not?

Moira sort of smirked, because everyone knew that Barry was awful.

9

'A woman's work,' said Gavin. 'But you're not taking the lovely Susan from our midst, surely?'

'Oh no. Susan's already been helping wonderfully. I don't know how I could have coped.'

'I only got out the knives,' said Susan.

'I couldn't have coped,' insisted Moira, as she scuttled out. 'It's been that sort of day. This morning we overslept, didn't we, Gavin, because of the clock. It boiled the tea to nothing. Everyone hungry?'

Everyone said mmm and starving, and Susan drank more gin.

'Not still on this macrobi-whatsname lark, are you Susan?'

Susan shook her head, and squatted on a pouffe. Or was it a camel saddle.

'No. It got too expensive.'

'Not good for you anyway, this health business. All this "this is bad for you" and "the other is bad for you" – *breathing* is bad for you, for God's sake, but what are you supposed to do? And as if *you* of all people have to look after your figure, Susan!'

'Well, it's not really about that, actually.'

'Always thought you were a shapely little thing,' confided Gavin more loudly than ever, cocking his head at Barry. 'Whoops! Shouldn't say that, should I, in present company. Jealous husband, all that.'

Susan shot a glance at Barry, who hadn't been listening.

'Oh, Barry won't mind. Will you, love?'

Gavin smirked. 'Nonsense. Barry'll know what I mean. Always been one for a trim ankle – hey, Barry?'

Barry said deadpan that he wasn't really an ankle man, and Gavin put his elbow on the mantel, a foot on the fender, and drank his drink when his laugh was over.

Moira flustered back, undoing a pinny that looked like a cut-down crinoline.

10

'You must be starving,' she gushed, her eyes open with real concern. 'Have a nut. It won't be long now.'

'Susan was just saying that she's chucked this diet lark of hers,' said Gavin.

'Well, I'm glad to hear it. As if *you* had to look after your figure, Susan.'

'Particularly as *I'm* the one busy doing that!' blurted Gavin, and laughed. Moira made a gesture of dismissal and held her nose and laughed, for Gavin could be awful too, but in a nice way, sometimes.

Barry was bored and hungry, and Gavin was going red from the fire and the whisky. Bloody Barry, he was thinking. Bloody passenger.

'Shall we hors d'oeuvres now?' suggested Moira, brightly. 'You must all be starving.'

Everyone trooped out, turned sharp left, and filed into the dining-room. When Susan had been getting out the knives, she had thought she would love to stick one in Barry, and now she thought of it again. Barry just looked on, while Moira directed everyone to his place, each of which bore a little stand-up card saying 'Barry', 'Susan', 'Mr' and 'Mrs'.

The table was sort of Sheraton, and the cloth was lacy white and a pair of candelabra had six red candles between them. Gavin applied a table lighter to each, and assured everyone that they made all the difference. A curious lighter, Barry observed, as Gavin put it down; like a shrunken Queen Anne teapot with neither spout nor handle.

On top of the tablecloth, each place was set with a maroon laminated mat portraying the ritual extermination of pheasants in tasteful sepia. On top of this was a plate – white, gold rim, probably sixties Rosenthal, Barry and Susan being not quite Coalport people – and this plate bore a folded triangle of Irish linen (a quite different affair from the napkin stuffed into the cut-glass goblet), fanned out to look like a party hat. On top of the linen, Moira now placed a side-plate holding a paper doily and a bowl. At the bottom of the bowl was a couple of spoonfuls of brown, and it smelt of fish and cheese.

'Ah!' said Gavin. 'This looks a change from those damn prawn cocktails and avocados that are all over the place now. Or *ad*-vocados, as the hoi polloi will have it.'

'Looks lovely,' Susan said.

Moira hoped everyone liked it.

By the time Gavin had begun his teeth-grating ritual of putting his infernal head just to one side and identifying the herbs, Barry had finished his. Moira had been right – he was starving, and there had been too little for him to decide even whether he liked it.

'Well Barry liked it, anyway,' said Moira through a smiling mouth, her eyes blazing jet and resentment. She flapped her napkin around and smoothed it over her knees.

'Mustn't get anything on this dress,' she said.

Susan was chewing something very odd, but she made the effort.

'It's a lovely dress.'

'Do you like it?'

'It's lovely.'

Moira nodded. 'I like it. Don't we dear?'

But now Gavin was fiddling around with his damn wine stuff. He had a thermometer these days, which was designed to tell him whether or not the bottle was at the same temperature as the room in which it was standing. He was sticking out his bottom at the table, as he insisted upon opening wine in the most bizarre manner imaginable, always keeping the bottles on their side – or as near, he would tell you, as dammit.

'I'm eager for this little Chablis,' he said.

He had even worked out a method whereby the Vinicool could rest at forty-five degrees. The claret, of course, had been opened for the prerequisite two and a quarter hours, and two bottles were laid in baskets made of tortured silver wire.

'Well,' said Moira, collecting the bowls, doilies and side-plates onto a tray, 'everyone seems to like escargots, anyway!'

'Oh, *that* was the escargots, was it?' said Barry. 'Very good,' he added. He did not want to peak too early.

'Shan't be a moment,' said Moira. Struggling with the door, she said she could manage. Gavin said he must just pop next door to check the video as he was taping a Spielberg which he found marvellous to unwind to. Barry and Susan were alone, as the sudden silence said.

'You are a bastard,' hissed Susan.

'What the hell now?' said Barry, knowing.

'You know.'

'Oh, shut up. Christ I'm starving. It's nearly nine o'clock. I don't know why they didn't have us at eleven-thirty for midnight.'

Susan blotted breadcrumbs with the pad of a finger. She knew what Barry meant about Gavin and Moira, poor souls, but at least they made an effort. It was easy to laugh, Susan thought, but some of the things they did were really nice. And they had a lovely home. And at least they didn't have to worry about money. They seemed happy.

Moira was in the kitchen putting miniature chef's hats on the leg-ends of poussins. A piece of her hair had fallen forward and she hit it back with a spatula, wondering frankly why she bothered sometimes. If it wasn't for Susan, she wouldn't mind never having them over again; it always seemed such uphill work with Barry and Susan. She always felt on trial. And now the hollandaise wasn't thickening and the damn knife had fused. But the braised prosciutto was out of the microwave, the new potatoes looked lovely, and the marron purée would save the day. She could really have done with more surfaces.

'Moira, have you been tampering with the video?'

'Don't be silly, Gavin. You know I don't know how to work the thing.'

'Well, somebody's been playing silly buggers. It's not taping. Damn film's nearly over now.'

'They'll have it on again, dear. They're always repeating that sort of thing.'

'That's hardly the point. I wanted to watch it after this dinner farce is over. Now I suppose they'll have to take the damn thing in.'

'Gavin, please. I'm trying to prepare a meal.'

Gavin's eyes shone with malevolence. 'Oh that's bloody typical, isn't it? My video can go to blazes!'

'It's not that, Gavin,' pleaded Moira, who knew she mustn't look up or she'd cut herself.

'Well just hurry up with it, that's all,' growled Gavin. 'Everybody's bloody starving in there.'

Moira looked at him with wet eyes, and the front of her hair fell over her face and she cut her finger.

'I'm being as quick as I can,' she said. 'If you could take in the gravy – '

'*You* take in the bloody gravy. I've got to do the wine.'

Gavin went back into the dining-room, and Barry and Susan stopped talking and looked away from each other.

'Everything all right?' beamed Gavin. 'Food's just coming. Can I offer you a Bordeaux or a Chablis, Susan? It's poussin.'

'Chablis, please Gavin. Lovely.'

Gavin poured it like a priest.

'Barry?'

'Claret please, Gavin.'

'Always were a claret man, hey Barry? I'll be interested to hear your comments on this one.'

Barry had thought he would. He just hadn't made up his mind whether or not to be nasty about it.

14

Moira wheeled in a bronze-brown hostess-trolley, and everyone said 'Ah!'

'Great,' added Barry.

'What have you done to your finger?' asked Susan.

'About time,' Gavin said.

Susan drank the whole glass of Chablis and thought, poor thing. Susan knew what it was like to cook for people, when you had to think of every little thing. And Moira really did do it so nicely. At least Gavin took care of the wine and was moral support – and this meant a lot, she knew. Barry was more likely to forget that anyone was coming at all and then miss out on starters on account of driving down to Waitrose to buy a couple of bottles of anything going. And it was always cheap because he said it made no difference, and that the sort of people they knew wouldn't know Lafite from gnat's piss, and it was only the label you were paying for anyway. And they both knew that Barry didn't believe this; it was just that he could not bear to be seen to take trouble. And he was mean. And Susan wished she could stick her knife in him.

'The Chablis is charming, Gavin.'

'I thought you'd appreciate it, Susan. Crisp, isn't it? Delivers well on the swallow. Did you hear that Moira? Susan is most impressed with the Chablis.'

'Could everyone help themselves to vegetables,' said Moira. 'Barry's glass is empty, dear.'

Gavin had only just begun rolling around his claret in a huge sommelier's snifter. He hadn't even taken that first, all-telling inhalation.

'To your liking, Barry?'

'It's fine,' said Barry, looking him in the eye. 'I was thirsty.'

Gavin poured more, and speaking more quietly than usual:

'I'm cautiously pleased with it. In Johnson it says it's going through a bit of a mute period.'

That decided Barry.

'Well,' he opined, drinking deep again, 'keep it coming, and we'll all be paralytic in sympathy.'

'Barry!' hushed Susan.

'It's all right, Susan,' said Gavin.

'Let's all have a nice evening, shall we?' implored Moira.

Cutlery clattered discreetly for a while. Everyone agreed that the poussins – which were cornfed – were very good indeed. Susan praised the chestnut purée, Moira passing all the credit to the Magimix without which, she insisted, she would be totally lost. The plates were collected and Moira announced that she could give them a choice. There was blackberry and apple pie – which, Gavin informed the company, Moira had made herself – a fresh fruit salad, or profiteroles and cream.

Barry said that he could only stomach fruit salad if it was tinned, but the profiteroles sounded marvellous. Susan also elected for the profiteroles, and Gavin thought that the fruit salad would be just the thing to freshen the palate. Moira felt she might try the pie.

It was at pudding that Gavin always brought out his Sauternes, and Moira started drinking seriously. Red wine she couldn't take, coffee made her not sleep, and cheese gave her nightmares; sweet white wine, though, was different. A whole bottle was not at all unusual, and tonight she seemed to need it.

'It's not d'Yquem,' Gavin said, 'but I think you'll approve.'

Moira drank it, and said nothing.

Barry was still drinking claret with his profiteroles, which Gavin thought frankly obscene. Susan had a smear of chocolate on her chin which Barry was damned if he was going to mention, which would drive her crazy later. The digital clock on the coffee-maker was malfunctioning, said Moira, which led Gavin to recall that his mother used to make the best coffee he had ever tasted outside of Istanbul – and she only

16

used a battered old jug. Then he cursed the wind-on curly candle on his cognac-warmer, opened another bottle of Barsac for Moira, and said with as much joie-de-vivre as he could muster:

'Liqueurs!'

Barry drained his claret and said: 'Brandy, please.'

'I have an old Armagnac,' said Gavin, more out of habit than anything, as he rather resented pouring any of it down the boor's bloody throat. Barry countered that Armagnac would do, if there was nothing else going.

'It came top in an Observer poll,' said Gavin, miserably.

'I'm sure it's lovely,' said Susan. 'I'd love some.'

Gavin dispensed the drinks, sat down heavily and said:

'Cooking is an art. Like driving. You're either good at it, or you're not.'

'Like sex,' Barry said.

'Barry!'

'It's all right, Susan. Barry's right. Driving and sex are the only two things a chap will never admit to being bad at.'

'Gavin's a very good driver,' said Moira.

'Advanced Motorist, actually,' amended Gavin, with a smirk.

'But he's not really a sex-man, are you Gavin?'

Gavin spilled Armagnac all over the cloth. He looked up, purple, and dabbed at the stain.

'Steady,' he said. Then rallying with a pained and brave grimace: 'Moira's joke for the evening. Well done, Moira. Too much wine.' He looked straight at her, and held the table. 'Too much wine,' he said.

'Oh but be fair, darling,' insisted Moira with charm. 'I mean, it's never really been one of your things, has it? Sex?'

'Ha ha ha. Shut up, Moira.'

Moira stared into her glass, and then poured more wine.

'Well I don't think so anyway,' she pouted.

Susan traced the rim of her glass with a fingertip, and Barry settled down to enjoying it all.

'Shall we go next door?' said Gavin, making apologetic gestures to Susan, and when she refused to respond, miming to an extent that conferred upon Moira total mental decrepitude.

Susan and Barry moved next door, taking the Armagnac with them, Gavin putting his hand on his wife's shoulder and saying 'All right, love?' and when they were alone 'I'll kill you,' to which he thought she replied 'I don't care.'

Susan fell into a peacock-patterned sofa, maddened more than she could bear by Barry's bloody face. She knew exactly what he was thinking.

'What are you thinking?' she asked accusingly. 'As if we both didn't know.'

'I was just thinking that at least you don't have any complaints on that score, that's all.'

'Oh no, no complaints. You're a wonderboy. It's just that you're not too fussy who you do it with, are you, you bloody bastard!'

'Oh Christ, if we're going to go through all that again – '

'Oh just shut up, you – '

'Oh shut up, Susan, will you?'

'Bastard.'

Susan cried. She cried and thought of Moira. She kept on crying and her face was splashed and streaky.

'Susan,' Barry hissed – he really hated this – 'I don't particularly want to smash a glass of this Christ-awful brandy in your face, but I'm telling you – '

Susan turned away and sobbed into the cushions, clutching her necklace around her throat.

Gavin came in and asked if everything was all right.

'She's fine,' said Barry. 'Just a bit – you know.'

Gavin nodded. Poor Susan, he thought.

'Do you know anything about videos, Barry? Can't understand what's wrong with the thing.' Poor Susan. 'Want to have a look at it?'

Barry looked at Gavin. 'No,' he said.

'Fine. I'll just see how the coffee's coming along.'

Gavin went into the kitchen really hating Barry and feeling very depressed. Moira was still drinking sweet white wine in the dining-room and Gavin really needed a Scotch, but was damned if he was going back into the drawing-room with that bloody Barry there. Poor Susan. Poor soul.

'Where are you going?' said Moira. She was up, tottering a bit, and still holding a glass of wine.

'I'm going to get the coffee, which is what you should be doing. Go and see if you can help Susan.'

Moira looked away. 'Who's going to help me?' she said into the back of her hand.

'What? What did you say?'

'Nothing. I'll get the coffee.'

'Well get a move on, can't you? Christ, what a farce! What a bloody evening! I don't know why we have that bloody man in the house. And now on top of it all the bloody video's gone!'

Moira smiled rather sadly. 'I'll get the coffee,' she said. 'The bittermints are on the music centre.'

In the kitchen, Moira looked with despair at the electronic coffee-maker. The grounds had bubbled up and poured over the sides, coating the clock and streaming down the fronts of the Smallbone units. There was no more coffee as she hadn't been able to get out to the shops, and if she brightly popped her head around the drawing-room door and said 'Anyone mind instant?', Gavin would kill her for sure.

'Everything all right? Coffee's just coming.'

'I think we ought to go, Gavin,' said Susan. 'I'm sorry about, you know.'

'Don't be silly. Quite understand. Course of true love and all that. Have another drink.'

'No, really, Gavin.'

'I will,' said Barry.

'You!' shrieked Susan suddenly. 'You!! That's all you've bloody done since we got here! You're supposed to be driving!'

'I'm perfectly capable of driving. And don't shout.'

Barry, Susan and Gavin all looked at each other, which they had not done before. It seemed that no one was inclined to speak. Gavin smoothed the fringe of a rug with his toe.

'Anyway,' he said, and coughed.

Barry stared into the electric fire, Susan stood up, and Gavin said:

'Bittermint, anyone?'

And then he sat down on a carver and thought why the hell should I bother anyway and where the hell is Moira?

'Well, if there's not going to be any more drink,' announced Barry, bringing down his Orrefors tumbler rather harder than necessary, 'we might as well be off. Only joking, Gavin. Coats.'

'We can get them,' said Susan. 'It's all right, Gavin. We can get them.'

Gavin made another effort.

'No no no. Not at all. Wouldn't hear of it. My pleasure.'

It was in the hall that Barry began to sway, thinking damn! I've got a meeting tomorrow.

'All right, Barry?'

'Oh shut up, Gavin.'

'Barry!'

'All right, Susan. We all know Barry.'

It was not until the front door was shut behind them and Gavin was hissing Thank Christ that Barry was sick all over the step. Susan hit him with the side of her fist before he had finished and he was crushed into a privet, retching.

'I still love you, Susan,' he hacked. 'Oh Jesus.'

Gavin heard it all and thought sod the bastard. He could drive off and kill the both of them for all he cared, the bastard. Except for Susan, poor soul. Anyway, she married the swine. A right filthy mess would be waiting for them outside in the morning, he supposed, but Moira could make herself useful for once and clear it all up. They were *her* friends anyway. Wherever she was. If she was still alive.

Gavin tried the bathroom door, after he found the bedroom empty.

'Are you all right in there?!' he intoned like a policeman. 'What the hell are you doing? Look, come on, woman! Open the bloody door, for God's sake! It looks like a tip downstairs.'

A very strange voice slurred through the panels, quite unlike Moira's:

'Fuck off, Gavin,' it said, and it was followed by the slumping of a weight and the tinkle of glass.

'Bitch,' he said, under his breath, and stumping back downstairs:

'I bet that's the bloody carpet gone too, now.'

Chapter Two

BARRY HALF-WOKE EARLY and wondered who he was. He could have asked himself where he was going, but even at that raw hour he recognised the impulse as being too mawkish for words. It was the few quick Scotches he'd had before going to bed that had maybe been a mistake; Susan had told him to think of his stomach lining and then she had cursed him. He had felt a bit more sober by the time they had walked to the car, but it had been a hell of a drive back and his eyes had hurt and the smell was terrible because he had skidded in his own coagulating mess. In the car, Susan was quiet at first, but she was a bit drunk too, Barry thought, and so she had cried a lot. She punched his knee at the lights, which nearly finished him altogether. He had even read a bit before switching off the light – *The Bell*, which he had always loved, and the new *Good Food Guide*. He liked Murdoch because, as he said, she was a *writer* and not just a woman writer, obsessed with ovaries and sensitive adultery. The *Food Guide* reminded him of all the places he could afford to go to before he got married; he could never quite decide whether he enjoyed reading the thing or not. He had looked over at the mound of Susan, once, in the night, and said Susan and she said don't touch me and when he touched her she hit him again and he said that he still loved her and she told him to go to sleep and then to hell.

It must be about seven, he thought; it was hard to say. He was damned if he was going to have one of those digital radio things in the house, but he always forgot to wind the little travelling clock and so he never knew what the time was in the bedroom. But it seemed about seven – or maybe not quite. He didn't feel too bad, considering. Bit of a head, but that was usual. It was a little cold because the heating had not yet come on, and Susan had all the duvet. She always managed this, but it had been the same with blankets. Barry thought he would get up, and lay still for twenty minutes, working it out.

1985 already: where had all the years gone, hey? He was thirty-five now, and the only way to go was towards forty; and that, he knew, was death. Look at Gavin. Mind you, Barry reasoned, Gavin had probably been born like that. But it was not that Barry was discontent; the reverse was probably the trouble. Most of the time he felt so absurdly pleased with himself for no immediately discernible reason. He had done nothing very much during the course of his life, but this failed to bother him unduly. What was growing into a sort of dread, however, was that this situation might become irreversible and that all he would ever have to look back upon was a fatly complacent void. And not for the first time, he vowed that things would be different. Now. From today. He would begin by bounding out of bed like they did in the toothpaste and cornflake commercials, and facing the day with a brave glad eye.

He stayed still for about ten minutes. Maybe at the editorial meeting someone would listen to him, for a change. Maybe he should wear something startling to get people's attention, and follow up the advantage with a new and meaningful contribution. Frankly, he smirked to himself, and yes – fearlessly. God what crap. Ah well, he sighed inside as he swung out of the bed, I had better be ongoing. First snide joke of the day. Well done.

Bathrooms were filthy places, Barry thought. They were never those wonderful powder-blue pleasure domes that you

23

saw in American films, with a brace of basins and a soft, high rainbow of velvet towelling stacked into a rattan obelisk: the sort of bathrooms where the soap never got wet and nobody splashed, water having been displaced by moisturiser in peachy and opulent pots, and the scent came in crystal phials too huge to handle. The plugholes in Barry's bathroom were always choked with Susan's hair. It was a mystery to him that she still had any on her head, there was always so much. Every morning Barry had to excavate half a greasy wig from the chromium interstices, which made him sick. Eno's made him sicker, and the whine of the Braun gave him a headache. Barry could enter his bathroom feeling in control, and leave it a nauseous wreck.

Nor did he enjoy exploring the more worrying crannies of his face. It was a pretty ordinary face, he had long ago admitted, and he was not, he thought, particularly vain – but at his age he hardly relished the prospect of getting old; not yet. In the seventies, he had toyed with the idea of growing a moustache so that he would look younger when he got rid of it, but everyone had them then, which rather put him off. And anyway, it wouldn't grow in properly and it was gappy and it itched.

His clothes were squashed into one end of Susan's wardrobe. She had an immense amount of clothes – most of them hideous, it was true – as she could not resist anything that was going cheap. Barry had long ago resigned himself to Susan's dreadful taste, but she only said that he had one helluva nerve in setting himself up as an arbiter of taste as he always looked like a tramp. Barry countered that taste was not a matter of personal vanity, nor of spending money; it was a sense of *style*, and a sense of *knowing*. Susan said that everything Barry knew could be copperplated on a flea's buttock and Barry told her to stop displaying her fathomless ignorance and vulgarity. Each hated the way the other dressed, but somehow, Barry believed, this was fitting.

Anyway, today he was going to wear an ancient kipper tie – Mr Fish, of course – and everyone would say Christ where did you get that thing and Barry would say it was retro chic. He would quite like to have been a sixties whizz-kid publisher, instead of an ageing and cynical editor in the grip of a recession, but at least he had a job. Which was more than bloody Susan did. She had gone through a succession of non-jobs: so-called PR, personal assistant, receptionist, that sort of thing – all of which amounted to being the painted-up tart who sat in the hall, so far as Barry could see. She didn't even do that now, actually stating that she was *looking* for herself, for Christ's sake, at which Barry suggested she sink to the bottom of the Thames and see if she was maybe down there, possibly. Susan had asked if he always had to be so *rude* and he said no he didn't have to be it was an optional extra and Susan told him to go and hang himself and Barry said he didn't know why he didn't and Susan said not to let *her* stop him and Barry said that was a laugh she'd be the bloody reason. Bitch.

She was waking up now.

'Oh God,' she said, which was her customary greeting to the promise of a brand-new day. She lit a cigarette, throwing down the packet into her bedside debris of blister-packaged contraceptive pills and cotton-wool balls. 'My head hurts,' she said.

'I am delighted to hear it,' said Barry. 'I'm late.'

'They won't miss you.'

'And I love you too, angel,' Barry cooed. But he didn't really feel smug or breezy. 'Actually, I do, Susan,' he said.

'Yes,' she said. 'Is the water hot?'

'Hottish, I suppose. Why – are you going to drown yourself?'

'Oh for Christ's sake, Barry. Why don't you just go to work?'

'Why don't you get some to go to?'

'Please, Barry,' she said.

They lived in Camden Town, which Barry would assure everyone was coming up. He always said it in inverted commas, though, making it quite clear that he was well aware what a worn-out load of garbage he was talking. Easy for town, though, he would tack on, which was true, but hardly the point. He got a taxi to Fitzroy Square that morning – a bit because he was late, but mainly because it built him up. Hopelessly bourgeois, he knew, but there it was.

'Morning, Mr Turville. Lovely day for it.'

'Morning, Len,' said Barry.

Len was the lift operator, and he always said that, and Barry always said that, and Barry hated him and Len – so far as Barry was a judge – had no views on Barry or indeed on anyone or anything whatever.

'Morning, Barry. On time for once.'

'Morning, Selina. Lovely as ever.'

Selina was the receptionist. She looked like a prostitute and had the wit of a child. Barry needed coffee now, but his secretary, a temp, always forgot the Blend 37 and Barry had to get down what was referred to ('in-house') as the shit from the machine. He suddenly did not want to be at work at all, and he contemplated 'flu. But no – all those contrived snuffles before someone suggested he would be better off in bed were too wearing to consider. And anyway, there was a meeting.

'Coffee, please, um.' Christ, he had forgotten her name. Jean. That was it. 'Jean.'

'Oh dear, I've forgotten to get it again. Do you mind the – '

'No. Just get it.'

The only good thing about the office these days was the revival of the miniskirt. It made Barry feel, among other things, young again. Not that Jean had legs worth displaying, they were so damn skinny. He had walked behind her in the street, once, and seen the Post Office tower between them. And she had globular knees like those starving children in the Oxfam pleas in the better Sundays. No, she wasn't too bad really, Jean, as temps went; he had believed her to be an imbecile at first, but it transpired that she was merely semi-literate and idle.

'Morning, Barry.'

It was George, from Publicity.

'Hallo, George.'

'Ready for the meeting?'

'Ready as ever. Is there a game going tonight?'

'I'm amazed you've got any money left.'

'Well,' said Barry, 'I've got a bit.'

'I should think we could make up four, then. Christ you are a devil for punishment.'

'Cliché, George. Too many blurbs aren't good for you.'

'Very droll, Barry. How's the delectable Susan?'

'Fine. She's fine. Do you care?'

George considered.

'Not especially. No, not really,' he said.

Barry smiled, which he didn't do that often. He rather liked George; bit flash, but all right.

'Let me go over these proposals, will you, George? I've only got a few minutes.'

'I'll see you in there,' said George. 'Christ – where did you get that tie?'

'Noah's Ark. Piss off.'

'Looks like it. Don't work too hard. See you.'

Barry always wanted an office like George's. It was on the sunny side of the building for a start, and all sorts of companies sent things to George – posters, mobiles, Unipart calendar. And he had a bloody good-looking secretary too, because apparently, according to George, in the publicity game you

27

need this. Barry's own office was much more editorial. It was partitioned, naturally, with the bloody Xerox on the other side. It was painted grey, with charcoal Heuga carpet tiles. There was an expiring rubber plant which no one bothered to dust, and galvanised industrial shelving. A bit of colour was supplied by Ryman – red file index, High-Tech perforated ashtrays, Anglepoise – but the general impression was one of drabness, this mainly due to the trussed-up mountains of typescript, all awaiting rejection.

An editor edits what the publishing director tells him to edit. Barry could not remember having commissioned anything in his entire publishing career, with one notable exception, of course. About four years ago, he had received in the post this massive unsolicited manuscript by Brian Somebody-or-Other, and Barry became convinced that with hype and then more hype it could really *be* something. He had appalling confidence in those days, and he pushed like hell. The Sales department, as usual, were the most impervious to his enthusiasm. 'Fat novels,' they kept repeating ominously. 'But it's got everything!' insisted Barry. 'Adultery. Adultery sells! Violence! Hate! It's a family saga. It's got everything, I tell you.' Sales said that a really big promotion would be needed as back-up. Production said that only a very large print order could halfway keep down costing. Publicity wanted assurances (up-front) that their efforts would be followed up by the reps, for once, and Editorial looked to big spaces in the qualities – 'Good for the house,' they said. Barry guaranteed everybody everything, with a positiveness that today quite terrified him, and he got his way, eventually. 'The Big One', he kept saying – (Brian Whowasitnow?) – would be no less than just that. This novel would be really *something*.

It turned out to be the biggest remainder in the history of the house. The shinier shops in Charing Cross Road and Fleet Street were soon awash with the thing. They could only take it at all, they said, if it was *really* cheap, and in the end they went for about a penny each. Literally. Even now there were bales of them still in the warehouse, Sales occasionally sneaking out one or two container loads to such outposts as Bangladesh and Milton Keynes, but according to Stock Control, it seemed as if they reproduced asexually in the night, for the piles never reduced. A few kinder folk had suggested to Barry that everyone would find the affair hugely funny, once the dust had settled, but nobody ever did. Nobody who mattered, anyway – just the *new* people, and temps, and typists, sod them. 'The Big One' had entered publishing folklore. As a result, the firm had not exactly fired Barry, although at the time one or two high-ups had intimated that they might be able to struggle on without him, but Barry – thank Christ – had declined to take the hint, as he knew that now he'd be lucky to get a job anywhere. And so he remained, four years on, subbing, scanning for literals, proof-reading, and identifying with the rubber plant. But maybe today! Maybe today Barry would come up with something good, for a change. Something fresh! Something startling! And maybe not. And now it was time. In fact, Jesus Christ, he was bloody late, bloody hell.

Margaret from the Art department was talking when Barry walked in. He did not bustle, but he was wearing his serious face in order to let the company know that he knew he was late, and that he would have moved heaven and earth to be otherwise. Margaret paused longer than she need have done – bitch – and then went on in the way that she did:

'Of course, the final decision rests with you, DJ.' DJ – the MD – nodded. As if it could be any other way, his eyebrows averred. 'But I should like it put on record that I think too explicit dust-jackets are not the direction in which we should be moving at this juncture of our development. Maybe,' she said, laying down her glasses and staring around blindly, 'we could get some vox pop on this.'

Margaret had been with the firm a long time. If anyone said anything with which she was known to disagree, she would stop sucking the arm of her spectacles, and smile cold and indulgent, lowering her eyes. 'I have been with the firm a long time,' she would begin – and it usually worked because she was rarely wrong, curse it, and eternally polite.

'Well look,' said George from Publicity. 'You know my views on this one, DJ. I'm all for punch. Pizzazz is what we need here, surely.'

'There is pizzazz,' warned Margaret, 'and pizzazz.'

'Margaret, you don't think you're just the weeniest bit in danger of the word "art" going to your head, do you?' suggested George – rather bravely, Barry thought.

'No,' said Margaret, 'I do not.'

Barry wished he could have said something then, but he was terrified of opening his mouth these days, and found himself looking sideways at DJ, along with everyone else.

'I'm inclined,' opined DJ, 'to agree with Margaret.'

George shuffled papers and muttered something dark.

DJ put his whole hand over his mouth and moustache, as if he felt that either or both was in danger of slipping. Then he started speaking.

'Didn't quite catch that, DJ,' said George.

'I said,' said DJ, his hands now joined in prayer, 'that the last jacket in the series I personally found tasteless in the extreme, and that if Margaret had been listened to at the time, it would never have got through. Bad for the house, George. We are not, and we do not pretend to be, one of those trendier Covent Garden set-ups, thank the heavens, and I do not take kindly to overtones of flagellation on our more up-market d/j's. Margaret knows *exactly* what's required.' He smiled. 'Queen of the d/j.'

'Thank you DJ.'

No one bothered to smirk any more. There were so many DJ jokes now.

It was going to be, it seemed to Barry, a very typical meeting. There would be a degree of gentle back-biting, the airing of various in-house jealousies, a joke or two, a couple of original suggestions which would be annihilated by one or other of the voices of experience, and a lot of milky coffee and yawning. Most of the departments were represented, with the accent on Editorial. Billy from Production sat, as usual, a little way away from the table; Billy thought that everyone thought him rather common, and Billy was right. Sydney from Contracts was on DJ's right – and DJ could really *talk* to him, he would tell you. And Roland was in the corner. Roland was the highbrow editor (no one ever understood even the nature of the books that Roland worked on – sometimes not even the titles) and Barry observed his presence with disappointment, for if Roland was there, it meant that Annie wouldn't be, and Barry hadn't spoken to Annie for what seemed like days, and he badly needed to see her. He could go up later, before the game. Just to smell the room she sat in was so bloody exciting.

It had started like a thunderclap, this Annie and Barry thing. She had joined the firm as Roland's assistant, must be over two years ago now, and from the beginning there had been none of the nodding and nudging in corridors, no Luncheon Voucher luncheons ending in large G and T's, no games, no – Barry was sure – smut. Barry and Annie had just – they laughed about it these days – *known*. 'Our eyes met!' Annie would deliberately intone like a bad voice-over. 'Crowded room!' shouted Barry, eyes wet with the glimmer of love and fun. 'Two hearts as one!' And he would cuddle her and laugh and they would drink more wine and her eyes shone and it was true, everything they joked about. God, she was so lovely Barry was pained by it, sometimes. All the old clichés – young again, acting like kids, the pain of parting – they had had all that. The ridiculous thrill of doing nothing at all, together. Barry had tried to analyse it – to break it down into comprehensible components – but he always ended up just thinking about her, and how everything she did she did so beautifully, and wanting her, and wanting her, and then came the glow when he knew he would see her again, very very soon. And then he wanted her more than ever, and it was his finger ends that felt as if they would burst from too much blood and he would 'phone her then, and just her first word acted as a cool narcotic, suffusing his veins – at rest only briefly until her laughter whipped him up into needing to share it, and to touch her and just to hold her so close to him. The peace and the pulsating excitement could madden him with delight, and they grinned beyond the control of their faces, and everything seemed tranquil and hotter than hot, and all he had to do was just *be* there.

'Are you taking in *any* of this, Turville?' he heard DJ say.

'Absolutely, sir. Of course, DJ.'

Oh God Almighty.

'Well if it wouldn't be troubling you *too* much for your views, Barry, seeing as from what we've heard this would appear to be your baby.'

'Yes, DJ. Of course.'

Barry's mind was in drunken confusion. That he had not the slightest idea what DJ was talking about was teetering upon the verge of becoming apparent to everyone. There could be only seconds before DJ's whistle of exasperation, and yet as Barry took in George's glance of concern and Margaret's implacability, his mind was just white and colours, and his mouth could only yammer:

'The way I see it is this!'

And his voice actually rose in pitch, and broke at the end. The silence became uncomfortable, and chairs were shifting.

'Are you quite well, Barry?' asked DJ.

Barry picked up his files, and made for the door.

'I'm awfully sorry, DJ. Not really myself. Might be a touch of. I think I should just. I'm really awfully sorry, DJ.'

In the passage, shutting the door on the rumble of wonder, Barry bared his teeth in a spasm of mortification, and his whole skull winced under torment. Even the corridor was moving in on him, and he just had to see Annie or he would die.

The four walls of 'the room' were killing Susan, and she had to get out tonight. The telephone rang just as she was about to pick it up, which annoyed her very intensely.

'Seven-two-six-four.'

'Susan.'

'Moira. How lovely.'

'Hello, Susan. I just 'phoned to say how awfully sorry I am about everything last night. I really am. Truly.'

'Oh, no, please, Moira. I meant to 'phone *you*. I really meant to 'phone. No, it's *me*, I, who am sorry, really. I'm so very sorry about Barry.'

'Oh no – we all know Barry by now. How is Barry?'

'Barry? Oh, he's fine. I'm sorry about all the mess, Moira.'

'Oh, nothing at all. We were all a bit – you know.'

'Yes, well, I suppose so.'

'Look, Susan, the reason I'm calling – you'll think I've got an awful cheek after everything, but Gavin's out again – you know Gavin, always working – and I just wondered if I could pop over for, you know, a short while. I'm a bit. I would ask you over here again, if you could stand it, but I know you don't drive and – '

'Oh, Moira – what a shame!'

'You're busy.'

'If *only* you'd 'phoned a few minutes earlier it would've been so lovely. I'm just going over to Hilary's.'

'Oh, Hilary. How is Hilary?'

'Fine, she seems fine. Oh, what a shame.'

'Oh never mind – there are other days. I hope you didn't mind, Susan?'

'Oh don't be silly, Moira. Any other time it would've been lovely. You and Gavin must come over for dinner soon.'

'We'd love to. You know we always love seeing you. Well look, I mustn't keep you.'

'Well I am just a little bit pushed, actually, Moira.'

'I know how it can be. Never enough hours.'

'Well thanks again, Moira. It really was a super evening. And we'll see you and Gavin very very soon.'

''Bye, then, Susan.'

''Bye. Bye-bye.'

Moira put down the receiver and thought Oh God Now What?

Susan picked up the 'phone very quickly and dialled Hilary's number. It was not that she suspected Moira of checking, it was just that that would be all she needed today – another crisis.

'Hallo?'

'Hilary? Susan.'

'Hi.'

'You in?'

'Mm.'

'Mind if I, you know?'

'Feel free.'

'Oh great.'

'OK. See you.'

'See you soon, then. 'Bye, Hilary.'

Susan thought thank the Lord for that. And now she just had time for a bath, instead of having to drag out the business

34

for the entire afternoon and evening. Good old Hilary. Thank God for friends.

'What the bloody hell was the matter with you this morning?' hooted George, but he appeared to feel something. Care a bit.

'Don't labour it, George,' said Barry. 'Have we got a four or not?'

'Oh sure. There are always people ready to drop their hard-earned money. Seriously, Barry' – George had dropped his voice – 'you OK?'

'Never been better. Come on, George,' Barry chided. 'You sound like a Jewish mother! Just get the cards.'

George did the mandatory 'My life, already' through his nose, and sauntered off down the corridor. Nice line in suits, George had. Man at C & A, but you'd never know it. Quite often when he was with George, Barry contemplated buying a few new clothes, but he never seemed to get round to it. And never mind bloody clothes – if the cards weren't hot tonight, he wouldn't even be eating.

It had been a very fraught afternoon. After the meeting fiasco, Barry had gone up to see Annie but she wasn't there so he just inhaled her cardigan, burying his face into it, and then dashed back down to his office to hide and think it out. He always had a half-bottle of Bell's in his desk, thank God, and he sucked in most of it like oxygen. Barry had little time for phrases like 'can't cope', but Jesus, sometimes he really felt like that. More so, lately. He had got through the afternoon without seeing anyone at all and he had sent Jean the temp home because if she had asked him if he was all right just one more time he felt he might have strangled her. He would have gone himself – not home – but this game was so bloody crucial.

'The Game' had been going on for about six months now, and it wasn't really a game at all. It was gambling at its most basic. No one much pretended to enjoy it; the whole point was simply to win money, or at worst to lose as little as possible. A pack of cards would be set at the centre of the desk, a stake would be placed, and a player would guess whether or not the card at the cut would be higher or lower than a six. And that was it. No skill, no fun. And that was the way everyone liked it. Only the winner smiled.

Barry had dropped a lot of money at the game; only George understood just how much. No one outside the firm – certainly not Susan – knew of its existence. Why should she? Barry had demanded of himself. None of her business. My money. Which was so, but during the last few weeks the inevitable had happened: Barry was losing heavily. He had laughed it off the first couple of times; can't always be lucky, he had said. And then he had started betting more than he could afford in order to make good his losses. Road to perfidy, George had said, but Barry didn't laugh. He was so annoyed by his own stupidity, but he had to acknowledge that he couldn't help going on with it. That was the trouble: he couldn't help anything, these days. But now it had become more a case of extreme financial necessity than any sort of gambler's compulsion, for Barry was damn near broke.

Standing Orders, unfortunately now for Barry, had no place in his life. He distrusted them, along with credit cards, Cashpoint dispensers and indeed any computer or its regurgitated print-outs. It seemed rather sourly funny now, but Barry had always liked to be in personal control of his finances, pay cash, and never at all by instalments. His attitude was seen by many to be suspiciously working-class – even *Northern* – but it was the neatness of the method that appealed to Barry. Paying the rent when it was due, having no wallet of collected bills – and so no red demands – together with the knowledge that everything that surrounded him at home (be it ever so vile, he quipped) was his own. Life – in this respect anyway – had been totally simple, and therefore very pleasing.

Barry usually had a fair amount of cash on him – for drinks and the like – and when he had seen a couple of the lads messing around with the cards, it had seemed a natural to dabble. To 'have a flutter'. He thought he even said that at the time, believe it or not. And of course, he won. It seemed to him now to be an evil and pre-ordained plan engineered with salacious relish by the gods. (Barry did not believe in God, but the gods, he knew, were everywhere.) He won quite a lot for a first-timer – forty pounds – and the very next time he played, he won again, even more. He began to earn quite a reputation for being good at it – as if, he would disclaim, one could be good or bad at it – and it was the image even more than the money that gratified Barry. And naturally it had been he who had suggested the upping of the stakes 'to make it more interesting', and he who countered all opposition to the change, and he again who almost immediately began to lose, encountering understandable resistance from his colleagues when he proposed returning to the original, and less expensive, system. Which, of course, had been a good deal more amicable too. It became a point of honour for Barry not to quit a loser, and so he played on. The rent money went first (he always drew out seventy pounds on a Friday for this) and then what he had earmarked for lunches. These days he just drew a succession of cheques to cover his losses, and two-thirds of his income was gone, usually before he had earned or received it. But now the bank had closed down his overdraft, Camden were threatening to sue for back rates, the landlord was talking about eviction, and Susan was forever grousing about her ever-declining food allowance, and accusing Barry of being a miser, and telling him that Harriet, or Hilda or some bitch or other had a brand-new fridge-freezer – as if Barry gave a sod what the hell Harriet had. Or Hilda, or whoever

37

the hell. It would be the bloody Fiat next, he could feel it. And without wheels, he'd be finished; if he couldn't get away from that damned flat when he had to, he'd be finished. Over. He told Susan he was saving with the bloody Woolwich, of all things. What for? Susan had wanted to know, and Barry had said rainy day and Susan had said what rainy day and then Barry said – why the hell had he said that?! – saving for a mortgage, little home, little house, and Susan had said really? And Barry had seen no alternative to nodding with misery and saying really, of course, surprise. Susan apologised then, and Barry shouted at her because he felt so sick, and now George was here with his secretary – gorgeous bloody bitch – and Billy from Production was hooking over a chair, and Barry was going to do the whole bloody thing again, God curse it, and please God believe in me, he thought, and let me win, please nice God, and I'll believe in you too. Honestly. She was wearing silk, he noticed.

'Ready for the slaughter, Barry?'

'Ready and waiting, George, ready and waiting. And the lovely Christine, I see.'

'Felt lucky,' said Christine, who, despite its being distinctly unfashionable, constantly wore too much, too dark make-up, and never seemed to suffer as a result. Painted tramp, older people said, but really it was difficult to take one's eyes off her. Damn woman. She was so all *over* the place.

'A little glamour,' said Billy from Production.

'Which, God knows, we need with you around,' said George, at which Billy made it clear that he considered George no oil-painting, and everyone said ha ha ha and everyone was as nervous as hell, but not as nervous as Barry. He had just sixty-three pounds on him – scrounged up somehow – which, with his Fiat, and his Omega watch and a couple of bits of furniture – represented the sum total of his assets. Pathetic. It was quite ridiculous that he should have come to this position, he well acknowledged, but apart from this accursed game – which in about a month had robbed him blind – there was no way that sixty-three pounds (damn near nothing these days anyway) might be made into more. If he could win, if he could just double it, he would be all right, he thought, until the end of the month, provided he paid no bills. As to losing – well, he just couldn't, that was all. No, bravado like that never worked. He *could* lose, he knew, and he was scared.

'So who's going to be first?' said George.

'Ladies first,' said Billy.

'Oh no,' said Christine. 'I doan mind.'

'Well somebody bloody be first for Christ's sake!' snapped Barry, who then wished he hadn't, when everyone looked at him.

'OK,' said George. 'I'll start. Or you can start if you like, Barry.'

'I don't mind starting,' said Barry, and everyone placed a ten-pound note on the table and Barry said 'over a six' and cut the pack and it was a nine and Barry pulled in the forty pounds, fast.

'Beginner's luck,' smiled George. 'Who's next?'

'My turn now,' said Christine. 'Zit still ten pounds?'

'Bet what you like,' said Barry, who suddenly betted her legs were silky.

'Well twenny, then,' said Christine. 'Dough nav too long.'

Barry threw down his twenty thinking no prizes for guessing where *she* gets her money from, bitch.

'Over,' said Christine, and then 'Oh!' when she drew a four. If only Barry had been sitting on her right; then he would have had the right to call. But it would have to be Billy, who said 'over' again, cut again, and drew a king, damn him to hell. Eighty pounds! And Billy didn't even have the taste to spend it on anything worthwhile, as anyone who mattered could have told you. Never mind. Barry was ten pounds up, Billy was fifty pounds up – look at his stupid grin – and George and Christine were thirty pounds down apiece, and each was making clucking noises of mock consolation.

'OK,' said George. 'My turn. I'll be brave.'

A twenty-pound note went down, and then George said what the hell and added another ten. The others followed, Christine saying that she had to go very soon, and George said 'Under, for a change' and drew a ten, which made him whistle.

'Jesus,' he said. 'Another thirty quid.'

Barry thought how bloody marvellous. It was his call now, and a hundred and twenty pounds was on the table.

'Under,' he said, and cut near the top of the pack. Everyone roared briefly when they saw the very same ten that George had drawn.

'Oh bad luck,' said George. 'What an amazing coincidence.'

Which was true; it didn't happen often.

Barry just stared at it.

'Oh bloody shit,' he said, really disgusted.

It was Billy's call again, and amid a welter of his usual drivel about streaks of luck, Barry gleaned through a daze that Billy was raising the ante before cutting the pack. He put down two more tens, and everyone followed, George saying he was nearly cleaned out, Christine saying that this had to be the last, and Barry saying nothing and thinking oh my God help me, another twenty!

'Under,' said Billy, and slowly – there was two hundred pounds on the table – he cut the pack. It was a seven. Hissings of disbelief and tension sizzled in the air only briefly, and then everyone became grim and silent. Christine tried a laugh, as it was her call now.

'Carn afford to raise or anyfink. So I'll just cut it. Oh God – I'll just cut it quick, shall I?'

'Just cut it,' said Barry in a very dark voice. His nails were really hurting the fleshy part of his thumb, but he didn't know it yet.

'Oh,' said Christine, ' – I'll say under again.'

And she cut, and she got a two, and she said wheeee and scooped in the notes like they do in the Westerns, and even clasped the stuff against her bosom and crinkled it. Barry was as pale as starch, and even George seemed to be finding it difficult to be *that* nice; he'd only brought her along to make up the four, for God's sake, and now she'd gone and won two hundred quid. Christine undid another silk-covered button on her blouse, in triumph. She thought, she said, she would stay on a bit, now.

George said he wasn't sure how much he'd lost, but he knew it was a lot, and here was his very last twenty. Barry knew exactly how much he had left – twenty-three pounds – and he put down four five-pound notes as casually as he could. He knew too that his only chance now was if George called wrongly; then it would be passed to Barry. And Barry had to get it right, or it wasn't at all funny.

'Well Jesus,' said George. 'Whatever I say'll be wrong tonight. If I say over it'll be a five. I don't know what's wrong with me tonight. Oh – to hell with it. I'll say under. I bet,' he said, cutting the pack, 'I bet it'll be a bloody seven now.'

It was a six. The air thudded out of Barry as if he had been kicked. A six meant nothing at all and George had to draw again, and Barry was not sure he could stand much more of it. He was gambling with his last twenty pounds in the world, Christ Almighty, and his legs felt so cold under the table.

'OK,' said George. 'I'll stick with "under". Here we go.'

He drew a nine, and said sod this then, I'm out of it.

Barry drew back his chin and chest. His call. He wanted to raise it, but apart from his three pounds he was finished. He couldn't raise it three pounds. Look bad.

41

'George,' said Barry. 'I seem to have left most of my cash in the car. You wouldn't care to sub me for, say, twenty, would you?'

George looked at Barry. He knew it was a lie, of course, and he knew that Barry knew, et cetera, et cetera. A face-saver for the others.

'And then you'll raise the bet, I suppose,' said George, only a bit jovially, still looking at Barry, and thinking I really *have* dropped a fortune tonight. 'And then I'll have to find another twenty to match it, I suppose,' he went on.

George tried to see in Barry's eyes what the blazes the bugger was playing at, but all he saw was pleading.

'Oh here – take the twenty, sod you!'

'Thanks, George.'

'And I'll expect interest!'

'Ha ha. OK, George. No problem.'

And then Barry thought, no more crap. Get it done, for the love of God. He put down the twenty, and it was matched. Barry's mouth was scoured and his eyes felt, what? Hot. He went for the pack.

'Hang on,' said George, putting out an arm.

'What the hell,' snarled Barry. He felt wild.

'Simmer down, for God's sake, Barry. You haven't said what, that's all.'

Barry stared at him. He didn't understand.

'What?' he said, with narrow eyes.

'You haven't said! You haven't called! Are you OK, Barry?'

Barry said ah, and shivered. He was standing now.

'Oh yes, of course. Sorry, George. Sorry, everyone. Um. Under. No. Over. Over. Yes, over.'

'Sure?'

'I *said* over.'

Barry stood still just for a moment. Right. Seven, eight, nine, ten, jack, queen, king. Please. Then he snatched at the cards and a couple fluttered out of his hand, but it was the one he flipped over that counted. The four of clubs. He clattered down the pack and lurched like a drunk. Got to go. Get out. Got to get out. The door seemed impossibly distant, and Christine looked frightened and Barry thought he might have heaved into Billy before he got his hands on the handle and he couldn't turn it, and he was shaking and rattling the thing, and someone said other way and he got out and he thought at last I'm out, at least I'm out, and where is Annie? Oh please God where is she?

He had spent a long time in the Gents; he held his open mouth over a basin, but nothing came. He sat on a lavatory with his head between his knees, but he didn't do anything. He did not dash water over his face, though, as this often made his headache worse, and puffed out his eyes. It was his eyes, mainly, that hurt like bloody hell. Barry just did not know what on earth was wrong with him. He hadn't even been drinking. Well, not like he normally did.

He 'phoned Susan then, to tell her he wouldn't be home. He always did this. She usually said so what, and then created hell the minute he got back. Or she wasn't in. He let it ring a long time but he got no answer. Must be out. Then he 'phoned Annie.

'Hello,' she said. Beautifully.

'Annie. Thank Christ.'

'Darling. Where are you? You're not all right, are you?'

Barry nearly grinned. God, wasn't she wonderful?

'Felt better,' he said. She would understand.

'How soon can you be here? I'll make you feel better.'

'Oh God I love you, Annie.'

'I bet that's what you say to all the girls,' reproved Annie, but Barry could tell that her eyes were dancing. It was all right.

'How the hell do *you* know?' Mock-indignant.

'You tell me.'

'Yes. Well. That's different. *And* you know it. Look, I haven't got any more ten pees – '

'Well just come over, for heaven's sake, and stop rabbiting on!'

'Oh, I love you, Annie.'

'Mother's not too well, but she'll be OK. I'll get her upstairs.'

'I'm leaving right now.'

'See you soon, my darling. Take care.'

'Oh Annie – I do love you, you know.'

''Bye, darling. See you soon.'

''Bye, angel. 'Bye.'

How could I do it without her, Barry thought. She wouldn't be pleased with him though. She wouldn't be pleased at all. Which was thrilling too, in its own funny way.

'I even get worried about the big things,' whined Susan. 'You know – nuclear threat, all that. I mean, the next war isn't going to be another Falklands, is it? London will be a hole as far as Reading. Is this Earl Grey?'

'Lapsang,' said Hilary. 'I don't know why you waste your time worrying about nuclear bombs. You can't do anything about it.'

Susan nodded. 'I know,' she said. 'Still.'

She had been at Hilary's for about an hour, and she had eaten three Chocolate Olivers and said that Hilary must think her awful and Hilary said don't be so daft.

'I'm eating a helluva lot at the moment, actually. Since I stopped the diet I can't seem to stop.'

Hilary was sitting on an old studio couch with her legs tucked up beneath her. It was covered in a blousy Morris print bought ages ago in a John Lewis sale, and Hilary usually wore black polos and smoked non-stop. It was wonderfully timeless at Hilary's. It hadn't changed since the very late Sixties and was so terribly comforting. Hilary must be what? Late thirties? Bit more? Maybe four or five years older than Susan. She had never married but she said she knew a lot of men and things, and Susan knew there was one who came over nearly every single Friday night. Had done for ages. She just didn't like going out much, that was all.

'Anyway,' said Susan.

'Was that Nicholas?' said Hilary suddenly alert.

'I didn't hear anything.'

Hilary's eyes veiled again.

'I'll go and check him in a minute.'

Susan drank tea and said:

'How old is he now?'

'Same as when you asked me last week. Ten. You don't have to keep asking, you know. I know you don't like children.'

'I don't *not* like kids. I just never know how to take them, that's all. Relate to them. I find it difficult.'

'You just "take" them like anyone else. They're people.'

'Oh I know, I know all that. You sound like a cross between Penelope Leach and *New Society*. I *think* it's Penelope.'

'You seem to know a lot about it.'

'Oh, I read them all a few years ago, when Barry thought we might. Spock – the whole lot. But he's supposed to be no good now, isn't he?'

'Never helped me.'

'Anyway, Barry's saving up for a house these days – did I tell you? Something, I suppose.' Grudging, but quite excited underneath.

Hilary was combing out her long hair with spread-out fingers, holding up the ends to scrutiny as she let the rest fall away.

'I'm glad I didn't get married,' she said.

45

'I'm glad I didn't have any kids,' said Susan. 'Really.'

'More tea,' offered Hilary. 'Vicar?'

'No, I'm fine, thanks. I've had three cups, I think. Oh God, I hate living, sometimes. I really think I have to get a job, you know, Hilary. I'm turning into a real bored housewife. And I want the money. I'm so sick of having to depend on Barry for every little thing. And he seems to be putting everything into this damn building society now – I never see a penny. Still, I suppose he's right. It's right, really. But it's so bloody *sensible*. We're all getting so old.'

'Speak for yourself,' said Hilary.

'I was,' said Susan. 'Hilary . . .?'

'Mm?'

'What do you think of George?'

'George is all right. Why – are you still seeing him?'

'I'm not seeing him. I was never *seeing* him. We just met a couple of times, that's all.'

'Well, that's *seeing* him, isn't it?'

'No – not in the sense you mean. He bought me this,' said Susan, holding taut the chain around her neck.

Hilary fingered the pendant.

'Pretty,' she said.

'You don't like it.'

'It's OK. What is it? Quartz?'

'Chryso-something. It's not expensive or anything.'

'No,' agreed Hilary.

'But you used to know George, didn't you?'

Hilary lit another cigarette and shuffled the packet over to Susan.

'I wouldn't say I know him, no. We slept together a couple of times. Had lunch.'

'Well Christ then!'

Hilary shrugged.

'George is OK. I suppose. Bit too much bonhomie for my liking. He's OK. Small doses.'

Susan sat on the floor, her back against a heap of *Listeners*.

'Just listen to the world-weary sophisticate!' she laughed. 'You are a fraud, Hilary! You're never that cynical and you know it. Or cheap.'

'It's nothing to do with *cheap*. It's a question of logic and freedom. I work, I earn my own money, and I bring up my own son. I'm not dependent on any man for my keep and that makes me very secure. I can be as casual as I like, because nothing has to be *important*. I am totally uncommitted to anyone – except for Nicholas, of course. I just take what I want – and believe you me, Susan, that's what men have been doing for ever.'

'Sounds to me as if you've got a bit of a chip.'

'A chip about what?'

'Well, about little Nicky, for a start!'

Hilary tossed her head away and Susan thought oh no I've made her angry and I need her just now. Susan was always making Hilary angry, she didn't know why.

Hilary just looked at her.

'*Nicholas*,' she reproved.

Susan blew out smoke, tapped off ash.

'Sorry. Nicholas. I meant Nicholas.'

And Susan looked away too. It was getting dark.

'Anyway,' she said.

All the way to Annie's, Barry was thinking how depressed he'd be when he came away. He used to be able to live for the moment, to at least enjoy whatever was going, but he couldn't seem to do it now. He had looked at a Pelican on Zen and, what was it, Seeing, but concentration was nowhere. Barry had really thought it might help him a bit, but he couldn't even read it. It wasn't that he failed to understand – he just

47

couldn't *read* the thing. Simply couldn't. Anyway, Annie was better than all the Zen in the world.

It was a pretty little town house in sort of Kensington, with a couple of steps up to the door. The fanlight warmed him, and when he rang the bell, he never had to wait, and then she was there for him. They never said anything at the door, but Annie's eyes sparkled welcome and love, and Barry drank it in as he was sucked through the doorway.

Annie kissed his hand – she always did this – and she started unbuckling his trench-coat belt, and all Barry had to do was just stand there.

'You OK?' checked Annie.

Barry shrugged.

'Is – ?'

'It's OK. She's upstairs.'

She always went to trouble. Her hair was newly washed, and the scent of her was sweet. She will have done all this when she put down the 'phone. A coal fire was burning although she normally didn't bother when she was alone, but Barry loved it. He sat down like a dead weight, and even said oh God what a day, and Annie knelt – she knelt, Annie – beside him and it was so wonderful that Barry was frightened it would end – and he even said so sometimes, but Annie just assured him it would never end, and a new sort of peace was warmly restored and Barry hoped to God she was right because he needed her.

A drink was there – Bell's, a touch of water – and Annie poured more when it was gone.

'Geisha,' Barry said.

'I love you,' said Annie.

'Oh Annie,' he sighed.

And his reef-knotted nerves were unclenching for the very first time since the last time. They stayed in silence for a long, long while, as Annie knew that he needed to. Barry tried to be

48

worried about money, to get his mind *around* the thing, but her eyes winked impossibly bright in the firelight and he thought what the hell, and suddenly he was enjoying the moment again, like he used to.

'Was it *very* bad today?' Annie said, eventually.

'Not too good. Doesn't matter now.'

Annie was so small. Her hand seemed so small on him.

'It matters to me,' she said.

'It's OK. Later.'

Barry needed her, but he thought they would not go up to her bedroom tonight. They didn't, always. And when he felt her fingers playing over his legs, he knew it. She could peel back his clothes with the efficiency of a nurse, and yet as subtly as an angel, and then her hands were cool on him, melting, then gently insistent, and her face shone love and honour. Dear, dear Annie; she was so good to him. He didn't even have to move.

'Turbo,' said Gavin. 'Makes a lot of sense.'

He was back. Moira had heard the front door. She might have been asleep. A Hammer film still glowed at her, and *Ideal Home* had slipped to the floor.

'Talking to a chap,' went on Gavin. 'Seemed a decent sort of bloke. Got one of those Saab jobs. Makes a lot of sense. It's going right *down* that pub, though. Bloody Space-What-Have-Yous bleeping all over the place. Like a bloody madhouse down there now.'

Alibi crudely established, Gavin poured a whisky.

'Thought you'd be in bed,' he said.

'I 'phoned Susan earlier.'

'Poor Susan. She all right?'

'She was going round to Hilary's.'

'Oh, Hilary. Women's Lib.'

'Single Parent,' amended Moira.

'Much the same. Drink? Oh, you've got. I'm tired. I'm off up.'

And he yawned extravagantly.

'Coming? Or shall I leave a light on?'

Moira looked up and Gavin thought she really looks old. Or maybe she had just been crying again. She didn't say anything though. Not a word.

'What the bloody hell's wrong now?!' demanded Gavin. 'God, I could bloody kill you when you're like this.'

'I'll kill *you*, you mean,' said Moira, so faintly.

'Look, if you're going to start your mumbling, I'm off right now. It's always the same. As soon as you've got a bottle of that sickly bloody wine inside you, you become all – what is it, what is it, oh Christ, I can't even *speak* now! What's the bloody word I mean? Respective. Introspective. That's it, introspective – and I can never bloody hear a bloody word you're saying. I expect you learned it off the television, along with everything else. Well it's not clever! It's not *amusing*, you know! It's just downright bloody silly, if you want to know the truth!'

Gavin held the door before thudding upstairs.

'You're bloody silly, Moira! I'm sorry, but you really are a bloody silly woman!'

It was minutes before Moira hissed into the room:

'I'll kill *you*, you mean.'

Chapter Three

GOD KNOWS what time Barry got in. Earlier on, Susan had been drinking gin and water – Beefeater, because she liked the label, water because . . . she didn't know why water, why not? She was feeling very let down by Hilary. Hilary always used to sympathise – empathise, they say now – and Susan was not at all sure that it had been worth the journey and she hated the Tube after dark and Camden Town always seemed so awful after Hampstead. Still. Problems of her own.

Obviously Susan had drunk too much; she was only opaquely aware of Barry getting home. He did not come to bed, and some time later Susan thought she might have heard him leave, maybe for work. It was now nearly noon, and she was getting ready ready ready, her head thumping like a heart, holding up a succession of scarves to her face. Meeting George for lunch at one. Charlotte Street Wheeler's: rather nice. She supposed she ought to feel bad about it, or *something* about it – George being Barry's, well, sort of friend, really – but she didn't. Not at all. Anyway, George had said he could find her a job, if she wanted, so it was almost business, if she looked at it that way. Maybe even Susan might contribute to this building society game, if all went well. Do her bit, sort of thing. Poor old Barry. Poor old soul. She supposed he wasn't that bad, really. Of course, Susan could easily do without him, live without him – and who knew? If she became independent again, who was to say what might happen? There was, Susan

further supposed, worse than Barry – had to be – but the thought of living alone did not scare her. Even the thought of living with somebody else. As to Susan's own behaviour – well, it was only *lunch*, for God's sake, and Barry had been no angel in the past. There had been a typist, once, and a couple of one-night stands at conferences, she thought. But she knew that these days he was faithful. Horrid word. All the red-eyed and vacuous appeal of a drugged Hush-Puppy. Did people still wear Hush-Puppies? No no no no no. It was just this sort of idle wandering that burned up Susan's days. Concentrate. She really must, if she wanted to get anywhere at all. Now. Get on the shoes. Get on the coat. Check the necklace. Out.

Susan was early, but George was there, thank God – corner table. She did not like sitting alone in restaurants and pubs. She liked people looking at her, but she could not bear to be *looked* at.

'Susan. Hello.'

'Hello, George. This is really nice.'

'Not a bit of it. There. Shall I just move the table in a bit?'

'Lovely. They're always a bit far away. Lovely.'

'Drink?'

'Mm. G and T, please.'

'Two large gin and tonics, please, Carlo – mine with Slimline. With those big wedges of lemon – you know the way I like them.'

'Of-course-sir-tenk-you-sir-tenk-you-madame,' said Carlo, with careless sycophancy.

Susan slightly hid behind a large yellow card menu and thought this is really nice.

'It really is really nice here,' she said.

'I like it,' said George. 'Use it a lot. Whitebait's great,' he added, pointing.

'Where's that?'

'There. Just there.'

'Ah. Not too keen on that, actually. Oo – they've got smoked oysters.'

'Whatever you fancy, Susan. And hang the expenses! You can be, what, *Sunday Times* literary editor, if you like. Does that appeal? Or would you prefer to be head buyer, W. H. Smith?'

'It's a bit of a twist, this expenses thing, isn't it? I mean – are you sure it's all right?'

"Course it's all right. That's what they're for. American Express – that'll do nicely. Just as long as I keep getting the right spaces in the right places. I only pray to God the firm never moves out to some Christ-forlorn plot like Warrington-bloody-Runcorn. A man could starve to death!'

Susan laughed a bit, as was polite after an exclamation mark, and drank her gin, which tinkled and was in a good, large glass. George was rather fun. She bet he had said all that before, though. This was something about George she had noticed: he was very easygoing and it all *seemed* perfectly natural, but at the same time rehearsed, if anyone could know what she meant by that. *She* did, anyway.

'I know I want sole,' said Susan. 'I think. I can't decide between normande and véronique. They sound marvellous. What are you having?'

'Just boring old grilled, I'm afraid. Waistline.'

And he actually patted it.

'Well I'm rather in the mood to be a pig,' apologised Susan.

'Oink away,' smiled George.

'Can't seem to stop eating, lately. I think I've decided. Yes. Smoked oysters, then, if that's OK, sole normande. Lovely.'

'Right, Carlo – I think we're ready. The lady will have the oysters, followed by the normande. Vegetables, Susan? Sauté all right? A few beans?'

'Lovely.'

'Right. OK. That. And I'll have the whitebait and the sole, my usual way – bit crunchy.'

'Of-course-sir-tenk-you-sir-tenk-you-madame.'

'And the wine-list, please, Carlo. No, actually – you needn't bother. We'll have that Niersteiner. Reliable.'

Susan looked around. It was rather pleasantly discreet, she thought, with the leaded lights and civilised hubbub.

'Really nice,' she said.

George nodded. 'Packed with publishers, of course. Otherwise it's all right. There's Simon over there. Do you know Simon? No, I don't suppose you would. With Cape these days, I think. Years with Deutsch. No – Weidenfeld, actually. Actually, I don't think it's Simon at all, just looking at him. Still. Doesn't matter.'

Carlo popped the wine – they always *popped* the wine – and poured George a dribble.

'I think we know this one well enough, now, Carlo. Pour on. I'm sure you'll like it, Susan. Reliable.'

'I'm sure I shall. Lovely.'

The food, the wine, and George's burnished pleasantries seemed to be going down well. The conversation grew dilatory, and then Barry cropped up. A relief, to be honest; he would not have stayed down much longer.

'He OK?' enquired George.

Susan thought she heard concern.

'Why?' she returned. 'What's wrong with him?'

'Nothing wrong with him. Nothing that I know.' George laughed, then. Try to laugh it off, he thought. 'Idle as ever!'

Susan fell silent before saying 'Barry', quite simply – near wistfully, she was not sure why.

'You rather like him, don't you, George?'

George chewed some wine as if it was a mouthwash.

'Good bloke,' he agreed. 'Hardly deserves you, though.'

54

'No, I know what you mean,' said Susan. 'What do you mean, George?'

'Oh. nothing. Nothing, really. Just a bad attempt at complimenting you, I suppose. Can I give you the other half of that glass? I think we'd better get in another of these.'

Susan did not protest.

'I'll be sloshed,' she said.

'I should be so lucky,' said George.

An eye-contact was maintained for a second or two, until George looked away thinking Christ I must stop this and Susan felt a bit let down. All rather obvious. It was not really what she wanted. Too trite. She ate a lemon sorbet.

'George. About this job.'

'Yes, well. Guy I know in the rag trade – top end, mind: no rubbish – and he was telling me he was on the look-out for, how did he put it, what did he say? Personable young – oh well, you get the gist, anyway. It boiled down to a good-looker with a brain who can actually speak English. Not a common combination, these days.'

Susan stabbed at the demerara boulder.

'I'm not *that* good-looking,' she said.

'So *you* say. I beg to differ. *And* you know it.'

'What would the job *be*, exactly? Who is this guy?'

'Name's Wiseman. Mark Wiseman. Rich as hell and never mind any recession. Money of his own, I think. Anyway – ah, can I see the cigars, Carlo? – anyway. What was I saying? Oh yes – Mark. Loads of shops up and down Oxford Street and that sort of area, but all under different names. This is apparently how it's done. Makes the stuff as well. Export – the lot.'

'Sounds interesting,' said Susan. Sounds like real money, she thought.

'Well, I said I'd pass it on. Yes, I'll have this little Bolivar, I think. No thanks – got a clipper. Susan, you won't indulge?'

'Haven't quite got to the cigar stage yet, thank you, George.

It's OK – I've got some cigarettes. Another nail,' she said, lighting one.

George ordered two Rémy Martins, and then said:

'Christ Almighty! Talk of the devil! Look who's just walked in off the street! It's like the Champs-Elysées.'

Susan wouldn't look round. Oh Christ, it must be Barry, she thought.

'Who is it?' she asked.

Oh *Christ* wouldn't it *just* be Barry, she thought.

'It's Mark. Bloke I was just telling you about. Talk about a small – hey! Mark! Hello – how you doing? We were just talking about you!'

'George,' said Mark. 'Nice.'

He slapped George's hand, which Susan thought odd – wasn't it just blacks who did that? George slapped Mark's in return, however, so presumably it was all right. Susan had clearly been out of circulation for quite some time.

'Business good?' urged George.

'It's a living,' said Mark, and Susan thought he rather parodied the shrug of the sort of people who said that, which might be a good sign, she didn't really know.

'Hello. I'm Susan.'

George smote his brow.

'Susan, Susan – forgive me! Whatever was I thinking of? Must be the Rémy Martin! Susan – Mark. Mark – Susan. Come and sit down, Mark.'

'Meeting a bloke. He's just come in. Some other time.'

'Sure, of course. Susan, Mark, is the girl I was telling you about.'

'You're joking,' said Mark. 'Coincidence.'

And he looked at her. His eyes twinkled and he looked not so much young as well cared for. About fifty, probably – maybe less. The suit was very pale grey, and Vinci or Principe or Leonardo or one of those types, Susan thought; Italian, anyway. And expensive. On his hand was darkish skin, little black hairs and a heavy gold Rolex Oyster; it seemed more on his hand than anything.

'Look, Sue,' he said. 'I hate to be rude, but call me. OK?'

And he placed a business card on the table, and shifted away. 'OK?' had not really been a question at all.

'He's very busy,' apologised George.

But Susan was not offended. In a way, she found it – him – rather exciting, even glamorous. Certainly, she thought, there was money there. And power. She carefully put the card into her bag.

George ordered more Rémy Martins, and Susan's legs were already fizzing below the knee. She hadn't really got over last night's bout. Still.

'You are looking *lovely*,' said George, expelling blue smoke.

Oh Christ, thought Susan. And then relented a bit. It was, after all, that stage of the meal. She half wished she felt just a twinge of lust, but if she was honest, there was nothing. Nothing at all.

'That little pendant of yours keeps catching the light. Suits you.'

'Like it?'

'I like it.'

Susan fingered the necklace.

'Barry bought it for me,' she said, thinking Jesus that was cheeky, I may be a little boozed.

'It's very nice,' said George. How the hell, he thought, can Barry afford to go around buying jewellery?

'Hilary,' went on Susan, 'didn't like it.'

'Hilary? I don't know any Hilary.'

'Well,' said Susan, 'she knows you. She says you knew each other. You did, didn't you?'

George looked honestly reflective.

'Well I'm very sorry. Don't remember any Hilary. Complete blank, I'm afraid.'

And Susan thought Christ, this world really does make me sick. You just don't know who to believe. What the hell ever happened to trust?

'It's getting to be so that living in London you feel a bloody foreigner!' cried Barry. 'God alone knows I'm not prejudiced – I mean I'd rather die than have anything South African as you damn well know, but Christ, Annie, these bloody Pakistanis really bloody get to me. I mean, wouldn't it be nice, wouldn't it be nice just once – just once – to go into a newsagent that didn't sound like a bloody discothèque and actually have them understand what the hell you're talking about! I mean, it's *English*, for God's sake! It's *these* things that are really *getting* to me, lately! Just this morning, I went into that one on the corner – Swami's, is it? Used to be called something like Smith or Jones – you know it? Sellotape, I wanted. Just an ordinary, straightforward roll of Sellotape. Nothing fancy. Not *difficult*, you'd have thought. Bloke directed me to some inferior muck and I said, no, Sellotape, I want Sellotape – it's the only one that *sticks*, and you have to bawl your head off to be heard in there because of this damn bloody heavy metal blasting through the shop – it's *shaking* with the noise, that place – and he says it *is* Sellotape, and I say no it bloody isn't mate, you just have to read the *label* and I say Sell-O-Tape like I'm talking to a baboon, which they behave like some of them, sometimes. It's a *brand*, I say, and he looks at me through his stupid bloody post-Imperialist moustache and like a zombie he says "Brown?" Brown! I mean I bloody ask you! Does "brand" sound like brown?! It just makes you give up! I just gave up, and now I still haven't got the stuff. I mean – a *language* problem, and we're in the middle of North-West-Bloody-One. And why *should* you just take whatever they happen to have on the shelves – all of it off the back of a lorry anyway, I shouldn't be at all surprised. It looked *terrible* stuff – I'd never *heard* of it. I mean, it wasn't as if it was Scotch tape, or anything. Anyway, that sort of thing really drives me mad. Oh God, Annie, I think I'm going mad, sometimes! But he's a real thicko, that Swami, bloody fool – and rude! They're really rude in there. They have no sort of manners whatsoever. I wouldn't go in at all, but it's near. Oh God. I mean – *look* at me, Annie! Just *look* at me! I've gone completely purple over a roll of Sellotape! I think I'm just cracking up. I must be. I don't know any more.'

Annie smiled.

'You sound like a completely different person when you go on like that. Try to calm down, Barry, please.'

'Calm down! Calm down, she says! Oh that's bloody funny, that is! Calm down! Calm down! I'd *love* to bloody calm down but you just tell me how it's done, that's all! I'm done Annie. I'm finished. You above all people should know that! I've told you about the money and everything. I can't go on taking hand-outs from you. Bloody bank manager wants to see me now – what did he write, bloody fool, how did he put it – oh yes, he said he thought it would be "useful" if we met! Well that's a joke for a start because I can't think of anything more totally useless in the whole wide world. He wants money – along with everybody else on this bloody planet – and I haven't got any. Simple as that. Anyway, I hate the man, silly sod, sitting there like a Dunns advert, curse him!'

'Angel,' said Annie, softly.

'Oh God,' snuffled Barry into her bosom. 'Oh God oh God.' She touched his hair.

'It will be all right,' she said.

'Won't,' said Barry, muffled. 'It won't. There's no reason it should be. Oh Christ, I owe everyone. I hate everyone, Annie!'

'You don't hate me.'

Barry's eyes hurt so much and he snivelled into Annie's breasts and held her tight.

'I hate me,' he said. 'I sometimes – oh, to hell with it.'

'What?' said Annie, suddenly.

Barry shook his head, but Annie insisted with her eyes.

'Oh hell,' he said. 'It's just that sometimes I feel like, well, *killing* my way out.'

'Killing?'

'Yeah, killing. You know – guns, knives, hate. Killing.'

He sounded offhand, even hard, but his mouth trembled as he searched her face. Annie looked down.

'I'll get you a drink,' she said.

'Large, please. Yes, I often think that. I think that a lot, actually.'

'You're not OK, are you, Barry? Not this time.'

He held her hand tight and looked up imploringly.

'I don't think so,' Barry whispered. 'No, I don't think so.'

And his face caved in and Annie caught his soul before it fell and she hugged him and hugged him and said there and there and there.

'Help me?' he asked.

'I'll help you,' said Annie.

'Don't leave me?'

'I'm here. I'm here, angel. Always here.'

'I love you, Annie.'

'Ssh.'

'Help me. Help me. Oh God help me!'

Barry whimpered and she held him, and much much later Annie heard the drone of sleep, and she held him fast. He flinched, and she held him tighter, and Annie's mother called from upstairs, and one leg was numb and then near breaking beneath her, but she wouldn't let go. She had said so, and she would stay.

It grew cold in the room. Barry was deeply unconscious

only because, Annie believed, he needed to be. She felt many things – love, mainly, but this could be dangerous, she knew, because it could blind her to likelihoods. She had urged him to help himself, told him that he was easily capable of such an act, because he was her man, and because she wanted him to be. It was always possible, though, that he could do no such thing any more; if this were so, then pressure would increase upon Annie, and she must be ready (could she be eager?) to bear it. Only occasionally did she resent this. Only sometimes did she smell her life like a stale and sickly scent, evaporating anyway. Really, though, she knew – life just *was* Barry. They were just too much of a part of each other for it to be any other way. She had hated him, sometimes. Hated him with a malevolence and an acid force of which she had believed herself incapable, but she found intolerable this feeling of hating him for long, for it became a sort of self-disgust that could fragment her. She did not think of futures, now. She did her job and she cared for her mother – but she *lived*, she *lived* for Barry. A bad, bad week with Barry was better than a single day without him.

Annie's mother was calling again. Dear mother. She was not an invalid, but it seemed that she saw little point in anything any more. She would stay in her room more now, and acted older than her years. Only seventy, but she kept saying to Annie that soon the house would be hers, all hers, but Annie really did not mind about this. She did not care for things, even valuable ones. And nor did she mind looking after her mother, although the poor old soul could be difficult with her aversion to any foods but white fish and poultry. Annie's job at the firm could bore her – but it didn't *matter*. Her mother, whom she loved, did not *matter*. Tomorrow, without Barry, did not *matter* at all. She did not know or care whether anyone would understand what she meant; only, she suspected, anyone who had ever felt the same. But Annie was not

61

a great talker. She did not enjoy the trade of conversation between two women, whereby the most personal and intimate became soiled like dark-edged playing cards, made commonplace and ugly by their interminable dealing. It was enough for Annie that she just felt; to part with the intense secrecy of an overwhelming joy, to confide the fears and doubts and pain would, to Annie, be not only vulgar, but the ultimate betrayal; of herself, really.

Her mother called out, but she would quieten soon. She was only lonely, and Annie had Barry to love.

'Life,' said Barry, when he had washed, 'is a terminal disease.'

'Glib,' smiled Annie.

'I know,' said Barry, and kissed her. 'Thank you, Annie.'

'Don't be silly.'

And then Barry just flared.

'Don't *say* that! Don't *say* don't be silly! You *always* do that! You always speak to me as if I'm a bloody child, or something!'

'Oh Barry, please don't start now.'

'I'm not *starting*. I'm not *starting* anything. I just said thank you, and you start patronising me!

Annie knew about this. She had to pay now, because she had seen him weak again.

'Have a drink, Barry. Please.'

'I don't want – *look*, I'm not a bloody alcoholic, you know! Have a drink! Have a drink! It's like sticking a tit in a baby! Just listen to me, can't you – look, look, don't walk away when I'm bloody talking to you!'

'I'm just going up to see how mother is.'

'Damn *mother*! Damn your bloody *mother*! *I'm* here now! You're supposed to be looking after *me*!'

'Oh am I?!' flashed Annie. Damn him, she thought. Now she was fighting back. 'That's my job, is it? That's what *I'm* for, is it? You've just told me *not* to. You really *are* a child, sometimes.'

Barry's eyes clouded dull with anger, and he caught Annie a scudding blow across her temple. She was knocked back into a chair and her eyes seethed at him, but she wouldn't allow herself to feel the throbbing.

'Don't *do* this again, Barry. I'm telling you – '

'*You're* telling me! *You're* telling me! I've got news for you, woman, you're not telling me *anything* any more because I'm going! You hear me? I'm off! You talk about *love*! That's about *all* you do, talk! You show me *nothing*. You *give* me nothing. Well to hell with you, then! Find somebody else! Get some other bored bloody bastard to keep you warm, you – '

'Barry – '

'Don't Barry *me*!! Don't bloody Barry me!! Just get out of my way, will you?! Just *move*!!' he bellowed.

He hurled open the door and it hit a table and he didn't care and he fought clumsily with the front door and near fell down the steps and someone in next door's garden looked at him and he didn't care and the hall yawned open to the cold and Annie closed the door, softly.

She sat by the fire and she thought I mustn't be hurt, I mustn't. He would need her more than ever when he came back in, and usually it took him only six minutes to walk around the block and ring the bell, but tonight he had fury within him, so say five, and by that time she must be ready because he was right, in a way: that *was* what she was for, and he was worth it, really. He just had to be. And anyway, she loved him.

George was in his office later on, looking at Christine's very sweet thighs and thinking I really ought to 'phone Susan, or maybe should I leave it a while? Sort of thinnish sunlight filtered through the vertical louvres, the dust dancing in its shafts and making the telephone grey. George often felt depressed after lunch.

She had disappointed him, really. He even admitted to himself that he felt a bit cheated, but the Lord alone knew what he had been expecting. Susan, it was true, had never led him to believe . . . and yet, and yet. It was their third meeting and their second lunch, and each seemed to be trying to preserve a detached and rather casual air – or maybe Susan actually felt that way? For George's part, he felt as guilty as hell about Barry – this was *all* the poor bugger needed right now, thought George. But wasn't he maybe being just a little old-fashioned? Christ, this was the *Eighties*, after all. And it was only *lunch*, for God's sake. But if this gelled, why had neither George nor Susan seen fit to tell Barry? Why, indeed, had George not asked him along? Because; just because: that's why. And while questions were being asked, why had bloody Mark Wiseman got George to arrange that Christ-awful 'coincidence' in Wheeler's? It had looked so clumsy to George. Why couldn't he have just given her an interview like anyone else? Wiseman had said something or other about always preferring to suss out a girl first – saves embarrassment, he had said, which was all double-Dutch to George, but as Wiseman had been giving off that man-of-the-world leer at the time, George had judged it ill-advised to say so; bad for the image.

A 'phone jangled, and Christine answered.

'Low. Publiss-tea. Nye hell pew?'

George fiddled with a paste-up while Christine tapped the receiver with a talon, newly japanned.

'Few, George,' she said, and George snapped a button and picked up the two-tone green.

'Ya. Oh hi, Gideon! Super. Ya. Oh you caught the ad, did you? Ya. Uh-huh. Ya. Glad! Glad! Terriff. Oh, nice one, Gideon – love it. Oh ya, surely. No problem. Wednesday? What, this coming Wednesday? Ya. No. No. I don't see a problem. Just hang on there, can you, and I'll just make doubly sure on this one.'

George guarded the mouthpiece and swivelled across to Christine.

'Wednesday. Lunch. OK?'

'Seems clear.'

'Hallo – Gideon? Hi. Ya. Wednesday's super. Joe Allen's, one – great. See you there, then. No. Ya ya, I know – don't you worry about that one Gideon. Leave it with me and I'll – ya – I'll – ya – I'll, I'll, ya I know, I'll . . . OK . . . OK . . . super. Lovely . . . lovely . . . OK, lovely, Gideon. Look forward to it. 'Bye. 'Bye, Gideon. Great.'

And he put down the 'phone and said bloody Gideon – why doesn't he leave me alone? And then he thought I'll 'phone Susan as soon as Christine swishingly uncrosses her legs and picks up her Rimmel cosmetic case and wanders off down to the lavatory again. Which she did quite soon, with a toss of her horse-blanket of hair, and her customary and bizarre enquiry as to whether George wanted anything while she was gone, to which he invariably responded:

'No thanks, Christine, love. I'm fine here.'

And today George noticed his own immediacy in snatching up the black 'phone and asking for a line. And he dialled. And it was engaged. Damn. And he asked for another line, and this time misdialled, and dialled again, and *still* it was engaged and Albert trundled in the trolley and dumped a mountain in the In-Tray and another 'phone was ringing and then Christine undulated back and answered it and said it was Fantasy Graphics and urgent. Damn damn damn. Try again later.

George was preoccupied that afternoon, but he worked as hard as an executive. He played with a pyramid of magnetic paperclips, tried with half a heart to mend his Newton's Cradle, and kept punching out 'Susan' on the Dymo. The best part of a pack of Marlboro had been ground into a recently pocketed Campari ashtray before he could finally stand it no longer. Every single time Christine went out (far more vanity than incontinence, George had long ago concluded) he had tried Susan's number – and surely to God no one could be on the 'phone for *that* long, and then he set to wondering whether she was all right – whatever that might mean – and then he thought of Barry, whom he had not seen all day, and he wondered if he should saunter down and have a word and then he thought Christ no, couldn't face him. Not that George had any idea *why* he wanted so much to speak to Susan, or even what he would say when eventually he did. He'd have to go round there, he decided. Oh yeah? (derisively) and what about Barry? What if Barry was in? Well then he'd just have to be *in*, George simply couldn't project at this juncture. He couldn't be expected to handle everything. All George could do at this stage was to introduce the toad to the lily-pad and see if it croaked.

Even when he was halfway there in the BMW, George wondered whether or not he was doing the right thing. He tried to coach himself into an *advertising* frame of mind, though unsure as to quite what he was selling. It was a very short drive, and he parked just a few doors down. Pocketing a grenade of keys on their big Michelin fob, George reached down and tugged off his driving shoes: very old and scuffed fake Gucci loafers, the wearing of which protected his semi-everyday shoes – also fake Guccis, though very much newer, and the snaffles still shone.

Susan came to the door in what looked like Barry's dressing-gown: stained, no cord. She didn't appear that pleased to see him, and George felt suddenly very intrusive. What the hell am I doing, he thought. It looks like I'm following up the fee for lunch. And what about Barry? And then, the dawning: oh Christ, the dressing-gown! What if she and Barry were . . . and that would explain his absence from work and no one answering the 'phone and oh Jesus, George wished he hadn't come.

'George,' said Susan.

'Hallo, Susan. I was passing and – '

'Come on up.'

'No, really. I was just passing and – '

And then Susan was irritated.

'George, it's bloody cold. Come in if you're coming.'

George stepped in and followed Susan up to the flat and he was still apologising, which was very unlike him, and he hoped Barry wasn't there – although he didn't say so – and he thought, no, she would have said, and her terry-towelled bottom looked pretty good from where he was standing and maybe it would be all right after all.

George was a bachelor and a tidy man and the state of the flat came close to sickening him. Plates and glasses, really dirty – days-old dirty – seemed everywhere and only one light was on and the stale air hung there and just the motion of bodies stirred up the dust into eddies. He had his 'don't be silly' ready for when Susan apologised for the mess, but she didn't so he said instead:

'Well.'

'I'm going out, actually, George. Thanks for the lunch. I meant to call. 'Phone's gone, though.'

George nodded, but it was off the hook, he could see.

'That's fine,' he said. 'I was passing anyway, and I thought, you know, drop in, why not.'

'Glad you did. Barry still at work, is he?'

'Haven't seen Barry, actually. Not today.'

'Oh,' said Susan.

Maybe she's right to leave it, thought George. He didn't particularly want to talk about Barry anyway. Susan smelled lovely – Chanel's Cristalle, if he was any judge – and she leaned across for a cigarette and the gown gaped open and she was wearing delightful peachy frilly little things underneath – either vintage Reger or, like George's shoes, something fairly close.

'I'd offer you a drink . . .' said Susan, and tailed off, indicating the spent Beefeater – on its side, which George thought looked a bit, well, sordid.

'You're having quite a busy day,' said George.

Susan swallowed smoke, but her smile was girlish.

'Not often like this, I assure you.'

George observed her bunching up her left sleeve and stroking her wrist, but he well knew a time check when he saw one, and said:

'I must be off anyway, soon.'

Susan felt a bit sorry for George. Poor soul. Bundled off like this. And he *did* buy her lunch, after all. And George did not quite wish to leave, and felt a little ashamed at saying that he had a bottle of Beefeater in the car, if she was interested, but a bit more encouraged when Susan responded:

'Oh Christ you haven't, have you? That would be absolutely marvellous.'

George flew down the road to the Victoria Wine, and tore off the paper halfway up the stairs.

'It was Gordon's, actually,' he said, just a bit breathlessly. 'Don't know what made me think Beefeater.'

Susan in the meantime had rubbed out a couple of tumblers with a yellow Scottie and had the air, as she cracked open the seal, of not really caring whether the stuff had been recently distilled in a fetid dustbin, just so long as she could get some of it into her glass and down her. She swallowed a shot, and suddenly felt awful about the dreadful mess in 'the room'. She would like to have everything done nicely like Moira, but when it came down to it, there just never seemed to be the hours in the day.

'Salud!' George said, but Susan seemed intent on just drinking the stuff. She did come back with 'Cheers', though, when she put her glass back down.

'Did you want tonic or anything?' she asked. 'I haven't got anything at all, I'm afraid.'

'Oh well, you know,' said George. 'Fine as it is. Hits the spot.'

Susan was drinking two to his one, and seemed gradually more relaxed. The gown fell away from a knee, but George could see that this was no contrivance, which hurt him a bit – or maybe it was a good thing, it was hard to say.

'Jesus!' exclaimed Susan, standing up. 'The time! God, I'm sorry George, but I really have to move!'

And gulping a mouthful of gin, she stage-ran to the bedroom and kicked shut the door behind her which lazily swung back open and Susan had thrown off the dressing-gown and Christ, she was actually wearing a full set of this gorgeous silky underwear even down to the stockings and *real* suspenders which George had only seen on a woman if he'd bought the things himself, and pleaded with her. It happened to be one of George's things, this get-up, and he just strode across and walked into the bedroom and it was clear that Susan was unaware of the open door, for a dress was now half over her head which arched her back wonderfully and her bottom and thighs were caught so tight in this skimpy gossamer and from the rear George just cupped her breasts like hard large eggs even before she knew he was there.

'Oh, Jesus, George,' Susan said into her dress.

George gargled a bit and stuck a hand right up tight between her legs as if he sensed that time was running out, and it was so plump and warm there and then Susan had wrenched away, curse it to hell, and the dress was on the floor, and her face was flushed, teeth slightly bared as she faced him, angry, and she looked so totally arousing by this time

69

that George just gulped and went for her with a low tackle to the knees which knocked her sideways and over the bed with her long, long legs in the air, and George just had time before he went down to wish she was wearing shoes.

Susan wrestled a bit – even beat the back of his head with her fists – and then there was a rip and that was that as far as Susan was concerned.

'Look Jesus Christ Almighty what the hell do you think you're doing, George! They cost a bloody fortune, these things!'

'Mmphlgh,' said George. 'Lovely. Lovely.'

'Look, get up – get up, you – get *up*, George!'

George was wild-eyed.

'I'm trying to!' he wailed. 'Oh God I'm trying!'

And then Susan had had enough, as she often did. She dragged herself free and yanked up George's head between her hands and squeezed and squeezed until George was worried and looked so much like E.T. that Susan laughed ringingly, it was all so absurd! She let him go, and George slumped over the bed, twitching, hiding his face and dribbling a fair deal.

Susan blew out her cheeks, and piled back her hair from her face.

'Jee-sus!' she said, and then, 'Phew!'

She walked back into 'the room' and filled two tumblers very full of gin, and brought them back into the bedroom. She kicked George's ankle, and clamped his fingers around a glass.

'Drink it!' she ordered.

George squirmed around, and avoiding Susan's eyes, drank deep. He sat on the floor with his back against the bed, and Susan found herself tousling his hair, like you would a dog.

'Oh George,' she sighed, in a hopeless sort of way.

George looked up, smirked stupid apology, and placed a

hand on her thigh, as if it were a paw, but it felt so good that he found himself gently stroking and the stockings were silk and Susan – who was drinking gin – raised her hand to hit him but it *did* feel good, with the silk and everything, and that was why she had bought them – the very same day she had bought herself the chrysophrase necklace.

The gin in her glass was gone, and suffused with warmth she just collapsed back onto the bed, flung out her arms and thought oh fuck it, what the hell?

Barry was in The Yorkshireman taking courage and stock of himself. It was so difficult to find a good pub, these days. All the decent Victorian stuff had been sold to Pimlico interior designers and replaced by the fake and ghastly 'Victoriana' – Ronsealed plywood and curtain pole-ends and burgundy Dralon and damn-near psychedelic stained-glass plastic. Nothing new, of course. The rot had been going on for years. Nowadays, most of the seating space had gone for the sake of those bloody computer games, and so irate was Barry with the whole caper that he had tried these sort of cocktaily wine bar places and Frenchified ghettos with names like Le Pub, but they were worse, if anything: phoney Art Deco and Tequila Sunrises and bloody Pina Coladas and witty damn funny Sloe Comfortable Screws, and all at about three quid a throw. Must be mad, whoever buys them. Barry had told most people that he would gladly have settled for a bon Scotch in le quiet corner, but none of this mattered tonight, because it was just a question of a very quick couple before he went round to see Gavin. What he had to do was not going to be easy, but Annie was right: *something* had to be done. And now.

Following his outburst, Barry had gone back to Annie's, as usual, head hung low, saying very little. He didn't know it, but his peremptory ring at the door had thrown Annie into a bit of a turmoil, because just a minute before, her mother had come down the stairs in quest of a jellied chicken breast and Annie had said oh God not *now*, mother, and her mother had said what do you mean, not now – it's my house, isn't it? And Annie had become arch and said that ownership of the property was not in question and Annie's mother had told her not to be so hurtful and not to *push* her, why was she *pushing* her, and she didn't *want* to go back upstairs, she had just come down, and Annie had said that it was for her own good and that she would bring up the chicken in a minute, honestly, and her mother had turned grudgingly back up the stairs, muttering that with Annie *everything* was in a minute and that usually meant hours, and Annie said oh *hurry*, mother, and her mother said she didn't see what all the rush was about, but she went up anyway because Annie was so very forceful when she wanted to be, and she hadn't really wanted the chicken at all, just a change of scenery, just a little chat. Then the bell clamoured and Annie gave her mother a final shove and answered it calmly and Barry slouched in and back to the room and fell into the chair and closed his eyes and when he opened them Annie was there, smiling kind, and so was a drink – very large Bell's, touch of water.

And he drank a few more of these now in The Yorkshireman, his elbow in a pool of keg – which, *damn*, he hadn't noticed – and thinking that Annie talked a lot of sense, and going over their mutual resolves, and also one or two other things that he had not discussed with her because she would not approve – and anyway, they might go wrong, which these days would not have surprised him in the least.

Sometimes, through drink, Barry could see everything so clearly. All the truth, all the fear, all the sheer gut-wrench of it stood stark and luminous and blinding, and it terrified him and so he drank some more and then he could be muddled and slurred like everyone else. Tonight, though, even Barry realised that this state of appalling illumination must not be so lightly dispensed with, but turned to his advantage. His position was dire – there was no other word for it – and with Annie's help, he was going to save himself. It seemed such a very worthwhile thing to do.

The very next morning, he was due to see his bank manager. He was overdrawn to the extent of about eight hundred pounds, maybe nine, and his monthly salary – not due for a week – would be swallowed whole and then what? Two things were needed immediately: cash – just to get him back on his feet – and then a promise of more, just to keep him there. And he had to cut out *this* stuff too, Barry knew, darting hate at his empty glass. That was where most of the money went, these days, and he was sure it couldn't be doing him any good. And even the Game would have to go. Particularly the Game.

Annie knew about his overdraft, but not about the gambling. Nor did she know that he owed other people money – George, mainly. She had given him another hundred tonight. I can't, he had said. Take it, she said. Oh God, he said, and took it. It was a start. Barry's plan – well, Annie's plan, really, but they both would call it Barry's plan – was to go and see DJ, and have a very serious talk. Man to man, Annie had said, to which Barry had responded oh my God in heaven. Tell him, she had said, that you feel quite frankly that you are not being used to your full capacity, and that no man can be expected to live under the shadow of one publishing mistake for the rest of his life. Annie broke off here to intimate that she was damn well sure that DJ had committed some blunders in his time, but then quite properly advised Barry to please not say so.

'As if I would!' snorted back Barry. 'But I'm sure you're right.'

'Get his backing,' Annie had urged. 'And I mean moral as well as financial. You've got to start commissioning again, Barry. You must make an impression on the list. Honestly.'

Barry had nodded eagerly – she had a way with her, Annie – and said he would, first thing tomorrow, and Annie had said, no, silly, not first thing tomorrow – there's the bank; and anyway – don't *jump* into it or you'll mess it up. It's got to be thought about. First, we've got to get a really good idea for a book. Or even a series. Or even – hey, Barry, what about this – an *imprint*?! And Barry had said oh Christ yes, inspired. An imprint! An entirely new in-house name with Barry as Managing Editor, dedicated to up-market but commercial titles specialising, um, specialising in the field of what, exactly, Annie? And Annie had said well, yes, exactly, that's what I mean. It's got to be thought about. She would think about it. Really she would.

'And don't make any promises you can't keep to the bank. Just try and stall them.'

And then Annie – God how he loved that girl – had given him the hundred pounds towards that end. And sitting in The Yorkshireman it was already down to ninety-five, but it didn't matter because now, right now, after another one, Barry was going to do the other thing, and ring up Gavin.

Moira's face was set like cement as she carried the tray from the kitchen, but she sweetened it specially as she entered the room.

'There!' she said, as if delighted by a child. 'I've got your very favourite tonight.'

'Sh,' said Gavin, indicating the television with an irritated hand. 'Just coming up to the end.'

'Thank you, Moira,' hammed Moira, rather recklessly. 'That was very kind *indeed* of you, Moira. How *thoughtful* you are, Moira.'

'Shhh!' hissed Gavin. 'Shhh, can't you?!'

Moira put down the tray, wondering why she bothered sometimes – or ever, even – and that blessed piece of hair

74

flopped over her eyes as the credits for the documentary were rolling.

'Mm!' approved Gavin, with satisfaction. 'Good programme, that. Knows his stuff, that fellow. Done his homework.' 'Course, without the Government grants . . . What the hell is this?'

'Cottage pie, dear. Your favourite.'

'My what? Since when was cottage pie my favourite?'

'You've always *loved* cottage pie!'

'I never said I *loved* cottage pie. I never said I *loved* it. I *like* it,' he granted. 'I quite *like* cottage pie but it's not my favourite, not by a long chalk. I *never* said I loved the stuff.'

'Well anyway. Eat it while it's hot.'

Gavin looked up at her.

'You always say that,' he said.

Moira looked back with open eyes.

'Say what, dear?'

'Eat it while it's hot. You always say that. I mean it's not as if I stubbornly sit staring at every plateful of food you ever put in front of me just waiting for it to coagulate, is it?'

'No, well, it's better hot.'

'I *know* it's better hot. I'm not *disputing* – Christ, Moira. Do you do this on purpose?'

'Do what, dear?'

'Do this – all this – oh, never mind! Where's the pepper?'

'There's pepper in it, Gavin.'

Gavin banged down his knife and fork, and slid up his eyes to the ceiling.

'God Almighty!' he implored. 'Can it never be simple? Just a straight answer to a straightforward question – is that *really* too much to ask?' And looking dead at Moira: 'I didn't *ask* if there was pepper in it, I *know* that. You *always* put pepper in it, I *know* that. I merely wanted to ascertain the whereabouts of the grinder so that I might apply more of the bloody stuff is that too much to ask Christ in heaven?!'

'Don't get excited, dear,' suggested Moira.

'You'd excite a saint!' thundered Gavin, and then more softly, and a little confused, 'No, that's not right . . .'

'I'll get the pepper,' said Moira, and when she was in the kitchen, 'He hasn't even tasted it, the pig.'

Gavin screwed at the grinder as if wreaking a terrible vengeance on all the little peppercorns in the world, and shovelled forkfuls of the pie into his mouth with a glazed, grudging expression on his face and an idly hunched back to demonstrate his indifference to the food, his anger with Moira, as well as a broad dissatisfaction with the world in general.

When the 'phone rang, Moira decided to take it in the room. Normally she hated speaking on the telephone in front of Gavin; it was somehow so inhibiting. But she couldn't be bothered to go into the kitchen again and anyway they might hang up if she wasn't quick and – who knows? – it could be one of Moira's girlfriends (Susan, namely) and so she picked up the receiver – onyx and gilt: pretty, but oh-so-heavy in the hand – and stated her number like an operator.

'Oh it's you, Barry. How lovely.' And aside: 'It's Barry, dear.'

Gavin drew in his chin in an approximation to the initial stages of heaving and stabbed his pie with hate.

'Yes, he is,' said Moira. 'Oh all right, then. Yes. Yes, I'm sure that would be lovely. How's Susan, actually? Barry? . . . Barry? . . . Hello?'

Moira walked back over to the table and picked up Gavin's plate.

'Funny,' she said. 'He seemed a bit . . .'

'He's *always* a bit something,' snarled Gavin. 'A bit bloody gone in the head, if you ask me. What did he want anyway? How's Susan?'

'He's coming over,' said Moira.

'He's doing bloody what? He's not, you know. Put him off. I don't want to see bloody Barry.'

'He's on his way. It's you he wants to see – *I* don't know what about.'

'Well,' announced Gavin, standing, 'he's in for a disappointment because I shan't be here.'

Moira looked up.

'You won't? Why? Why won't you?'

'Out. Work. I told you.'

'You didn't tell me. You didn't say anything about going out tonight. That was *last* night.'

Gavin kissed her forehead.

'*And* tonight. I told you. You don't listen, that's your trouble.'

'Oh, Gavin – do you *have* to go out tonight?'

'*Work,* love. Got to keep the wolf from the door. Must keep my lady wife in all her accustomed finery, mustn't I? Hey?'

'But just *one* night, Gavin!'

Gavin spread his fingers and opened his eyes very wide: totally sincere, out of his hands.

'I gave my word,' he said.

'But Barry!' said Moira. 'What am I going to do about Barry? At least wait until Barry gets here.'

'I have no intention of waiting until Barry gets here. The advent of Barry would only serve to hasten my departure from anywhere on earth. How was Susan, by the way?'

Moira heaved her chest once, without sighing. He was going to go out, and that was that.

'He didn't say,' she said.

'Typical,' tutted Gavin. 'I don't know how she sticks him. Right! I'd best be off.'

And then Gavin touched his midriff.

'God, I feel odd,' he said. 'Do we have any Rennies?'

'In the middle drawer. You eat too quickly, Gavin.'

'I'll pick some up on my way. Can't stop now.'

'Are you sure you'll be all right?'

'Of course I'll be all right. Just a touch of indigestion, that's all.'

'But what shall I say to Barry?'

'Say what you bloody like to Barry. I would suggest "goodbye" for openers. I don't know how she sticks him, I really don't.'

The front door slammed and the Rover revved and the sense of alone came over the house. Which was silly really, Moira admitted, because Gavin was no company at all. Still, at least *someone* was coming over tonight, even if it was only Barry. Anyone was something, these days.

Barry's plan had been to go back to the flat and freshen up a bit – maybe change his shirt, if there was one – and then drive on out to Gavin and Moira's. He started rehearsing what he was going to say, while the Panda was idling at the lights, and then thought no, this is wrong, if it comes out too pat he'll be suspicious; probably will be anyway, as soon as the word money is mentioned. Better just let it happen. On impulse, Barry drove right past his flat, thinking the sooner the better, and then he could have sworn – no, couldn't have been. Was it? He had thought he had seen George coming out of the house. Well, it could have been. George was all right – Barry always said so – and it would be just typical of him to look in and check that Barry was OK. Barry sometimes felt very humbled by George, because Barry would never have thought to look out for anyone but himself. He was lucky to have George around, he concluded – and not just because of the Game and the money and everything.

Barry's plan was a bit wild, even he had to admit, but desperate measures, et cetera. It all centred around Barry bombastic, boneheaded vanity, which seemed to Barry so unconquerable as to render the whole scheme foolproof. It was risky – Barry did not want to jeopardise his job – but he felt sure, reasonably sure, that he could pull it off. And it was not illegal; or at least he didn't think so. And anyway, even if it was just a little bit, it didn't really matter because nobody was going to know. Everything hinged on the fact that so far as Barry was aware, he was the only person on earth who knew that Gavin nurtured a secret and quite preposterous desire to write his autobiography. Even now as he drove through the drizzle, Barry could only smirk. Gavin was a boring minor public school snob, a businessman, a boor, and – what else? Not much, as far as Barry could see. As to culture, Gavin actually prided himself on the fact that unlike inferior people, he did not experience the *need* for books, or music, viewing both of them as crutches supplied by lunatics for the benefit of inadequates. Painting began and ended at the Athena sale, and his views upon anything remotely avant-garde were quite what Barry would have expected. And yet Gavin was only about, what, forty-two? Forty-four, maybe? But he behaved like an old colonel – seeing these silly old philistine bastards as 'class', or something; Barry could never quite work it out. Still, he had better not get too carried away by his contempt for Gavin. After all, he needed him now.

As soon as Gavin had discovered that Barry was 'in the publishing game' as he often put it, he had loudly disclosed that he had often thought of – what was that bloody phrase? – 'penning his memoirs', that was it. Really? Barry had said, for he was considerably more polite in those days. And Gavin had spoken in that maddeningly irritating way of his which suggested that he could not quite decide whether or not to treat the world to such a miracle as the story of his deadly existence, and nowhere was there any hint that he might anticipate problems with either the writing, or the finding of a publisher. Barry carried away the impression that Gavin would have lined up the most eminent in the field and selected the one who grovelled and appeared truly appreciative. 'And it would sell!' he assured Barry. 'A human story. People like that.' Men like Gavin always knew what would sell. Men like Gavin never bought a book from one year's end to the next. 'So if you want a sure-fire bestseller,' Gavin had blustered through whisky, 'you know where to come!'

Joking, of course. Just making conversation. And apart from laughing his head off at the very idea, Barry had never again thought of it, till now. And then there was the clever bit: the point of it all. Stage one was to do what Annie had said: get DJ back on his side – get back the power to commission, plug this imprint business. It was Annie's scheme that had really crystallised the whole thing in his mind. Stage two: commission a couple of sound books by good people and get them cheap. There were always good writers going cheap, you didn't have to look very far. Then slip in Gavin's book – or at least the proposal – even write the bloody synopsis himself if he had to, which he probably would, knowing the sort of long-winded crap that Gavin was likely to submit. And then the chancy bit: explain to Gavin all about the principle of subsidies. Tell him about huge printing costs, and their defrayment. Tell him the cold facts about the economics of smallish print-runs, and then – the clincher, this – tell him about the cost of publicity. Yes Gavin, he would repeat, *publicity*. Barry might even pull George in on this one – a couple of dummy ads, a counter-pack, something like that. At least he could trust George to keep mum. Gavin would be foaming at the mouth by then, Barry just knew it. Suggest five thousand pounds. The businessman in Gavin would be unable to stretch beyond three. Settle for four, publish in the normal way, keep the money, end. And a few drinks for George. The book would bomb, of course, but not until it was published in well over a year's time, and maybe by then Barry could cobble together one or two more successes to cover the deficit – and anyway, to hell with a year's time, Barry needed the money right *now* – and yes, the little light was on in the porch, and as Barry scrunched over the gravel his mouth was pulled with pleasure as he thought right Gavin, you lucky lad, I'm going to make you famous.

'Barry,' said Moira. 'How lovely.'

'Hello, Moira. Christ it's cold out here. You look radiant.'

'Let me take your coat. You feeling all right, Barry? You're not – well, you know, drunk or anything, are you, Barry?'

'Not yet, Moira, not yet. But after a couple of shots of Gavin's malt – you know, the one he hides at the back – who can say?'

Moira elongated her mouth into the putting-up-with-him smile, and said: 'Yes, well, you're very welcome to a drink, Barry, but I'm afraid you've missed Gavin. He's out.'

Barry just stopped in the hall.

'Out?'

'I'm sorry, Barry. He's just gone this minute. You've just missed him.'

'Out? But you said on the 'phone he was in.'

Moira wrung her fingers.

'Well, he was, then. But he had to go out. I forgot. He told me, of course. It's just that I forgot. I'm awfully sorry, Barry, but I had no way of contacting you . . .'

Barry grunted. He was completely and utterly ruined now. He felt so bloody stupid standing in the middle of the hall and Gavin wasn't there. God, he could have done this really well tonight. What a mess.

'Well. I'd better go, then.'

'Well have a drink anyway, Barry,' said Moira.

It looked to her as if he had already had quite a few; it

wasn't that she particularly wanted Barry to stay, but the alternative seemed even worse, tonight.

'OK, then, Moira. I'll have a drink, why not.'

Barry lay on a peacock sofa and thought how much more acceptable the room appeared without Gavin all over it.

'What did you want to see him about?' queried Moira. 'Or shouldn't I ask?'

'You shouldn't ask,' shot back Barry, and then he laughed – more out of pity for Moira than any other reason, poor soul. It was so *easy* with Moira, and she always looked so *hurt*. Mind you, married to Gavin, what did you expect?

'Only joking, Moira – of *course* you should ask. Your house – your husband, after all.'

'I didn't mean to pry.'

Oh God, thought Barry, she's so pathetically humble. What has that man done to her over the years?

'It was about money, Moira. Money money money. Any chance of another drink?'

'Yes, of course, I'm so sorry.'

Barry felt a genuine pang for Moira.

'That's all right, Moira,' he said. 'Aren't you having anything with me?'

'Oh you know me, Barry. I'm not a spirit-person.'

'Well there must be some of that syrup you drink around somewhere. Why don't we open up a bottle?'

'Well . . . I wouldn't mind just a little, as it happens. If you look under the sideboard . . .'

And Barry did, and it was chock-full of the stuff. He opened what looked to him like a good one – why not, poor old Moira; and Gavin was paying – and they sat on opposite sofas and drank. Sort of like old friends. Except that Barry was now drinking towards the blur; the lucid had become chilling and offensive, and he had no further need of it. If he stopped to think, if he stopped the drink, he would become inconsolable.

Moira felt nervous, but more about what she was thinking than anything.

'Well, Moira,' said Barry.

'Well, Barry,' said Moira, who felt she might be getting the hang of this sort of exchange – it was so silly anyway – and they both came quite close to a giggle, which was silly also and, to the best of Barry's recollection, quite without precedent, Barry being not over-given to giggling, and certainly not with Moira, of all people in the world.

'Oh Barry,' sighed Moira. With affection, really. 'Maybe it's just lots of people.'

This sort of chat suited Barry well. He felt comfortable just now with the meaningless.

'What's just lots of people, Moira?' he filled in with ease.

'You know. Not getting on. Friction. I mean – like now. We're perfectly happy, aren't we? I mean, getting on, I mean?'

Barry felt quite expansive. Gavin would be livid when he found all his Glenlivet had gone.

'But we've *always* got on, Moira. Two peas in a pod.'

Moira drank wine, and touched her nose too.

'You're laughing at me,' she laughed.

'Moira, Moira!' – mock chiding – '*would* I, *could* I ever laugh at you?!'

'Oh, Barry!'

'I know, I know – I'm *awful*.'

'Well you are.'

And then, God help him, Barry giggled again, which was plain ridiculous, and Moira joined in and they were looking at each other, a thing they never did.

'I'm sorry about Gavin,' she said.

'Oh you needn't apologise for the existence of Gavin,' waived Barry. 'The world needs Gavins. Salt of the earth. Pillars of the community. I expect he'd have some other phrases as well.'

'No, silly – I mean about him not being here. You knew what I meant – you really are terrible.'

'I am, aren't I? Oh, don't you worry about Gavin. I don't much care about that any more. I'll speak to him sometime, I expect.'

Barry clicked his thumbnail over the diamond ridges in his glass, put it back down on the table, and poured more whisky.

'Oh yes. I'll talk to him.'

'Barry . . .?'

'Hallo?' said Barry, but he hadn't liked the sound of it at all. It was one of those female it's-just-occurred-to-me-can-I-ask-you-a-question-you-won't-mind-will-you lead-ins. And yes, he was sure of it now, because wasn't it just followed up with:

'No. Doesn't matter.'

Now he had a choice. He could either say, well, if it doesn't matter, and tail off – his usual course of action (although in his experience this only led to well it's just that, et cetera, et cetera – they'd say it anyway if they really wanted to, curse them, bitches, law unto themselves, women) – or he could say no, come on, tell me. Say it.

'No, come on, tell me. Say it.'

'Well, it's just what you said earlier. You know.'

'Earlier? What I said earlier? What did I say earlier, actually, Moira? That was a hell of a lot of booze ago.'

'You know.' And then Moira forced out the word. 'Money.'

'Ah!' Barry was all comprehension. 'Money, yes. Root of all evil. Filthy lucre.'

And then the whisky crushed his cheeks and he looked tearful and whispered:

'Christ I wish I had some. Oh God I do.'

Moira sat forward and concern was on her face, but also something else as well – Barry was damned if he knew what the hell. Her eyes were bright. It almost looked as if she was scheming something or other – unthinkable, of course. Moira was all right, innocuous, but a perfectly hopeless dullard. Naïve. Didn't see things head-on, the way they really were.

'So you're a bit short, are you?' she said.

Barry drank.

'About five-foot-nine. Pretty average.'

'Barry, don't be silly. I mean it. I'm being serious. Maybe I can help.'

Barry smiled and he felt small. A hint of the old acid crept back into his voice.

'Are you *very* rich, then, Moira?'

Moira plumped up cushions, which meant that she was going to behave as if she was offended until Barry apologised or at least became serious.

'Sorry, Moira,' said Barry. 'Only joking.'

'But I really *do* mean it, Barry. I mean, I'd hate to think of Susan – I mean, you and Susan – '

'Oh! Susan!'

'And you, Barry.'

'No, not me. Nothing to do with me at all, really, is it, Moira?'

Moira threw a cushion full at him, which was an amazing thing for Moira to do because she always said she couldn't bear them wrinkled.

'What the hell?!' yelped Barry, very amused except that he had beaten off the thing and knocked over the bloody Sauternes.

'Oh Christ I'm sorry, Moira.'

And then to Barry's disbelief – he hadn't drunk *that* much surely? – instead of clucking around with a J-cloth and saying that Gavin would be furious, Moira marched over with purpose, sat right next to Barry on his sofa, actually got his face in her hands – in her *hands*, for Christ's sake, he'd never felt her hands – and said:

'For the last time, Barry, I *mean* it. I can help you. We can help each other.'

'If you say so, Moira. You're hurting my face.'

Moira did not let go, but slackened the compress. A finger idled beneath Barry's eye.

'Tired?' she said.

'What?'

'Are you tired? Your eyes look tired.'

What the hell was this now? Barry was guarded.

'Quite tired, I suppose. No more than usual. Don't sleep much these days.'

'Poor Barry,' said Moira.

Barry sensed the hairs in and around his ears growing away from him, and not just because Moira was teasing them; or maybe wholly so, he didn't know.

'What are you doing, Moira? I mean, what exactly do you think you're doing? That wine's going to ruin the carpet, you know – leave a mark. What the hell are you up to Moira?'

Moira put her hand flat on Barry's chest, and drew it down to his stomach and pressed, which proved very uncomfortable as Barry was all hunched up and the whisky was playing merry hell anyway. Acidic.

'I've got money,' she said.

Moira's eyes were glistening with a quite ferocious intensity and her face was so close to Barry's that he had to try to pull away just in order to be able to focus. Her features swam and shifted and yet he felt impaled upon those white lights in her eyes. It was really most extraordinary.

'I've got money,' she said again. 'Lots of it. How much do you want?'

Barry made an attempt: 'Oh, lots will be fine.'

And then she hit him. She did. She drew back her arm and it came down on him unbent and his mouth was open in disbelief and Christ her entire palm and wrist caught him a ringing blow all down the side of his head and his brains were rattled and his eyes were red-hot with a boneless and bulging pain.

'Now just shut up,' commanded Moira. 'And listen.'

Barry was rubbing his face and babbling badly.

'Jesus, Moira, Jesus! I mean Jesus for Christ's sake Moira, Jesus!'

'I *said*,' she repeated with intent, with damn-near cruel eyes, '*listen!*'

And Barry felt awesomely and deliciously defeated. How very strange, he thought.

'I'm listening,' he said, overtly subdued.

Moira nodded, and moved a little away.

'I have got money. Plenty. You appear to need some. Take it.'

'Very kind,' muttered Barry, more scared than he could ever remember.

'All that I require – '

'Look, Moira, I've got to go. I think we've both probably drunk far too much, it's very late, and let's just forget that anything happened and I'll just – '

'Barry,' said Moira quietly. 'I'll kill you if you interrupt me again.'

He felt so drunk and amazed. He said nothing at all.

'You,' went on Moira, 'must service me.'

Barry sat up and she pushed him back.

'I must what?!' he shrieked, urging himself forward again.

'You heard,' said Moira simply. And she pushed him back into the cushions. 'I have one thousand pounds actually in this house. In cash. It's yours. Just earn it. You can *earn* it, can't you?'

Barry had stopped the outrage. It was silly, and only a convention, anyway. He supposed, if he was honest, that he had understood sentences ago. What the hell did this make him, then? And now they were discussing the price.

'Of course,' Moira went on conversationally, 'I have a lot more than a thousand. Gavin,' she sighed, 'has been very generous.' She looked up. 'I'm lonely,' she said. 'But I expect you knew that.'

Barry was caught by the new tone, now.

'Well, I didn't, actually, Moira. I always thought that you and Gavin – '

'Yes, I know. Everyone does. Captain of industry: little woman. Sickening, isn't it? Anyway.'

And she put her hand back on his stomach, wriggling two fingers under his waist band and Barry shifted – for his own comfort really – and this helped Moira and she got her fingers around him and lifted his hand up to her breast and their faces were close – and suddenly, nothing happened at all.

They looked at each other, Barry and Moira, and the whole situation seemed lost. Fat tears welled up in Moira's eyes and Barry was more scared than touched.

The spattering crackle of gravel hitting the window sobered Barry like a douche and he was up and startled as an animal. The car door slammed and the front door clattered open and Barry thought oh God save me and Gavin lurched into the room crippled and ugly and God, he looked so *green*. His face was bloated and blotchy and his eyes were nearly closed and puffed out like bubbles of flesh and he was holding on to his stomach as if it would fall away. Barry had got him under the arms but Gavin could not tell him what was wrong and Moira was shaking and concerned and they carried him upstairs and he was so heavy and he grabbed at Moira's pearls to save him falling and they exploded and ricocheted everywhere and Barry near broke his neck by treading on them and it could have been the end if he had lost his footing. Gavin just lay stock still and cold in his bed, save for his chest which was heaving like a bellows.

Barry's fingers were glycerine and he couldn't control his

breathing. Moira was on her knees by Gavin, smoothing his face.

'Christ!' expelled Barry. 'We've got to get a doctor fast. It looks like – Christ – it looks like he's *dying*.'

Moira looked up like a staff sister.

'You go off now, Barry. I'll see to it.'

'But Christ – '

'It's all right, Barry. Not the first time. I can deal with it.'

Barry hovered.

'Go, Barry!'

'But – '

Moira turned on him.

'Get out of here, for God's sake! I can handle it, I tell you!'

Barry backed off, more jangled than he could say.

'And Barry!' Moira called back at him, quite like Moira again, 'don't forget. Don't forget, will you? We've got plenty to give each other.'

If he had stayed another moment, he would have fallen over. He had no recollection of the stairs. The front door clanged behind him, maybe not shut. He drove the Panda far too fast, the lights boring ahead of him as white and cold as moonbeams.

After the street-lights began to blind him, Barry pulled into the forecourt of a pub. He ordered a large Drambuie: a perfectly preposterous drink in the circumstances, but it was an impulse thing that he did sometimes; sure to make him sick later on. He had not lingered. Sleep was what was needed. He thought he would not go to Kensington because Annie would know that something appalling had happened and she would ask and ask and ask about it and Barry felt so weak he'd end up telling her and that would be too dreadful to contemplate. Anyway, Camden Town was nearer and he really did need sleep. He was not going to think – couldn't anyway. He'd had it all worked out. What the hell had happened? And Gavin! Christ – his face! Barry had never seen anything like it. And Moira. What could Barry possibly think about Moira? Or himself, for that matter. What would Barry have done if – no, he was not going to think about it. Couldn't anyway. Sleep – that was the answer. Don't think of today, and don't have time to dread tomorrow. Sleep. Just sleep.

Halfway up to the flat, Barry knew that apart from anything else he felt, he was very, very, drunk. Which was welcome, just now. He'd be unconscious within minutes, and tomorrow could look after itself. It *would* just happen, then, that Susan was still up when Barry walked in. All the lamps were on in 'the room', which was unusual, and Susan was standing in the middle of the floor (odd) and there was a lovely smell – what was it? Scent? And that too was very odd and what the hell was that on Susan's face? She looked, what – stunned? Yes, stunned. And pale.

'Susan?' Barry ventured.

Susan just stared back at him, blanched and rigid. And was she shaking? It was not cold in the room. Then she sat down and then she stood up. She was wearing something long and satin that Barry had not seen before and she held onto her arms just above the elbow. She seemed very frightened. *Did* she seem very frightened? Barry was so terribly tired. He wouldn't even try to work out this one. He would just go to bed. Go to sleep.

Screwing up his eyes in anticipation of the abrasive lighting in the bedroom, he turned the handle of the door and oh God *why* wouldn't it turn and he turned it the other way and nothing happened and Barry thought oh *Jesus* will this day never end? Why must even the inanimate be so goddamned bloody difficult?!

'Susan,' he groaned. 'What's wrong with the door?'

Susan smoked a cigarette, her fingers white and stiff as sticks.

'Barry, why don't you take a walk? Just a short walk? Please, Barry. Come back in ten minutes.'

Barry gazed at her, and his mind just clouded into stupidity.

'What? . . . Look, I don't know what's going on here, and I don't much care. I've had one hell of a day and I just want to get some sleep. You can stay up all night if you want – *you* take a bloody walk!' And then the anger came. '*Walk*?! What the hell do I want a bloody *walk* for?! I've been wandering around like a nomad all day and I just want to get some sleep in my own bed in my own bedroom – right?!'

And Barry renewed with clumsy energy his attempts to twist open the bloody door.

'What the *hell* . . .' he hissed.

'It's locked,' said Susan, coldly.

Barry turned around, feeling so outside *understanding*.

'It's what? It's locked?'

Susan nodded curtly, thrust one fist into a pocket, and smoked hard, the burning end becoming a long hard glowing coal.

'Well . . .' murmured Barry, lost until the logic came. 'Well, unlock it, then.'

'No.'

'What do you mean – no?'

'I don't want you to go in there.'

A filtering gauze of something cancerous seeped into Barry's brain, just behind his eyes. His stomach revolted within him, and his whole body became tensed against more.

'Who's in there?' he said, the echo of it hitting him.

Water spluttered straight out of Susan's eyes, and her teeth closed over her lip.

'Please, Barry! Just five minutes! Just come back in five minutes and it'll be all right, I swear it!'

91

Barry could not get even a part of his mind around this, so it could not be happening. But he boiled with coldness in his very guts and felt sober and demented and savage.

'You little bitch . . .'

Susan wailed like an animal.

'You fucking little *bitch* . . .!'

Susan's arms were up and flinching as Barry hurled the telephone across the room, the cord tugging it back in the air down into a table where it fractured open and clattered across the dented surface, the receiver purring placidly, and cutting off, dead.

Barry snorted like a maddened bull, and turned back to confront the door. As if his eyes were bleeding he tightened them against the scarlet blur. He thudded his body sideways again and again against the panels of the door until he was damn near spent and Susan was scrabbling at his legs and he was roaring and then he thought of *George*, then he remembered *George* in the street, *George* – not *George*, not bloody *George*, the two-faced bastard! And more force came from somewhere and he'd kill him! He'd kill him! He'd kill him! The door splintered open and Barry spun drunkenly into the room and that bastard was hiding under the sheets, the bastard, and Susan clawed him back as he snarled and spat and near choked in his effort to reach that bloody bed he'd kill the bastard when he got to that bed and he tore the sheet into the air and collapsed with raised fists into the bed and wrenched around the fucking bastard's shoulders and glowered with seething hate and an insane confusion at a face that he had never before seen in his entire bloody life.

Chapter Four

BARRY SPENT THE night in the Panda. He held on to the wheel, only knowing how cold it was. The night spat at him, gobbets of rain slapping the windows and heavily pounding the roof. He sat for hours without moving, awash and alone, trapped in some mad child's tin drum. The window seals were oozing and the din turned to a pummelling drone and he woke soon after dawn, his chin hard up against the dash. He drove to the office, which was closed, and he waited. He had never seen the big oak doors swung open before. It was just after eight, and Barry was grateful to move, and yet reluctant to leave the car. Clucking his mouth to rid or assimilate the taste, he walked stiffly up the steps and through to the lift, more deeply asleep than ever in the night. He didn't even feel terrible.

'Morning, Mr Turville. Lovely day for it.'

'Morning, Len.'

Every office on the floor was empty, thank the Lord. Barry went straight to the lavatory and his eyes looked so swollen and hurt, asking him all sorts of questions, and his mouth wouldn't shut for dryness. He dabbed a bit of water on those poor old eyes which stung and even made him cry a bit and his lips trembled with – what? Hurt? More injustice. Bereavement.

George kept a cordless Philishave in his desk, Barry knew, and he made for it now. There was George's desk, just as always. Dead packets of Marlboro and shiny hand-outs. Christ, Barry felt bad about George. How could he have thought that of dear old George? But then, it had been one hell of an evening. Nothing was unbelievable, really, and yet giving credence to any single thing seemed more than naïve – it seemed stupid. Illogical. Truth had become at least an unlikelihood.

Barry crushed up the polystyrene cup after quickly swallowing the coffee – shit, it really *was* shit – from the machine. Either he had punched the wrong button, or it was not delivering sugar. The sugar helped out, usually.

He must have slept at his desk. He remembered a scuffling in the Xerox room, but everything else seemed quiet and so he eased back his mind into a quirky oblivion. A bang startled him, and then there was whistling. Maintenance. Maintenance on the Xerox. And that could take all morning, Barry knew. It was the whistling that killed him. That damn trill, near operatic warble as the man went through snatches of an eclectic repertoire, with those smug little twiddly bits beloved by people who did that. Barry thumped the partition, which stopped the cretin in mid-bar, and then came a falsetto 'Allo?!' and then again like a toucan 'Allo?!' and Barry hugged his whole head in his arms before the next 'Allo?!' and 'Allo?!' and 'Allo?!' and Barry's mouth was full of sleeve and he couldn't cry.

'You all right, Mr Turville?'

Barry looked up like a drunk, but he wasn't drunk.

'What?'

A typist, or a junior, or a temp, or some such thing, looked down at him. She was wearing the expression that she had seen on American television, used to denote gentle concern. Her head was cocked to one side as if she was trying to understand a kitten, and she kept one hand on the door. She looked so young, Barry thought, with her mail-order Thai silk and

94

thin silver jewellery. One-size tights and 4711. Boots No. 7 and Dr Scholl. Green apple and Loseley yoghurt. Season ticket and Luncheon Voucher. Boy called Dave and late-night Thursday shopping. Benidorm and Je Reviens.

'Mr Turville? Shaw yaw OK?'

'Who are you?'

'Shirley's had a baby.'

Barry screwed down his eyes. Either his forehead was heated or his fingers had died with the cold.

'What?' he said. 'What?'

'Shirley. Little boy. Seven and a half pounds.'

Even Barry was forced to twist away a corner of his mouth at the cruel, silly humour of the thing.

'Not guilty,' he said.

The girl tightened her grip on the handle.

'I'm sorry?' she accused, with nerves.

'I say that that is one thing for which I may definitely not be held responsible. Never even met her.'

Barry was yawning with words, but it was waking him up. The girl flicked back her hair. Harmony and Carmen Rollers.

'Silly!' she chided. 'Shirley's in Sales! I'm getting up a collection. For the baby!'

'For the baby,' repeated Barry, flatly.

'Most people are giving fifty pee,' suggested the girl.

'Then most people must be bloody mad!' shouted Barry suddenly, with a lemon-peel of a smile again when the girl twitched with shock. 'I've never heard of Shirley. I don't know who Shirley *is*, and nor do I have the slightest doubt that she remains in total ignorance of me. I for one find that state of affairs to be perfectly excellent. I would not wish to poison so splendid a working relationship with a paltry fifty pee. Go, wish Shirley and her baby well, and shut the door quietly behind you.'

95

The girl's eyes were like soup-plates, though infinitely more frightened.

'*Shaw* yaw all right, Mr Turville?'

But already she was rehearsing her stifled guffaws over that loony Turville down the passage, and anyway, Barry had tired of RADA, and the pain was seeping back. He dropped his eyes and sighed. He had to be rid of her now.

'Oh, go away,' he husked, more from his throat than his lips.

When he was next awoken, the hum of the office was well established. All those noises of work had been activated by some programmed mainspring, it seemed to Barry, and yet computers almost certainly possessed no component so comprehensible as a spring, he supposed – or was all this nonsense? And then a bustle and a rustle of papers right outside, and Barry's neck was upright and he opened his eyes like a disinterested teller and glanced through the in-tray – disinterested, but professional. It was Annie.

'Annie! O God, Annie!'

'You're back!' said Annie in surprise. 'I just came to leave you a note. Rather soppy, really.'

Again Barry's skull was stuffed with foam. Back? What did she know? How could she know?

'Back?' he said.

Annie nodded eagerly and then she smelled something and looked at him with half her eyes.

'Oh Barry! You didn't forget? You *can't* have forgotten?'

Barry flattened his brow with a palm and tried very hard to concentrate. If only he could ring her back on this one. But he just could not get hold of it, and all he could do was look up for help.

'Annie, I'm awfully sorry, I just don't know what – '

'The bank! The bank, Barry! You *can't* have forgotten!'

Barry shut his eyes tight, opened them, and looked at his watch. Ten past eleven. Appointed at bank: ten a.m.

'Christ, Annie, I'm sorry. I'm just – look, it's a long story – '
'Oh, Barry!'

Annie was close to tears with disappointment. What she knew – what she hadn't told him the night before – was that his job, his whole future, was hanging on a thread. She had heard talk. If he didn't do something soon . . .

'Anyway,' she rallied. He did look pretty rough, poor thing. No sense in going *on*. 'When have you booked to see DJ?'

Barry bit his lip.

'Ah,' he said.

'Oh God, Barry – you don't mean you haven't done that either! I just don't understand you, Barry, sometimes! Last night you *agreed*. You *know* how important it is! How *can* you back out now? What's *wrong* with you, Barry?!'

'Oh God I'm sorry, Annie – it's not like it looks. Honestly. I've really had a hell of a time, really. Look – as soon as I get back, I'll go straight in and see DJ's secretary – June, isn't it? Really, love. I swear it. Honestly.'

'What's wrong with now?' pouted Annie. Why didn't he *see* how important this was? What was *wrong* with him?

'Well, actually, I was just slipping out for a half of Bell's – '
'Oh – Barry!'

Annie turned in the middle of her shriek of exasperation and collided with George, who affected having been winded and said:

'Whoops! Sorry! Lovers' tiff. Bad timing.'

Annie walked right past him, and Barry sat down hard in the chair.

'Oh Christ, George,' he said.

'Sorry, Barry. Just wanted a word.'

'Can't it wait, George? There are a couple of things I've got to – oh bloody hell, George! Why is everything . . . why does everything have to be so . . .?'

George nodded and felt worse.

'Yorkshireman?' he said. ''Bout one?'

Barry nodded and said: 'Thanks, George.'

George tightened his mouth and hustled out thinking Christ, George, I hate you, you bastard. How could you do this to Barry? As if he didn't have enough on his plate, poor sod.

'Oh Hilary!' whined Susan. 'Hilary, Hilary, Hilary!'

Hilary was seated in the lotus position on a Conran dhurrie in the centre of the room. She stared at TV-AM, the sound turned down. Vivaldi played into her Walkman, the yellow pads comforting her ears. She wanted to hear Vivaldi, she didn't want to listen to Susan, and she was suffering from a physical congestion that heralded the feeling that she always experienced the very day before she was due to undergo severe pre-menstrual tension. She sliced another triangle of Lymeswold and put it into Nicholas' mouth.

'I've still got banana!' he spluttered through a yellow mess.

'Cheese is good for you,' said Hilary, who hadn't heard.

Susan was miming at her, and the Vivaldi was ruined anyway, now. Hilary removed the headset, and sighed.

'I don't know what you're making such a fuss about anyway!'

'Fuss! Jesus, Hilary, you can't be serious! Barry saw! He saw him! He was there!'

Hilary deliberately lidded her eyes into laziness.

'So?'

Susan was stung with anger and hurt. Her face twisted away as if it had been slapped.

'No good talking to you at all when you're like this. You can be so cold.'

Nicholas looked up through a heavy fringe and John Lennon glasses.

'I think it's hot in here,' he piped.

98

Susan snapped on that taut smile that she used for children, wishing Hilary would say Not Now, Nicholas, or Don't Interrupt, Nicholas, or – better still – Go and Hang Yourself, Nicholas, but she didn't. She wouldn't. It would stifle him, Hilary said. Susan had wanted to, often.

'Barry'll simmer down,' said Hilary.

'Oh for God's sake, Hilary! Why do you have to *be* like this! You can't be as sophisticated as all that, you just can't. I dare say I'm being very bourgeois about the whole thing – '

'Bourgeoise,' corrected Hilary. 'Yes.'

' –*geoise*, then – but Christ, this is a – thing, what do they call it – *crisis* – *watershed*. I felt so cheap – is that wrong? I mean it's one thing to be unfaithful – '

'What's unfaithful?' asked Nicholas.

Why doesn't she shut that brat up, thought Susan with bitterness.

'In this particular context,' explained Hilary, with just the approved pedantry, 'unfaithful means when a husband or a wife sleeps with someone other than their husband or their wife.'

Nicholas wrinkled his nose, and put a finger into it.

'Sleeps?' he enquired, puzzled.

'Oh God,' said Susan.

'Well,' went on Hilary 'not *sleeps*, exactly . . .'

'Oh I know,' burst in Nicholas with pride. 'You mean fornication!'

Hilary beamed with pleasure as Susan was nearly sick into the muesli.

'Good, Nicholas!' approved Hilary. 'Very good!'

'But Hilary!' pleaded Susan, trying to ignore this new and surreal element. 'What should I do?! O God, I'm so – I feel so – oh Christ, what should I *do*!?'

'Nothing,' said Hilary.

'Lego,' suggested Nicholas.

99

'That's not what Susan meant,' said Hilary.

'I see,' nodded Nicholas, who seemed to.

'Have some more tea,' offered Hilary. 'For God's sake.'

'Yes, thanks, I think I will. Is it Lapsang?'

'Darjeeling.'

'It's very good.'

'It is rather. Yes.'

And Susan started crying, just as Hilary feared she would. It was difficult enough in the mornings without all this. Nicholas was up and grinning.

'Kleenex, anyone?'

'Go and get your shoes on, Nicholas,' said Hilary. 'Stop it, Susan.'

Susan wailed and dabbed her eyes on the tablecloth, which upset the milk.

'I've *got* my shoes on,' said Nicholas.

'Well coat, then,' from Hilary, who was thinking oh, bugger this. She supposed, though, she ought to make some sort of effort on Susan's behalf. Just take one look at her, poor soul.

'Nicholas will be collected by Ariadne soon,' soothed Hilary. 'It's her week on the rota.'

Susan nodded, and sobbed her gratitude for that, at least. A hooter hooted outside and Nicholas shouted from the hall:

'It's Ariadne with that ghastly child of hers!'

'Off you go, then, Nicholas!' hailed Hilary. 'Have a fruitful day!'

'Goodbye, Hilary!' called back Nicholas.

"Bye Nick,' said Susan. ' –olas. I meant Nicholas – honestly I did, Hilary. Don't hate me – I need you.'

The front door slammed.

'Have some tea,' said Hilary. Here we go, she thought.

'I'm bursting with tea,' drivelled Susan with misery. 'I feel so – oh God – I feel so – '

'Oh Christ put an adjective to it, for the love of God!'

snapped Hilary. This social work thing, she recognised, really wasn't her line. 'You've been saying "you feel so – you feel so – " since you got here. About two hours ago,' she added deadpan. 'You feel so *what*, for Christ's sake?!'

'Oh Hilary!' screamed Susan. 'Oh Hilary, please! Be nice, please be nice, Hilary. Be nice to me, be nice!'

'Be quiet,' said Hilary, who felt a bit bad about it, actually, but it was plainly Susan's fault. Everyone knew that Hilary was no good at all, first thing.

Susan lit yet another cigarette, and the smoke cut into a throat rasped by choking sobs and a night of gin. She shivered a bit, and smoked more slowly, her eyes on her hand as she consciously regained control, then flashing up in momentary apology.

'It's OK,' acknowledged Hilary.

'I wish I could be like Moira,' said Susan. 'She's so very happy. Bit dull, I know – but she has everything she wants. She always seems so *contented*.'

Hilary nodded. 'Ignorance is bliss,' she agreed.

Susan dabbed her eyes upwards – more to save the black liner than blot the wet – and she sort of laughed.

'Unlike you to use a cliché,' she sniffed.

'I thought in this case,' Hilary smiled, 'apposite. Nothing, but *nothing*, could ruffle the calm of Moira's little world. The middle class begins and ends with Moira.'

'I know what you mean,' conceded Susan, becoming really rather conversational, 'but I mean – well, we're *all* middle-class, really, aren't we?'

'*You* may be,' grunted Hilary – rather offended, Susan thought.

'No – I didn't mean, I didn't mean to – I mean – oh, you *know* what I mean, don't you, Hilary?'

'No,' said Hilary. 'It's not so much a question of background these days as *attitude*. It's all a matter of approach.'

'Well, yes, no, I see what you mean. But less semantically speaking, if we discount the, well, working class – which we are not – '

'Right,' agreed Hilary.

' – and the upper class – Queen and so on – well, everything else is in the middle, isn't it? And that's us.'

'There is middle – ' began Hilary.

'Oh I know! There's middle and middle, of course. But still, broadly speaking, it probably means everyone we – well, I – know. Don't you think?'

Hilary shifted. The conversation was stupid anyhow. Susan was getting carried away with herself – but Hilary had ways to deal with that sort of thing.

'Anyway,' she said abruptly. 'What has all this to do with your getting screwed?'

Susan's face deflated. Good. Hilary could not bear it when she became so bloody pedagogic. It was as if she thought Hilary was a child, or like *her*, or something.

'Oh, Hilary! What should I *do*!'

This was much more like it.

'Leave him,' said Hilary.

'Leave who?'

'Well, I meant Barry, of course. But the other bloke, if you like – I don't know. How should I know? What did you say his name was?'

'I didn't.'

Hilary stiffened. 'I see,' she said. 'Well of course, if you don't *trust* me . . .'

'Oh it's not that, Hilary – it's just that – '

' – you don't trust me. Quite.'

'No!'

'Sounds like it to me.'

'No really it's not. I do, of course I do. Of course I trust you, Hilary. I don't mind telling you his name – '

'Seems you do. Anyway, I'm not that interested. One man is much like another. Is he rich?'

Susan looked down.

'You're not helping me, Hilary.'

The smoke of a Gitane filtered up through Hilary's teeth.

'I don't care,' she said.

Susan felt a child again. And in the wrong, somehow.

'I'll go, then.'

Hilary crushed and bent over the Gitane into a Mason's saucer.

'You do that,' she said.

Susan near-shuffled out, feeling so grubby and dejected. The only thing that had got her through the night was the thought that she could talk to Hilary in the morning. But it just wasn't *soothing* at Hilary's any more. There wasn't that sense of peace. Sometimes it seemed almost as if Hilary resented her presence and it never used to be like that. Susan *knew* that Hilary had problems too – who didn't? – but this was really a time when a friend should help out, wasn't it? Or was it? Was it wrong of Susan to burden Hilary with her own self-doubt? No, surely not. That was what friends were for: everyone said so.

Hilary just watched her go. It crossed her mind to call her back, but Hilary really didn't want her back. Susan was all right, at times, but she never recognised anything outside her own tedious little universe, as far as Hilary could see. There was no conversation any more with Susan. Their talk took the form only of a catalogue of her dreary doings or else something too damn close to a Roman Catholic confession. Hilary felt, well – *used* by Susan, these days. And she was frankly getting a bit fed up with it. And what did Susan care about Hilary's problems? Or did she think she didn't have any, if she thought that far at all? We couldn't *all* be like Moira, happy and blind in her own double-glazed Dralon little world.

Hilary scooped back her hair and started stacking up plates, putting a thumb in the Vintage Oxford – a thing she hated doing. God, that Susan could really drink tea. There was never any left when Susan had been. Hilary pressed her stomach inwards and then upwards, probing with her fingers. Yes, the little bastard was still there, hard as a stone. And now the man she had been seeing every single Friday night for as long as she could remember had suddenly announced that he didn't want to any more. Just didn't want to. Oh well. No loss. All men were the same. But she'd miss him. And Susan didn't know *his* name either – so there. Oh sod. It was such a fearsome world. Maybe Susan was right to worry about the Bomb and the future and so on, Hilary didn't know. Or maybe the Bomb would be a *cleansing* process – scouring the world of all that was foul. The prejudice. Apartheid. Oppression. And then there was Nicholas; his future was important. He was proving so very *responsive*. And yet, did she wish him to grow up in an ugly, cruel and violent society, where every motivation was towards money, and greed, and the urge to destroy? Oh sod. Why didn't people see sense? Where was reason, art, beauty? Why was everyone's first thought one of destruction, one of negatives? Oh sod. Sometimes Hilary felt she'd like to blow the whole planet to buggery.

'Large gin and Slimline, large Bell's, please.'

Barry had said that a few times now. Five, maybe. Had someone enquired rhetorically 'Who's counting anyway?' Barry might have become indignant – even bellicose – and retorted 'Not me, that's for sure!'

'I've given up making cocktails,' he said, in a profound yet at the same time distracted sort of way, which implied to George that he was talking of something other; but then, George was very much on his guard. 'They just don't seem to work. Anyway – can't afford all the stuff, these days. I find that the best thing you can add to a whisky is a little more. A little bit more.' Barry's mouth turned down. 'God, I hate the stuff. It must be killing me.'

He added a touch of water and swallowed the Bell's in two, thinking just one more and should I tell George? How do you *tell* somebody a thing like that? That you walked into your own bedroom and . . . ! Even now Barry could barely believe it. Each time he had woken up during that dreadful morning in the office, his mind had awaited the delicious relief when a black and ugly demon recedes into the clammy dark, only to be double-damned by its reasserting itself with kicks and needles. Should he tell George? Why, though? What *for*? What good would it do to tell George – or anyone, for that matter? He couldn't help. It would only embarrass the man. What could he say, poor bugger? George didn't even *know* Susan – they'd only ever exchanged a couple of words. No. He wouldn't mention it. It wouldn't be fair to burden him. No. He'd keep it to himself. Work it out. Be a man.

'Oh Christ, George, what am I going to do I've got such an awful bloody problem I'm so bloody distraught oh Christ oh Christ oh George!'

George put down his gin and started whispering comfort and enquiry, but had to raise his voice over the lunchtime pub-din.

'Hey hey hey, Barry!' he roared. 'What's this, what's all this? You tell your uncle George. It can't be all that bad. If it's money – well, I'm a bit short, but I can stretch, say – '

'No,' gasped Barry. 'Not money. Well, yes – I do still have the money thing, of course, oh Christ – I'm broke, but that's not it. That's not it.'

George thought Oh Great. Not with malice – but the chance of helping Barry out was too wonderful for words. Make him feel better about yesterday. Oh God, he felt so bad about yesterday. Good too, though.

'What is it, then?'

'I'm not sure if I – maybe this just isn't the place.'

'What?'

'I said maybe this just isn't the – oh, never mind.'

'What? I'm sorry, Barry, but I can't hear a word you're saying. Maybe we should go back to the office.'

'No. No, not the office. I don't want it getting all round the office.'

'Well *tell* me then, for God's sake. It's clearly getting to you, whatever it is.'

'It's Susan,' said Barry.

George had been looking at Barry with concern, but he had to look away now thinking Jeeeeeeesus what do I do now how do I handle this one think boy think but hang on he can't know because if he knew why would he be telling me oh Christ I'd better say something what I mustn't be is *nervous*.

'What?' said George.

'Susan,' mumbled Barry.

George had not heard that either, but he got the gist.

'What about Susan?' he probed. 'Your wife, you mean?' he added, feeling at least two things: shit of the year, and really very confused. Was Barry *testing* him? Barry couldn't be *testing* him, surely?

Barry formed the words:

''Nother man,' he said.

Game's up, then, thought George. Bloody hell. It wasn't a very *long* game, was it? And yet, why would Barry . . . ? He *wasn't* testing him, was he? No, you just had to look at his face. He needed a friend now, poor old sod. He obviously knew, but he didn't know who. What should George do? What *should* George do? What would make him look best – or at least not too bad? What could he *say*?

'Have another drink, Barry.'

'Oh, I don't know. I feel a bit – oh, OK. Just the one. Make it a large one, could you George?'

George meddled around at the bar, flying a fiver and trying to think think think. What were the possibilities? Had he left something at the flat, maybe? Lighter? No, he had his lighter. Cufflink? No, George never wore cufflinks. Had Susan confessed to Barry? Surely not. Why should she do that? To hurt him, maybe. Or maybe she was drunk; she had been, quite. What seemed clear – and it was about the only thing that did – was that Barry didn't know who. Could George bear to string him along? Could he do that to a friend? Well. Yes. He supposed so.

'Here we are, Barry. I put in a touch of water.'

Barry stared at the glass.

'Bloody stuff,' he said. 'Anyway, George, there we are. Fact. You're lucky being a bloody bachelor, you know. I wish to God I was. But I don't really – that's the trouble. I love Susan, George. Damn her. Damn the bitch. I mean – oh God I'm sorry about this, George – really agony page muck. I really mustn't do this to you. You don't even *know* Susan.'

George had never before felt like he felt just then. He *had* to tell him. He *had* to tell him. Make a clean breast. He just *had* to.

'Maybe you're wrong about her. About it all,' he said.

Barry shook his head in misery.

'Not wrong,' he said. 'I saw.'

George swallowed gin. It was coming, then.

'Saw what?' he whispered.

'What?'

'I said – saw what? What did you see?'

'Christ, George – this is painful enough for me, you know. You don't have to be so *crude*, do you? What do you want – a blow-by-blow account?'

George was muddled. He did not want to say too much, and yet he felt rather outside all this. Cross-purposes.

107

'Sorry, Barry. I didn't mean ... I just meant ...' Christ almighty what *did* he mean? 'Look, if you don't want to talk about it ...' Oh shit.

'No no, George. It's just a bit raw, that's all. I find it hard to ... it's very difficult to say it, you see. But if I don't talk, I'll go mad. I really think I might be going a little mad, you know, with this on top of everything else.'

And Barry turned to George, his eyes imploring assurance that what he was about to say was a lie.

'I *saw* him, George. I was *there*!'

'You were *there*!' repeated George, shaken white. He *can't* have been there! What did he mean he was *there*? He *can't* have been!

'I saw him,' repeated Barry, more dazed than drunk. And then, as his eyes began to weep without tears: 'I ... *touched* him.'

Was Barry mad? Was George going mad or what was going on?

'Barry, I don't understand,' rasped George. His mouth trembled with helplessness and a sort of grotesque wonder. 'When *was* all this?'

'Last night. Late. I *touched* him. Stared at him. And then he ... I don't know. Must have bolted. I don't know where the hell he went then. Christ knows who he was. Where he came from. I don't believe it.'

George couldn't believe it.

'Barry – are you *sure* ... ?'

'Christ, George!'

'Sorry, Barry, sorry. Of course. Sorry.'

A cracked bell clanked, and George got in another couple, fast. Neither seemed too inclined to drink them, and they stared ahead thinking it through, both concluding nothing, neither understanding, and yet they were completely estranged.

'George,' said Barry. 'I couldn't spend the evening with you, could I? You know – few drinks. Show, maybe?'

George hissed through his teeth, for this was becoming a little bit horrible.

'Christ, Barry – any other night . . . I really *can't* tonight, Barry, I've got this really urgent – '

'It's OK.'

'I mean any other night, Barry – '

'It's OK. It's fine. I'm fine.'

Barry just walked out of the pub and George was in bits, but God thank God he'd gone. What in the name of Christ was going on? One thing was sure, when George met Susan that evening, he'd bloody well find out because this was getting weird.

Barry ignored Selina the receptionist when he came back to the office and Selina had thought odd, that's not like Barry at all. He had walked very quickly back to his office although he dreaded the thought of the place, but he felt so vulnerable just walking around.

'Oh – Barry!'

Go away, thought Barry. I cannot hear you.

'Barry!'

No!

'Barry! Barry! Didn't you hear me, Barry? I was calling you.'

Barry turned round. It was June. June was DJ's personal secretary and Barry hated June and June had nothing but the basest contempt for Barry, whom she considered to be not *serious*, not *reliable*, and not really anything at all that she could put her finger on; nothing worthwhile, certainly.

'Hallo, June,' slurred Barry.

June snapped her rubber-band smile. Her voice twanged, and everyone knew she wore elastic stockings, but they looked fairly normal.

'Annie was telling me you wanted to see DJ urgently and I explained to her that DJ was completely chock-a-block this afternoon, but she was most insistent so I've managed to slot you in at four. That *has* to be convenient, I'm afraid. And *do* try not to keep him longer than necessary, Barry – he really is up to his eyes today, poor thing. And he has to see Sir Charles at half-past so do be prompt, won't you, Barry?'

Barry grinned. 'Hallo, June,' he said.

June sniffed the air like a pointer.

'Liquid lunch?' she enquired, with arch distaste.

Barry's grin broadened. God, he hated June.

'Very,' he agreed.

'You will be all right, won't you, Barry? Maybe we should leave this over till tomorrow when you're more ... when you're not quite so ... are you listening to a single word, Barry?'

'Every word, June, every word. I am perfectly all right, June, though it's sweet of you to care. And I promise not to assault DJ. Promise. And thank you for slotting me in.'

June's lip wrinkled in frank disgust.

'Do you have to be so flippant *all* the time, Barry? Why don't you just run along to your office and – what was it Lilian said – get your *act* together. Silly expression.'

Barry sucked in a gust of temper. The devil of it was that everyone was so bloody *nice* to June because you *had* to be nice to June because she was the only one who had any pull whatsoever with DJ and because people had been so nice to June for so long she actually seemed to believe that she really *was* nice, or that people *liked* her, or some such bullshit, whereas really everyone knew that everyone hated June because she was so bloody neat and prissy and efficient and officious and awful and even if everyone didn't exactly *hate* her (bloody good secretary!) Barry certainly did, and rarely more so than now. And yet he couldn't be rude because if he was rude she would cancel his appointment with DJ and if she cancelled his appointment with DJ Annie would hate him and DJ wouldn't hear his plan and Gavin couldn't be taken for thousands and Barry's life would be in ruins and even through all the whisky Barry saw that the very last thing in the world he must be was rude to June and yet he told her to go and fuck herself even before he knew it was coming and she went indigo and spat *right*, Barry, you just *wait*, Barry, and she stumped off and Jean the temp caught the end of it and said what's up with her and Barry said oh, it's just June, Jean, and Jean said oh and Barry thought oh Christ now what and Jean had forgotten the Blend 37 and Barry couldn't face the shit from the machine and the Bell's tasted awful this time around and his stomach really pained him with no food and spirit and he thought Annie's got to work out this one. Annie'll have to make it OK. Dearest Annie. God, I love her.

George had got back some time later. He had driven his BMW like a dodgem down to Camden Town because he couldn't wait to know and Susan wasn't there. He was stopped on the way back for not wearing a seat-belt so that was another bloody fine – Christ, the dash was crammed with tickets as it was.

'Way view been?' queried Christine, when he bustled in looking urgent.

'Out. Why?'

'Hadda lotta cause. *Bookseller* says will you ring.'

George nodded. There was some pressing copy on his desk, and some routine blurbs which he initialled and threw into 'out'. He sent Christine on some fool's errand and started dialling Susan. No answer. Where was she then? Hell. He snatched up the 'phone in anger when it rang.

'Yes. Publicity.'

'George.'

'Susan! Where've you been? I've been trying to get hold of you. I came over. Look, what's going on, exactly? I'm a bit – well I'm a bit, more than a bit puzzled, to be perfectly frank. Look – not to put too fine a point on it, Barry told me – '

'I don't want to know what Barry told you. It's none of your business anyway and I don't want to talk on the 'phone.'

'Well tonight, then. I'm really confused about all this. Either Barry's gone nuts or I've gone nuts or *something's* bloody strange.'

'George, I can't see you tonight.'

'What? You can't? Oh hell. Oh hell, I was really looking forward to that, Susan. I mean, apart from all this funny stuff, I really wanted to see you. Are you sure you can't make it, Susan? I thought we'd go to Gavvers and then possibly – '

'I'm sorry, George.'

George shrugged surrender. What could he do?

'OK. OK. Well – I'll 'phone you, then.'

'Fine. I don't know how much I'll be around in the next few days, actually, but OK, fine. 'Phone me. Is Barry all right?'

'Very far from it, I should say – and who can blame him, poor bastard. But look here, talking of Barry – how did he know? I mean – *does* he know, or what?'

'I have to go now, George.'

'Susan!'

''Bye, George.'

'Susan! Susan! Susan! Oh shit.'

George banged down the 'phone thinking two can play at that game, girly, and he snatched it up again and got a line and was dialling fast.

Hilary was stir-frying prawns and bean-shoots when the trimphone bleeped.

'Hilary? It's George. Look, don't say a word. I've been thinking things over, and I think I behaved a little rashly when I – you know, said what I did. I'd miss you too much.'

'Well,' drawled Hilary, thinking soya, where did I put the soya?

'Well,' continued George, thinking Christ, she could make it a *bit* easy, 'well – today's Friday.'

'Clever boy.'

'Oh come on, Hilary! I *always* come over on Friday. How would you like a nice bottle of champagne? A magnum, maybe – let's go mad. Taittinger – your favourite. How about it?'

If only, thought Hilary, he wouldn't *apologise*. If only he wouldn't *ask*. Why can men never be men about it and just turn up and *take*? That was never what she said; but that was what she thought.

'No, I don't think so, George.'

George was angered. What did women *want*, for God's sake? Bloody jeroboams?!

'Come on, Hilary. Don't give me a hard time.'

'I don't intend,' returned Hilary, thinking lovely – what a gift, 'giving you any time at all. Goodbye, George.'

She depressed the plastic bar on the trimphone and left off the receiver because he always 'phoned again and became increasingly whingeing and it was a nuisance. And anyway, someone else was coming over soon – a girlfriend, actually, but she'd never let George know that when she saw him the following Friday. Yes. Hilary would let him come over the following Friday because she really rather missed him, the ineffectual dolt. Shame about the champagne, though, but these people really had to be taught a lesson. But it was true what George had said: Taittinger *was* her favourite. It had such class.

Annie had calmed down June and had been pretty severe with Barry. Barry didn't mind: quite liked it, sometimes. He was waiting for a buzz. Then he'd traipse in and see DJ and then what? He couldn't think. He couldn't think about anything, he was so stewed in alcohol and so very deeply *upset*. What *did* one do at times like this? Murder one's wife? Seek names, facts, explanations? Sue for divorce? And how did any of that stop this dull, undulating pain throbbing down in his guts? Better just to keep on drinking. It didn't hurt so much in the long run. Well – short run, anyway. And what would he do tonight? Not Annie. Annie would go on and on and on tonight; she could be like a wife, sometimes. And he couldn't go back to the flat, that was for sure. That would be just dreadful. He wasn't quite sure if he could ever contemplate going back to the flat again, but he supposed he would in time because he had to, really. Barry supposed he would in time because it was just a question of getting *over* it, and that at base, most issues came down to necessity, and this simplistic little thought rather lifted him, but then that dark blade of pain and even fear cut again into his stomach, slicing to the spine.

The 'phone buzzed, which made Barry start like a woman.

'Yes, June,' he responded, with what he hoped would pass as responsibility, or at least comparative sanity.

'Barry?' enquired George.

'Oh George,' said Barry, thinking sod, I wasn't ready for George, I was ready for June.

'Look, Barry – I've been having a little think and you seem in such a state over all this you-know-what business, I thought maybe we ought to have a bit of a knees-up after all. Sort of see you through, if you know what I mean.'

Barry felt so good to hear it.

'Great, George. Terrific. Thanks a lot.'

'Don't be silly. Least I could do.'

Oh great, thought Barry, when he'd put down the 'phone. That was tonight taken care of, anyway. Good old George. Christ it was good to have a friend. But he hadn't said what time. Six o'clock? No – probably five-thirty in The Yorkshire-man. The 'phone buzzed again and Barry picked it up feeling a hell of a lot better and said I know, George – I've just worked it out for myself: five-thirty in The Yorkshireman, and June said DJ will see you now Mr Turville, and her thin little mouth underlined *now*, and although Barry could barely believe it himself, in that short space of time he had actually *forgotten* that he was awaiting any summons at all. Gone completely out of his head. It must be the strain. Pressures. And the booze. Barry was sure that stuff was killing him. He sucked a Polo and strutted off to see DJ thinking right, here goes, and envying the people in the corridor who were just on their way to do ordinary things and didn't have to see DJ at all, and wishing that he had had time to see Annie even quickly so that she could tell him again that everything would be all right, and he wished that she could do the whole thing for him – not only because she'd do it so much *better* than Barry, but also because he could then get out of it altogether and just wait for the verdict, the whole affair blissfully out of his hands. But it wasn't to be like that and June was looking at him like a lime and opening a communicating door and then another door and then she was gone and DJ was looking at him.

'Barry,' he said.

'DJ. Good of you to see me. Short notice.'

'Seat?'

'Prefer to stand, thanks DJ. No, I will sit down, actually.'

But he didn't because he couldn't immediately locate a chair and he faltered and damn near dithered and thought don't dither or you'll be too useless to go on and then he saw about four chairs right in front of him and thought Christ how did I miss them but the moment had passed and so he remained where he was. He leaned on DJ's desk, but then he stopped doing that because it didn't seem appropriate. But he'd be all right. He'd be all right. Barry would be all right so long as DJ didn't ask him if he was all right and then Barry thought damn I shouldn't have thought that because now he will; he's bound to now.

'Are you *sure* you won't sit down, Barry? Much more comfortable if you sit down, I should have said.'

'Think I will, actually. Thank you, DJ.'

And Barry sat on one of those chromium chicken-wire efforts that afterwards left you feeling dropsical and scourged, but Barry was sufficiently aware to realise that how he would feel when he eventually arose was to be very largely conditioned by what occurred between now and that moment and did not depend upon any chair in the world, chromium or otherwise, and that if he did not fairly soon subdue this kaleidoscope of prattle in his head, tame his thoughts and actually *say* something he might as well give up before he had even begun.

'Time passes, Barry,' suggested DJ.

'It certainly does, DJ,' agreed Barry with gusto, 'and I am not going to waste any more of it. That is to say I realise you are a very busy man, DJ, and that it's frightfully good of you to see me at all and so I intend coming straight to the point and lay before you the reason for my visit. Without more sort of, you know – ado or anything.'

'Oh get on with it, Turville,' sighed DJ.

'Of course, DJ. The way I see it is this!' And his mind blacked out. Barry shut his eyes in dread, and then a bit of it came to him, thank heaven. Concentrate. 'Now, DJ, I know I don't have to remind *you* of all people of this commission of mine some years ago – well, let's not beat about the bush, we all know what I'm talking about, "The Big Thing" – '

' "One",' interjected DJ, with, Barry thought, asperity.

' "One", quite, DJ. "The Big One", as you say – and I

freely admit as I did at the time that sales were, well, disappointing – '

'Disappointing,' repeated DJ.

'Beneath market expectations,' conceded Barry. 'And I think my apologies were profound at the time, and I must repeat them now. On the other hand, DJ – and this is my, as it were, point, DJ – on the other hand, I really don't think, that is to say I really do believe that it is wrong to expect a man, a publisher – someone in publishing, that is – to live under the cloud of one – severe, admittedly severe, DJ – ah, error. I mean, publishers *are* human. They do *err*. Every publisher, every editor has at some time or another committed some appalling blunder or other. I mean, I'm sure even *you* – '

DJ looked up sharply.

' – will acknowledge the truth of that, DJ,' continued Barry, with barely a break, thinking Christ Almighty be careful.

'And?' said DJ.

'And,' repeated Barry, a bit breathless and off his guard, for he had assumed that it would be DJ's turn now to have said something – something more than 'and', anyway, but they could get away with that sort of thing, managing directors. They could do what they liked. 'And, I am here to suggest that I am once more invested with a degree of authority and, well, power. I really do believe, DJ, that I have learned from my mistakes. And over the years, I have watched with fascination the machinery of this very fine organisation – and in particular the faultless precision with which you yourself, DJ, run the entire operation. DJ!' announced Barry, really warming to the thing, 'under your directorship, and always with your guidance, I really feel that I could achieve great things. My idea, sir, is for me to captain a totally new in-house imprint, sir. A new direction. A new vista.'

'You sound like George,' said DJ. 'When he wants something.'

Barry knew what he meant. It had been a little, well – overt. But he had to sell it, just had to.

'But anyway,' said Barry. 'What do you think?'

DJ cradled his jaw in a hand and spun a green Pentel around the blotter.

'The scheme is at least ambitious,' he said.

A smile hovered, but just hovered, at the edges of Barry's mouth. What was one to make of that? DJ always spoke in this very flat, emotionless way – could even be out-and-out sarcasm, for all Barry knew. It was certainly very professional.

'I must say, Barry,' went on DJ, 'I have been less impressed with your performance of late than – ah – than I should have hoped to be. Of course you have heard that there is due to be this internal reorganisation within the firm?'

'No,' said Barry. He hadn't.

'Really? Grapevine must be breaking down. Yes – a sort of, what should I say? Rationalisation programme. Boosting, streamlining, and cutting down on the – ah – dross. Capitalisation and change, as one might say.'

'Oh yes? No, I didn't know that, DJ. But certainly what I have in mind would fit in well with such a scheme, don't you think, DJ? A sort of up-market, slightly *elitist* imprint – more, well, *literary* than the average. Not that our list isn't literary, DJ, far from it – far from *not* being it, I mean – but commercial as well, of course. Oh yes, very commercial.'

But Barry was losing DJ's attention, he knew. Whatever was or was not going to be done within the house was already planned and probably in hand. As was to be expected, Barry had nothing at all to do with it. He felt gauche and inept and a little bit annoyed. But he would go on with it.

'Very striking d/js,' he said. 'Six-colour.'

DJ nodded, but he was gazing at a defecating pigeon on the window-sill. He scratched his cheek and swivelled around to Barry.

'No,' he said. 'No, I don't think so, Barry. Money's committed, you see. Something of the sort you envisage – takes launch, takes money. Just not there, Barry, I'm afraid.'

Barry flexed his hands.

'Wouldn't take that much DJ. New logo – some sort of hand-out or competition for booksellers to get the thing going. After the first few successes – '

'Barry, Barry, Barry,' intoned DJ, on a descending scale of avuncular indulgence. 'Don't you think that such things have been thought of? Discussed? I am fully aware that other houses have had great successes with imprints such as this – high-quality trade paperbacks, lamination, fashionable artwork, educated youth market – feminism. I know exactly the sort of thing you mean. But it's all a question of *identity*, Barry. House image. We would appear as grotesque as some pot-bellied financier squeezing into a sports car.'

'Which many do,' said Barry, he didn't know why. The cause had strayed anyway; he might as well *talk* to the man. 'Those Mercedes, usually.'

'Quite,' agreed DJ. 'But not us. That is not for us. We are more a vintage Bentley of a machine, if you will forgive me, and that's the way I should like to keep it.' DJ coughed. 'However . . .'

It seemed that the chatty bit was over. Barry should not have come, he saw that now. And if underlining were needed, it was provided by the character of that 'however'. They were moving to the particular.

'Yes, DJ?'

'We have never liked – it has never been our policy – to hold back a go-ahead young editor, while neither do we wish to alter the status quo for his own personal benefit. Not you in particular, Barry, you understand. I am talking,' said DJ, 'in general.'

'Yes I see,' said Barry, thinking but you're not, are you? You're talking about me. Aren't you.

'And so, Barry, if you – or indeed any other member of the organisation – feels tied down by a fuddy-duddy, yes, I suppose we are rather fuddy-duddy – ah, management, then that man – or woman, or woman – must feel free to move on to pastures new.' DJ sat forward. 'And believe me, Barry – the firm *never* takes exception to such action.' DJ reclined again, and looked at the ceiling. 'We like to feel,' he concluded, 'we *understand*.'

Barry wished he had phrased the whole thing differently, approached it from an alternative standpoint, not talked *down* to DJ – selling it like a rep. He wished also that he had never walked through the bloody door, and now that he was here, that he had not drunk quite so much beforehand.

'But DJ,' he tried. 'While I quite appreciate all that you say, you surely see no objection to my, well, commissioning, or no, I should say – submitting for your approval one or two titles somewhat outside our usual range? As an experiment?'

'But then we have been tripped up already over such "experiments". Haven't we, Barry?'

It was bloody, this. Just bloody. Everything was being turned against him. How was this happening? DJ had a reputation for being a bumbling old sod who couldn't publish a book to save his life, so why couldn't he damn well *act* like it? Barry felt utterly trounced. His time was up. There was nothing else he could think of to say.

'On the other hand,' conceded DJ, 'any MS that you show me, or propose at the meeting, I shall give every consideration to, of course. Having come through the filter of a reader and one of my editors.'

'Thank you, DJ.'

'But that has *always* been the case. As you know, Barry.'

'Yes.'

Which, if Barry had ever bothered to work it out, was true, of course. He felt clumsy: all head and nose and legs. He had brought attention to himself in quite the wrong way. The results of this little meeting could be disastrous, he saw that now. A wincing pain caught his left eye. This was the beginning of the blinder that came when he drank too much and then stopped. He could either suffer through the afternoon, or take another shot.

'Are you all right, Barry?'

Of course this was all bloody Annie's fault. If she hadn't *pushed* and *nagged* and gone *on* and *on*. If only Barry could have got to this in his own time and not after being up all night and boozed and living with the thought of Susan oh God Susan it was quite incredible and so painful and yes here it was that blood-coloured heaving of an indigestible wall of heavy anguish and if he swallowed hard and kept on swallowing he could keep it down but if he took his eyes off his hands or if he shifted in his chair it would well inside and up to his gorge and splatter all over his brains and out onto the floor and his hands were shivering but that didn't matter so long as he didn't take his eyes off them for a single second.

'Barry! Turville – are you all right?!'

It was the buzz of the intercom that broke it, whatever was gripping Barry cold and hard.

'Sir Charles for you, sir.'

'I'll go, DJ. Sorry, DJ. Thank you, DJ.'

Barry saw the man's eyes as he left. There was all the schoolmaster's insinuation, and the chill of suspicion. The relief he felt outside the door was a weak and flimsy thing. Closing a door was now only a prelude to opening another. Barry was strung between the fear of enclosure and the need to run. Or was he dramatising all this? Making too much of it? He didn't feel too good, that was the truth. Maybe Jean would get him a drink. Maybe he should write it all down, what he felt, and get DJ to publish *that*. No. Pseuds Corner: done before. Anyway, he couldn't. And he couldn't think now anyway. Just a quick Scotch, get the head together, and try and work it out. Try to understand, or at least to tolerate. Barry didn't mind admitting to himself that the very business of breathing, of dressing, washing, eating and all the rest of it was becoming an impossible burden. And yet he did very little, these days; everything was such a mess. Even sex. He could not remember when last he had even wanted to. Even thought about it. And yet Susan – oh no I can't feel that any more, thought Barry, as the broad blunt teeth of agony ground down on him again and there was nowhere to hide. He thought he had to sit down, and he thought he must get a grip, and he thought that if he was not careful he could become ill, or worse, and he told Jean to pour him a Bell's – interrupting her shaking performance with the injunction to *pour* it, woman – and she looked at him in that way that people appeared to these days – nervous, but for themselves, and questioning, and wanting to get away, and she asked him if he was all right and Barry answered no, quite without qualification, which he didn't do, not normally. Dying did not seem a terrible thing just at that moment; there were no alternatives to being dead. And yet a burning within him twisted him elsewhere. When he felt that, he wanted to kill his way out. In a coldly logical way, it seemed the same thing. Means to an end; that was all.

Life, thought Susan, was a funny thing. Which was the sort of sentiment she had felt free to express to Hilary, until lately; now, she wouldn't have dared. 'Hilarious', Hilary would have said, or 'sidesplitting', and then Susan would have had to go through all the no-not-*that*-sort-of-funny-you-know-*exactly*-what-I-mean business, which was a trial, and rather childish of Hilary, which she could be, sometimes. Susan couldn't *talk* to Hilary any more, just as she couldn't *talk* to Barry. What was *wrong* with everyone these days? Anyhow, no matter how banal the reflection, Susan considered it had been quite a twenty-four hours, what with one thing and another. Apart from the Barry problem – which, frankly, she didn't quite know *how* to handle – Susan at least had something positive to show for it. She had a job. Yesterday it had just been an idea, and today a reality. 'You sound like a novelette,' Hilary would have said. Or Barry. It was getting so that Susan didn't dare open her mouth. But they didn't matter now. Not really. Well – Barry *mattered*, of course, poor soul – but she couldn't do anything about him just at the moment. And anyway, the job thing was more exciting, right now. As for George, he was already proving a bit of a pain. Susan wished she hadn't, now; and anyway, it had been so odd, the way he did it.

The job was the thing. She had been aching to tell Hilary all about it, but Hilary had been so unsympathetic about the Barry business, it really seemed a waste of breath. Anyway, she only would have been beastly, damn her, whereas only a short while ago she would have been full of praise and encouragement, and when Susan would have said oh but Hilary I don't know if I can even *do* the job I'm quite unqualified, Hilary would have said nonsense, rubbish, of course you can, you can do anything if you put your mind to it, and that's why it had always been so great at Hilary's and it was horrible now.

Susan was standing in front of the built-in dressing-table, her knees painfully bent because the mirror was too low if you stood up properly, and if you sat on the silly little buttoned stool your face was truncated at the bridge of the nose. Making up eyes was a farce, as one was constantly screwing them up against the white glare of the striplight, the chaos of these units rendering the whole business of dressing a thoroughly exhausting affair. It was such a dreadful room.

Really, Susan's existence had become so shabby, so sordid, and she had barely noticed until now. Still, maybe life would revive. Maybe things would change. Maybe everything would be all right after all.

She had been in a quandary as to what she would wear for this evening, and she had kept looking at her watch. Tanya – did he say Tanya? Yes, she thought he said Tanya – was going to drop in the keys about five. Have a look over the shop at the weekend, he had said. Get the feel. Quite ridiculous, really. Susan had never before worked in a shop, let alone managed one. But what with her PR and everything, she reckoned she knew what was wanted. Bluff; that was what it all came down to. Along with everything else. Until you knew the ropes. And then it was OK. So Tanya would drop in the keys – she was late, wasn't she? – and on Sunday Susan would go and have a look. He had been vague as to the exact nature of the clothes on sale, but she imagined continental and quite fashionable. 'High-class leisure wear,' he had said, and he had given her a couple of samples: a pink towelling track suit with double stripes in white snaking up the sleeves and across the shoulders, and a glazed cotton sort of blouson in greeny-blue. 'I like the epaulettes,' she had said. 'Fashion pointers,' he had said. 'Name of the game.' Susan had said that they were very nice clothes and he had smiled – nice smile – and said 'Merchandise – garments – units – lines – in this business we say anything but "clothes". But you'll catch on. Bright little thing like you.' 'How did you know I was a 10?' Susan had asked. 'When you've been in the game as long as I have,' he said, 'you could spot a regular 10 blindfold.' And the money seemed good, too – ridiculously good, actually, but Susan wasn't complaining.

The trouble was what to wear this evening. There was a sort of pleated longish skirt, charcoal, with a thin gold line in it, quite classy, and a pale grey Viscose top, but this had been a standard outfit for years and Susan was very sick of it, not least because she always had to wear the same Wedgwood cameo which exactly covered a stain made by crème brûlée one dinner party because the dry cleaners had treated it as silk, as instructed, and then had remonstrated with Susan when the stain remained on account of the garment *wasn't* silk at all, was it madam? No, she couldn't wear that: too depressing. What else? A candy pink Fifties revival cocktail dress. No: too short, now. She shouldn't have bought that, but it was very cheap. Well what the hell, then? Tanya would be over with the bloody keys any moment and Susan wasn't even dressed. There must be *something* decent to wear in this damn bloody wardrobe – Christ knew there was enough stuff. She picked out a fairly simple A-line dress, kingfisher and black. That, with the black patent shoes, black tights, should do it. Bloody well have to. She would have washed her hair, but there wasn't the time; wrap it up like a pirate's in a Jacquard scarf, and trail a couple of ringlets. Face looked a bit tired – and Susan hardly wondered at it. Still, a brushful of Maybelline and a coat of lipgloss, a bit of blusher and a squirt of Rabanne: voilà. It was really just a question of application.

'Answer the 'phone, Nicholas, could you?' called Hilary.

'In a minute.'

'Don't be trying, Nicholas, there's a love. Just answer the 'phone. Hilary's had a draining day.'

'I said I would,' protested Nicholas, 'in a minute.'

'Be rational, Nicholas. It won't be *ringing* in a minute.'

'Well then,' said Nicholas.

'Nicholas! Answer the 'phone right now! Or no chess after supper!'

Nicholas picked up the receiver and Hilary felt bad about having been bullied into a blackmail situation, which was defeatist and ultimately negative. She would have answered it herself, but this was her time for relaxation.

'Good evening,' said Nicholas into the telephone.

Oh Christ no, thought George; it's that bloody kid of hers.

'Hello, Nicholas. It's George. Might I have a word with your – is Hilary there?'

'I don't think she wants to be disturbed, actually, George. Can I take a message?'

'Just tell her it's me, will you, Nicholas?'

'Hold on please. Hilary! Hilary!'

'There's no need to shout,' sighed Hilary, through half-closed eyes. Her very pores seemed sensitive tonight. 'Who is it?'

'It's George.'

'What does he say?'

'He says to tell you it's George.'

'I don't want to speak to George.'

'I said that. Hallo – George? Hilary doesn't want to speak to you, George.'

'Look!' bellowed George. 'Just get her on the bloody 'phone, will you?'

Nicholas wandered into Hilary's room.

'He's becoming profane,' he said.

'Just tell him no,' said Hilary. 'And hang up.'

Nicholas went back to the telephone.

'Hello – George?'

'Yess!' hissed George.

'No,' said Nicholas, replacing the receiver. He scratched the lens of his spectacles as if it itched. 'Should have left it ringing,' he said, and as Hilary came into the room, he took off the receiver again and left it purring. Hilary beamed her approval.

'Babes and sucklings,' Nicholas said, wending his way to

126

the kitchen. 'Can I have some grissini with my Laughing Cow?'

'Who was that on the 'phone?' grunted Gavin, dabbing a napkin to his lips. 'Decent soup, that.'

In fact he had enjoyed it very much indeed. If anyone but Moira had made it, he would have pronounced it really bloody good.

'Don't you go worrying yourself about 'phones,' cooed Moira. 'I'm glad you liked the soup, dear.'

'Don't keep talking to me as if I were in a kinder-bloody-garten, woman! I'm not an invalid. I merely have a gastric complaint. My mind remains unimpaired. I was not *worrying* about 'phones – I'm not *worried* about it, I merely asked to know who was on the other bloody end of it when it rang, that's all! I mean, I am *allowed*, aren't I? I mean, this is my house, isn't it? Or am I very much mistaken?'

Moira sounded like a mother.

'Don't be *silly*, Gavin.'

Gavin threw down his napkin and sat forward in his bed. He glared at Moira with accusation.

'You *do*, don't you?'

Moira's smile was unshakeable.

'Do what, dear?'

'Do it on purpose. Don't you?'

'Do what on purpose, dear?'

'Do *what* on purpose, dear, do *what* on purpose, dear – I just *knew* you were going to say do what on purpose, dear. You *always* do that. You always twist it about and throw it back at me, you always do that. And if you say twist *what* about, dear, so help me Moira I'll maim you! Now for the last time, will you just simply tell me in words of one syllable who it was on the bloody 'phone!'

'You're not well, dear.'

Gavin looked for judgement to an invisible jury.

'Is it fair? I ask you – is it just? Why do I have to put up with this? I mean – *why, why* won't she just give me a straight answer for once in her life?!'

'And all this shouting's not good for you. You were really quite bad last night, you know. Are you sure I shouldn't fetch a doctor, Gavin?'

'Don't want any bloody doctors.'

'But Gavin – '

'I told you I don't want any bloody doctors. Now just take away this bloody awful soup and – oh Christ!'

Gavin had suddenly tightened his mouth and a hand had gone down to his stomach. He hissed in pain.

'Christ, it can be a swine, this. Get me a – Jesus! Get me a Rennie, could you?'

'I'll bring one up with the pudding,' said Moira. 'Fresh pineapple – all right?'

Gavin nodded curtly, his face gently relaxing as the spasm subsided. He could her Moira flip-flopping down the stairs and he thought oh God I wish I didn't feel so bloody awful – I'd love to get out of this house tonight but I doubt if I could stand. Just think – Rover in the garage, London at his feet – and here he was trapped in this bloody room under a pink quilted bedspread with bloody Moira popping in and out like an epileptic almoner, plumping and cooing and smiling – forever that bloody smile – and all because his stomach was cutting him in half and all he was eating was soup and fruit and he hadn't even had a drink all day long. Gavin felt furious, and he suddenly got too hot, and threw off the bedspread in temper and punched the pillow next to him. He lay on his back and roared to the ceiling:

'And who was on the bloody *'phone*!!'

'Just coming, dear,' called Moira from downstairs.

And Gavin said much more quietly:

128

'What's the use? What's the bloody use anyway?'

At last Annie had got Barry to agree to come over. For a short while, anyway. He wouldn't say anything on the 'phone – why he was in such a state, what DJ had said – nothing. He was drunk, of course, but Annie was used to that.

'Well come over this evening anyway,' she had said. 'And we can talk about it then. What would you like to eat? Is there anything special you'd like?'

'No,' muttered Barry. 'Not tonight. I really can't tonight. I promised George I'd go out with him tonight.'

'But Barry – we've hardly spoken all day. What's *wrong* with you? Why won't you tell me what's going on? Why do you have to go out with George tonight? You spent most of lunch-time with him, from what I hear. Don't you think we've got one or two things to discuss? Come on, Barry – I'll help you. I'll look after you. Shall I get some steak?'

'Look, Annie, I can't talk now,' gabbled Barry, glancing wildly around his empty office for a reason. 'Someone's just walked in. Anyway, I can't let George down. He's depending on me.'

Annie did not often become shrill, but now she did.

'And what about *me*?!' she demanded.

'I can't talk.'

'What about *me*, then?! Hey?! Don't I count any more? Why is it so easy to let *me* down?'

'I can't talk now, Annie.'

'*I'm* depending on you too, Barry. More than George. I *love* you, Barry. I *need* you. I'm nothing without you – you *know* that.'

'Annie – for God's sake – '

'There's no one with you at all, is there?'

'No. Oh God.'

'Barry – please come. You love me, don't you?'

'Of course I love you. You know I love you.'

'*Please* come, Barry.'

Barry hissed with frustration. What could he do?

'Look. I'll come over for a drink just before, OK?'

'No. No that's not OK. Stay with me.'

'I *can't* stay with you, for God's sake! I've given my word to George!'

'Barry – !'

'Look. Look. I'll tell you what. Oh Christ if only my *head* didn't hurt all the time. I'll call straight after work, after I change, and then I'll come back later. About eleven, OK?'

'Promise?'

'Angel, I don't have to promise. I love you.'

'Promise anyway,' said Annie.

'All right, Annie. I promise.'

'I love you, Barry.'

'And I love you, Annie. Don't worry. I'll see you soon.'

''Bye, Barry. I love you.'

''Bye, angel. 'Bye.'

Annie put down the 'phone with new hope. She would make everything extra-special for him tonight. Make him feel important. She loved him so much. First thing she'd have to make sure of was that her mother stayed upstairs, quiet, and well out of sight. That would be *all* Annie needed – her mother coming down in the middle and spoiling everything.

Barry had stared at the 'phone for a long time after he hung up. He needed Annie, this was true – more so than ever, now – and yet it was just that sort of exchange that made him feel more oppressed, more under stress, than almost anything. To have denied her would have been to welsh upon a vocation. His love and duty combined with his need, and all of them nailed him down. Barry hated promises, he hated appointments, and he was frightened by Annie's intensity. And yet he needed to be needed, and would not have been without the thought of seeing Annie later . . . but still, but still. It was just that he wished he didn't *have* to go round because he had *said* he would. But he supposed that that was rather selfish.

He had been sitting in the Panda – filthy, just look at it, must get the inside cleaned out – waiting for Susan to leave the flat. He had seen the shadow of her bobbing to and fro behind the Luxaflex blinds in the bedroom, and firmly harnessed this thought into Christ she's taking a long time Christ I wish she'd hurry up, because he felt weak with lack of sleep and hurt and worry and alcohol and his brain had put up a last-ditch defence. Had one more round of agony entered him now, he would have lost his mind for sure. Barry sometimes believed that he sensed his mind near afloat in his skull, circling elliptically upon a precarious pivot. He saw this quite literally as the 'balance' of his mind, and he strained to keep his head upright in the face of fatigue, so delicate was the hairlike mechanism. Nonsense, of course. But real enough when everything seemed a little mad.

It was gone six, and Barry was getting stiff in the legs. It was beginning to rain again, and half of him regretted his date with George. He had only about forty-odd quid – what was left from Annie's hundred, God save him – and all that would go for sure. And he'd get wet, and drunker, and even more tired – if that was feasible – and the next day he would feel even worse and he would smell inside and out. And yet George had sacrificed a lot to be with him tonight, Barry knew, and he supposed that the whole evening might yet be rather enjoyable, in a blind sort of way, once he got into it. Evenings like this were usually successful because they were necessary and one's sheer desperation would not allow them to fail. Even late, when the last drink was drunk and the lights were flicking out, that morose and stale-mouthed sadness was largely self-induced; at its simplest, a blend of tiredness, drink, and conscience, but often a belated and self-important display of independence and maturity. Why didn't he just go to Annie's then? Because she wanted to talk, and Barry had never in his life less wanted to talk; he didn't want to say a word. But he'd go, as he said, when he had changed this reeking shirt – if he could ever get into the flat. What was Susan *doing* up there? (No, don't think of that, think of the shirt. Think of Annie.) And then he'd go and see her when the bender was done, when no one on earth could have made him talk, not even Annie. But she could comfort him, then. She'd feel sorry for him, he expected; he'd look such a sorry sight by then, if all went well. Probably did already. Her lips and her fingers would then be sensed through a slumped and deadened pain, and alcoholic vapours might almost be seen to rise as he would nuzzle that scented neck of hers. Yes. He'd look forward to that.

A couple of hours earlier, Barry had hit upon an idea; well, more of an extension to his original idea, really. It was a bit chancy, he acknowledged, but as George for some reason or other seemed so much on Barry's side just lately, it had seemed only sensible to Barry to make use of the situation. What, he had thought, if Gavin could be persuaded to join them tonight? What if Barry billed it as a West End meeting between publisher, publicity director and prospective best-selling author? Surely Gavin would overcome his hostility to Barry if such a chance were dropped into his lap. And yet, the effect of a 'phone call would be far less strong and convincing than would have been personal contact, had all gone well – when was it? Christ, less than twenty-four hours ago. Still, worth the chance, Barry thought. But he wasn't going to go out there again, not tonight. So he had 'phoned, praying that Gavin himself would answer and not Moira, and Moira had answered and had just kept asking Barry when he was going to come and see her, and whispering that if it was *money* Barry

132

was after, why did he keep bothering about Gavin when she, Moira, was offering him all the money he wanted? And Barry – who had not thought Moira would *do* all that on the 'phone – had blustered and said that this was hardly the time or somesuch, and if it wasn't too much trouble could he please talk to Gavin. Then her voice turned – just as cream is said to – and she told Barry deliberately that Gavin was asleep, and anyway far too ill to come to the 'phone and Barry had thought oh Jesus yes, because he had entirely forgotten that Gavin had been ill, forgotten that he had dragged him up the stairs, forgotten that he had looked close to dying. How is he, enquired Barry, and Moira told him that she had just told him how he was and that she was frankly worried and maybe Barry could visit and Barry had said oh good heavens no I'm sure I'm the last person in the world that Gavin would like to see if he's feeling dreadful I'll wait till he's better and Moira said but *I'd* like to see you, Barry, and for the umpteenth time that day Barry felt that it was all beyond his control and he started his must-dash-goodbying noises and Moira wouldn't co-operate and so he more or less put the 'phone down on her and he was so shaken afterwards that it took the rest of the half of Bell's to set him right.

And so now Barry was half-paralysed in the Panda in Camden Town with a haze of rain outside and pondering this new and ultimately rather important problem of Gavin's illness, and Moira's, as it were, impenetrability. And yet, maybe he *was* going about this the hard way; if Moira really *did* have all the money she claimed to . . . but then there could be terrible complications later – this last reflection appealing in a grotesque sort of a way to Barry's sense of the ironic: as if there could be any *more* complications. Ha!

It was clear that Susan was going somewhere tonight – the jerky silhouette of her kept coming back to the wardrobe area – and Barry supposed, as far as the could think of it at all, that this hardly surprised him. She would be eager to get out of the flat in case Barry came back. But no. Susan would be driven by no such negative: she was clearly going *somewhere*. Barry acknowledged this with helplessness, and yet a spark of last night's anger ignited his eyes. He must not stoke it, though, for when fury like that died down he would be left with the coals burning through his eyes, and that pregnant nausea heaving below. But when the front door slammed and he saw her hurrying into the street looking better than he could remember, he could have run across and chased her, and caught her, and throttled her, and she wouldn't have looked so bloody lovely then! Susan was in a taxi now (where was the money for taxis? Where was Susan getting money for anything?) and Barry caught her profile in the back as she pouted her face into a little mirror. This was at least what he had been waiting for, but Barry felt very reluctant to move, now that he could. The flat would smell of her. All the discarded clothes would be over the bed and the floor. The stubs would still smell of cigarettes. There would be talcum powder on the rug.

Barry walked slowly across the road, and then he cantered. If he didn't get in soon he'd be soaked, and whereas the chances of a fresh shirt were fair, any hope of pressed trousers was negligible. And wasn't it amazing, he reflected, mounting the stairs, that he could even think like that? The human brain would keep homing back to the little things, the old things, the things it *understood*; for which, Barry supposed, he ought to be grateful. It would be truly terrible, otherwise.

Barry had by now built up his dread of the flat to such a degree that he found himself stumbling around the rooms with his eyes tight shut, while his mind ran amok behind them. He barked his shin quite badly against something in 'the room', he didn't check what, and opened only one eye while rummaging for a shirt. He found a tattersall Viyella that

134

looked all right, and he decamped with it to the bathroom, which seemed the least offensive place to be. All her damn little tacky pots were out, though – she never put the top back on anything – and the basin was foul with hair and grime. It amazed Barry how women could emerge immaculate from a room leaving such a cess of a mess behind them. He washed a bit, and the cold water felt good. He smacked some birthday Eau Sauvage into his face and under his arms, and got the shirt on quick. He combed his hair, knocking a bit over his right eyebrow; he used to think this made him look raffish, but now it served to cover the lines. Right. That would do. There was an open lipstick on the dusty glass shelf in an impossibly unsuitable magenta sort of a colour and Barry snatched it up and held it poised over the mirror. He suddenly, desperately, wanted to scrawl something over the mirror, like in films – but something immediate, something from the heart, something he felt – but he could not think what, and he caught sight of himself and he thought how sad, how silly, and he nearly cried he felt so sorry for himself and then the fat sticky smell of the lipstick caught him, and he puckered his mouth in a puritan disgust and looked for the cap and snapped it back on.

Barry walked out into 'the room' forgetting that he did not want to see it, and there was an open bottle of Gordon's on the table and he thought he could do with a jolt of Scotch before he left because he never drank gin as a rule and he had a quick look around, each flicker affecting him badly, and he had to get out and he couldn't see any Scotch and so he picked up the bloody gin and swigged at that and screwed his mouth away from it – it was so bloody *surgical* – and he had a last pull at it and straightened his tie and slammed the flat door and ran down the stairs thinking right, that's that. Now let's have a good time, for God's sake. Annie first – and then who knows?

The front door flew open just as Barry reached it, and so

under threat did he feel just now that he was sure that here was an attack from hell. It turned out to be one of those liquid brown-eyed sensuously lovely *rich* girls who exude a tactile luminescence and one preceded by a fabulous scent and all this Barry took in immediately because he had seen it before but only *seen* it and sometimes – once in Harrods – he had got into a lift ascending to God-knows-where just to be crushed a little closer and they always looked away, these girls, but they looked down first which was such a very aware thing to do and although it was *overt* and although it was all built around *money* and *sex* and *silk* and *fur* it moved Barry to his roots, always had, and the reason for this was that he found rich girls clad in silk and fur and sex and money very alluring indeed and they even had fake beauty spots, some of them, and their hair was carefully and expensively rumpled and tumbledown, and hanks always fell over their eyes and some-times it was highlighted and often reddish-browny-black and they affected that this glorious mane was the bane of their lives and they lifted up handfuls of it and it always fell back, just as they knew it would, and here in front of Barry was a prime example of the genre and her eyes shone as if through glass (could *be* through glass) and she looked only about eighteen and yet her clothes suggested a sophisticated lady of maybe twice that mainly because they were so deliciously expensive and her hands were white and the nails were bur-gundy and long and immaculate and what with the scent which was far too much Barry just wanted to touch her which was absurd, but just to hold her waist through that fur and slide his hands under to the crêpe de Chine and over around her hips would be an almost drunkenly divine experience and the scent was so strong he felt he might even already be doing it and since this sublimely elegant earthy thing had walked through the door maybe a second had passed and just by being there her red mouth was kissing at him and it opened and inside was pink and white and warm and he was sure he hadn't heard a word she had said.

'What?' he said.

'God, I'm out of breath,' she said, spreading a hand flat on her bosom. 'Have I missed her? Bet I have.'

'I'm awfully sorry . . .' groped Barry, who was winded in more ways than one, and terribly angry with himself for coming across like a stunted clerk.

'No, I'm sorry,' smiled the girl, and already she was flirting, Barry was sure of it. But you never could tell with this sort of girl because they *always* seemed like that. Even when they were with their fathers. Sometimes more so, then.

'My name is Tanya Wiseman,' she went on.

'Barry,' said Barry.

Tanya put her head on one side. She had studs in her ears.

'Hi, Barry! I'm looking for Susan. God, I *am* late. My dad'll kill me. I've got these keys, you see, and I was supposed to be here ages ago.'

'Susan?' queried Barry, perplexed. Could this be a friend of Susan?

'Yeh. Susan Turville. Do you know her?'

'I know her, yes. I can give them to her if you like. She's out now. What are the keys for, actually?'

Tanya hitched up her white shoulder-bag and looked rather hesitant. Even more attractive, that, because her eyes were full, and her mouth not quite shut. And Barry thought oh what the hell, she'd find out anyway.

'It's OK,' he said. 'I'm her – husband.'

'Oh – you're *Mr* Turville. Well, that's OK, then. Didn't she tell you about all this, then?'

'Well, no. I've been away a bit, actually, and – look, why don't we go and have a drink somewhere and talk about it? I'd ask you upstairs but – well, it's a bit depressing up there, frankly. You wouldn't like it.'

Tanya's hand went to her hips, and she became mock-arch, her eyebrows up in irony.

'And how do *you* know, pray, what I would and wouldn't like?'

'Well I don't,' admitted Barry. 'But I'd like to.'

And the game was on. How could he ensure that this fabulous piece of another world did not immediately slide back into it? Barry was wearing his class like a weighted cloak. He didn't even feel he could decently ask her into a pub, she looked so outside that sort of thing. Even the thought of her in Camden Town was wrong. She was more St John's Wood. Marylebone. Not Camden Town.

'Maybe we could have a drink,' suggested Barry anyway. 'In town,' he added.

'I'd like to, Barry, but I've got my car outside. I'll tell you what – the flat's quite near. Come back for a drink and I'll clue you in. I expect Susan's really annoyed at missing us both.'

'I'm sure,' agreed Barry. Jesus, he thought.

A bronze Porsche Carrera stood outside the house, glistening in the rain. Thank Christ that bloody Panda is around the corner, thought Barry, hating himself for thinking like that, but he always did, he always did. The car was perfectly new and immaculate; it was *paid* for, but Tanya hadn't paid for it. It shone, but Tanya hadn't polished it, and that was thrilling. It was cool and leathery inside, and the passenger seat was strewn with tastelessly loud disco tapes, and some old Motown, along with a packet of Kent and a Cricket lighter. There was a Browns carrier bag in the back and Barry clunked on his seat-belt and he felt he had always wanted to be here and Tanya was so carefree and rich and confident and rich and to her this was no big deal, it was just a girl and a man in a car going off for a drink. And then she thudded a cassette into the Panasonic deck and something Negroid and pounding filled the car and the ignition snorted like an ill-tempered and poky animal and her long white fingers on the stubby wheel pulled away the car with power and on the straight she lifted up her hair with one hand, her mouth pouting to the beat of the music. Her hair fell back down and she glanced to her left. Barry was looking at her already, which she knew. Her eyes softened, and yet they were glinting lights as she said, almost laughingly:

'Hi, Barry!'

'Hi,' he said. Automatic reflex.

Tanya executed a swift and coolly competent racing change on a tight right turn and smiled into the mirror at a stymied driver left behind. Barry's mind hummed with a fat and child-ish glee. He didn't feel tired any more.

The flat was in an opulent block just off Baker Street, built in the early 1930s, Barry guessed. The main doors were glass and strap-iron, the vast foyer the usual cocktail of mirrored alcoves and fluted uplighters, the closeted and expensive silence broken only by the clang of the gold lift-gates. There was a short fat man dressed as a security guard; he was uni-formed porterage, and aware of it.

'You weren't long, Miss Wiseman,' he said.

'Hallo, Dennis!' Tanya called brightly. 'Did the flowers come?'

'They're upstairs now, miss. I took the liberty.'

'You're sweet, Dennis. Thank God they came. My dad would've killed me.' And then to Barry: 'Coming?'

Barry just padded on behind, and although he always hated men who did that with this sort of girl, now he was with this sort of girl, he thought he understood why they did it. And all he could think was well, at least I washed and changed my shirt.

There were one Chubb and two Banham locks on the main flat door, each in line with the raised and fielded panels. Tanya had all the keys, saying:

'No one's here at the moment.'

And Barry was given to understand that this was unusual. It was a mansion flat, with the accent on mansion. The sort of flat where maybe three, four, five people lived. And there would be a cleaner, maybe two, an occasional cook for dinner parties, and no doubt there had been a live-in nanny, at the time. One could never tell, in context, whether 'no one' meant no one at all, or merely no one of any consequence, but had not the flat been utterly empty, Barry doubted whether Tanya would have mentioned it at all.

The hall itself was rather small, and hung with ice-green moiré. The floor was black and white marble and it shone like it was wet. A one-legged gilt rococo console supported an Attic urn berserk with hothouse flowers, every one carefully graded, while leaves and gypsophila filled in and straggled upwards. Two bergère chairs flanked an elegant Regency pierglass, and a large pair of ceramic leopards looked doleful in the corners. The hotchpotch of periods and colours was not wholly successful from Barry's point of view, but he had never in his life seen anything so *clean*. The crystal ashtrays positively defied the thought of smoking, and the chairs would *not* be sat in. So far as this went, the hall could not be said to be welcoming, but it warmed Barry through and through because every object was so *expensive* and so *designer-approved* and the owner of this flat (Tanya herself?) had *not* hung the pictures, had *not* decorated the walls, had *not* arranged the furniture, had *not* removed the dust; the owner had merely *paid* for it all, which was so appallingly exciting to Barry that he almost loathed the idea for its decadence, but he wanted more. He got it when Tanya threw – threw – her lynx jacket onto one of the chairs and it slithered off onto the shiny floor and she left it and so precious and so feline a thing so beautifully destroyed the *perfection* of the hall that Barry actually felt sexually aroused, but he also acknowledged that he felt a little faint, and that awful sick fatigue swept over him again, but he must not let it be seen. He *must* be all right, tonight.

'Drink?' said Tanya.

And Barry clutched the word to him.

'Please,' he said.

Barry stepped with care – the air was of a museum or show-room – reflecting that Tanya, at least, was not so bourgeois as to avoid saying the word 'lounge' – 'You go into the lounge,' she had said. 'I'll be through.' But the snob in him knew that Tanya had never realised that she *should* avoid saying 'lounge' – which was all to the good, he defended her. But she didn't seem terribly educated. Stupid to say that after a few minutes, he supposed, but you could always tell, somehow. Still, he thought, looking around this newest mirage, who cared? And what have the fatuous little Noblesse Oblige hangovers to do with education anyway? Or real life, come to that.

The room – lounge – was very long and broad. The far end near shimmered in the distance and Barry could hardly tell whether the painting over the mantel was a landscape or an abstract. He approached soundlessly on the powder-puff carpet and made it out to be a sort of sub-Monet lily pond. Or maybe it wasn't sub-Monet; hard to tell, here. There were lithographs all over the flanking wall – Lowry, Hockney, Flint – no one Barry hadn't heard of. The room was pearly and peachy and pink and very much 'designed' in the American taste. The imposing bureau-bookcase had rather too many too-small panels on the drawer-fronts, the fretwork pediment was over-broken, the dark veneer distressed to the point of angst. All the sofas (there were six) stood in pairs, and the attendant tables were wide and squat and low. More chunky ashtrays and Dupont table-lighters for those who dared. The curtains Barry was sure were called drapes, and could well have serviced one of the old Odeons. What was striking, though – Christ where was she with that drink – was the dearth of real personal possessions. The books behind glass were elaborately bound, and all hundred (Barry counted: one hundred, exactly) were Masterpieces of Literature, with the accent on things like *Huckleberry Finn* and *Moby Dick*. None had been opened, Barry would swear. He doubted whether even the protective doors had ever been penetrated. Possibly the bookcase had been delivered complete. What knick-knacks there were – a little octagonal Cartier clock, a walnut cigar humidor (not Tanya's flat, then) – had the air of having been impressive gifts rather than intuitive purchases. So affluently stark and Hiltonic was the place that Barry found himself sliding open drawers – a thing he wouldn't do, normally, well, probably would, actually – while cocking an ear for Tanya's return.

At least it wasn't so neat in the drawers. Old invitations, bits of a watch, candles. Then one drawer was completely empty. And then in the next one there was a pack – a double-pack – of bridge cards, and also a gun. Barry stared at it. He had never been so close to a gun before, and yet he was in no doubt at all that it was the real thing. He desperately wanted to touch it, to feel it, to weigh it in his hand, and yet absurdly – hangover of a thousand films – the warning word 'fingerprints' flashed across his mind. Ridiculous. He remained quiet. God knew where Tanya had gone. Barry looked down at the gun. He had no idea what sort it was. His knowledge of guns was confined to the six-shooters in Westerns (this was much shorter) and what he had read in the Bond books. What were they again? Smith and Wesson, Lambretta – Biretta, was it? Something. Barry's hand snaked into the drawer and he felt it. Surprisingly warm to the touch. His nerves tingling with the daring, he picked it up and it felt so right in his hand, so heavy, so fitting. His finger curved into the trigger as naturally as if he had been holding guns all his adult life. It was more blue than black. Ugly and beautiful and charged and powerful, and just think, just think.

Something moved somewhere in the flat, Barry was sure. There was just a shift of air signalling change and he slid the gun back into the drawer without a clatter and closed it all in one movement. He ran yards over the carpet to the mantel and he leaned against it and stared fascinated at the cornice and he still had a minute or two before Tanya came into the room. It must be a catacomb of a flat, Barry thought, and then all thought left him as he looked at her because she looked so bloody *physical* and somehow glossy American and she was carrying a tray that already looked sumptuous and she said:

'Sorry I was so long. I was dying for a glass of champagne but then I felt tacky and changed. I thought I'd do a special drink. Hope you like it. Are you hungry?'

She was wearing a dress, a shift thing, that was truly unremarkable in any sense, but because it was silk – *everything* was silk – and because of the way she moved inside it, Barry's throat was stopped as if by a thud. She was swaying towards him, holding high the tray and smiling not one of those miserable simpering *boring* little smiles, but a fully-fledged slash of the pleasure of living, with eyes, teeth, everything. Barry held on to the mantelpiece for more than effect now because suddenly that scent was everywhere and he felt sick and hungry and excited and also a bit grubby and he had just been handling a gun.

Tanya knelt on a kilim and tinkered around with the things on the tray. Her hair was auburn, but little golden hairs glowed on her forearm, and a heavy cloisonné amulet once tight above the elbow clunked down to a nimble, bony wrist. She bent to what she was doing, and now she threw back the weight of her hair like a young impatient colt. Barry must stop thinking of physical imagery if he was going to get through this at all.

'I hope I've made them right,' said Tanya. 'Champagne

cocktails. I made them in the kitchen because I hate people looking.'

'I love them,' said Barry.

He had always wanted to taste a champagne cocktail. It was the one in his book that he kept coming back to. But the bloody ingredients were so bloody expensive and people always drank that sort of thing and wanted another, so he had never dared. Not only did these *look* beautiful – they were in the right glasses for a start – but there was a bottle of Krug standing alongside, with a bottle of Hine.

'You never used these to make a cocktail!' said Barry. He almost gasped it. He was learning – just in the last hour he was learning – just how very middle-class he was, and used to being poor. Tanya looked up in beautiful, young alarm.

'Isn't it right?' she asked. 'I'm sure that's what it said.'

Barry smiled. Fond as a father, and yet there was a mounting well of protection that was encompassing in quite another way. Interesting.

'No no. It's right. They look fantastic.' What, thought Barry, am I doing here, actually? 'Very good of you,' he said, 'to go to all this trouble for a – well, I would say for a perfect stranger, but nobody's *perfect*. Ha ha.'

Tanya laughed a bit, which meant she was either polite or the only person in England who hadn't heard that one.

'Oh, don't get carried away by it,' she smiled. 'I always like a drink about now, don't you? I would've done it anyway. Well – maybe not *cocktails*. That's just me showing off. Anyway, they're awfully nice. Terribly bad for you, I expect. They taste *terribly* wicked. Anything that tastes so gorgeous is bound to be *awfully* bad for you. Don't you think?'

She was cocking her head on the side again, but the act of ingenuous naïve was a little too perfect. She was acting all the time. But it didn't matter. It was such a good show.

'What's all this key thing about?' asked Barry. It had been

bothering him a bit, this – he didn't know why – but he tried to make his request sound casual, not alarmed, not snooping. Conversational.

'Ah yes, that. Well – I expect you know Susan's got a job with my father? Well – his firm, anyway.'

'This cocktail is marvellous.'

"Tis good, isn't it? Well, this shop she's going to manage has been done up recently and Daddy can't bear keeping them closed longer than he has to – only three days, this one – so muggins here was given the job of shooting round with the keys so that Susan could – I don't know – do whatever she wants to do in the place over the weekend, and open up on Monday. She's got a couple of helpers, though, so it shouldn't be too bad. Then I go and see this absolutely *terrific* dress in Browns – God, I've left it in the car – and so I was late, as usual. Anyway.'

'I see,' said Barry, thinking good Lord Susan's got a job at last and she never said anything well I suppose there was hardly the time to say anything lately Christ I don't understand that woman any more she seems to be changing out of all recognition what was *wrong* with her for God's sake still thank Christ for the money oh God I wish I wish I wish she hadn't done what she has done and then it could be all right again because I love her really.

'What sort of shop is it?' he asked.

Tanya waved in the air.

'Oh, you know, usual.'

'Ah,' said Barry. He couldn't, he thought, affect *total* ignorance. Find out later.

'Delicious,' he said, draining the glass. Pink sugar coated the sides.

'Great, aren't they? I can't be bothered going through all the palaver again, though. Would just a glass of champagne be OK?'

145

Barry smiled. 'I think I could put up with that,' he said. 'But don't make a habit of these slovenly ways. Bad for the soul.'

'You're laughing at me,' she chided him.

'Not at all. You're making me happy, that's all.' Barry dropped his voice, only a bit for effect. 'I haven't been very, lately.'

Tanya nodded with a childlike emphasis.

'I know exactly what you mean! I've been a bit fed up lately too. I didn't get up yesterday, I was so fed up. There's never anything to do – do you find that?'

'Well,' said Barry. Christ, he thought. Another world. 'I know what you mean, I suppose – I've felt it, yes. I felt that when I was younger. But my problems are a bit different now.'

'Just listen to you!' hooted Tanya, pouring Krug into the sugary glasses. 'When I was younger! You sound like an old man!'

And Barry supplied the inevitable:

'I sometimes *feel* like an old man.'

'Oh you mustn't talk like that. That's horrid. I really hate it when people talk like that. It must be awful to be old. Anyway – I don't know what you're talking about. *You're* not old.'

'Older than you.'

'Oh, *me*. Simply *everybody's* older than me. Boring.'

Oh God she's not *that* young is she, thought Barry, while his vanity led him on to:

'Well how old do you think I am, then?'

'Oh gosh no I'm not very good at this. I can do stars – you know, astrological signs – I can do those, but I'm hopeless at ages.'

'Roughly,' Barry urged.

Tanya screwed up her nose and put her head on one side in a pastiche of concentration.

'Hmmm. Well. Let me see. You're over twenty-one . . . !'

Barry grinned. 'Correct,' he said.

'And under . . .'

146

Tanya was getting playful. One of her long fingernails was on her lips. How cheeky can I be, asked her eyes.

'Careful,' Barry warned, with mock foreboding. Christ, he felt good.

'Under . . . seventy-five!'

'Ha ha.'

'No no no. Seriously. I think you're about . . .'

'Yes?'

'Thirty-five.'

Barry's face must have fallen a bit.'

'Oh gosh I'm wrong, aren't I? Oh gosh, look I'm most awfully sorry if I've offended you I said I was no good at this sort of thing. Have some more champagne.'

'No no. You're right. Dead on. Well done.'

'Oh gosh. Really? How great. I'm usually awful at this. Well I'll tell you what – I'll tell you your sign now. This I know I can do. Are you into all that, by the way?'

'Astrology?'

'Yes.'

'No.'

'Oh. Well. Anyway. Doesn't matter. I think you're one of the power signs – the strong ones. You're either Leo, Aries, Aquarius or Taurus. Now. Which one? I think – Leo!'

Barry shook his head. 'No. 'Fraid not.'

'No? OK – Taurus, then.'

'Not Taurus.'

'Aries? You don't seem like an Aries.'

'Nope.'

'And I suppose you're not Aquarius either! You must be – Aquarius.'

'Not Aquarius either. I thought you said you were good at this?'

'I am, usually. Are you *sure* you're not one of those?'

Barry threw up his arms. 'I should know,' he expostulated.

147

'Yes. Well you must be Libra, then. Or Gemini.'

'Keep going.'

'Oh no gosh really? Oh gosh. What's left? Oh hell I don't know what you are. What are you?'

'You want to know?'

'Yeah – go on.'

'Pisces.'

'Pisces? Really? *You're* Pisces? Gosh. I wouldn't have thought you were Pisces. Oh I don't know, though. Yes, yes, I suppose you *could* be Pisces. Yes. There's no more champagne left. How depressing. Oh God, and another evening to fill. Hey – are you *terribly* busy this evening? I expect you are.'

Barry looked at her.

'No, not really. No, I don't have anything on at all, as a matter of fact.'

'Oh how super! You don't fancy taking me somewhere divinely delicious for dinner, do you? I'm starving.'

'Sounds marvellous,' said Barry expansively. And then he thought Jesus – money. 'Trouble is, I've left all my cash and cards and stuff back at the flat. I've got a few notes on me – thirty, forty pounds. That's all.'

'Oh don't worry about that. There's usually a bit knocking around here somewhere. Or we can charge it to my dad – he won't mind, old thing. Well, he might – but he never finds out. Where shall we go? You think about it and I'm going to change. I get so bored with clothes, don't you? Shan't be long. Oh great. How exciting. You must think I'm an awful child, but I just adore going out, I really do.'

'No, not at all. So do I.'

When she'd gone Barry admitted that he *did* find her rather juvenile, but it was all quite appealing. Refreshing. Different. Could drive you mad, though, too much of it. He resumed his perusal of the room. Down at the far end was a magnificent grand piano that shone like a car. Steinway; would be. And a clutch of photographs in engine-turned frames on the top, and another cascade of flowers, this time in a silver rose-bowl. One of the photographs was of a sort of party – anniversary, maybe? Wedding? Something like that. And there was Tanya looking tanned and voluptuous. God, Barry was looking forward to this evening. Life was so strange. And look at everyone else in the photograph. They all looked so fit and rich and happy and well-dressed and rich and confident and all of a sudden Barry's neck snapped taut and he felt all the blood in his face drain away to the centre of the earth and his eyes stared hard at the photograph and Tanya swished back into room and said ready hey Barry I'm ready are you all right Barry what's wrong is something wrong and he said as easily as he could manage no I'm fine sorry million miles away admiring your pictures who's this man? And Tanya said who? Him? And Barry said yes, him, and Tanya said that's my dad and Barry said oh that's your dad is it, fine-looking man, let's go if we're going shall we? You look wonderful. And out in the hall Barry found his ribcage trying to burst out of him and his stomach heaved and pushed and he was near blind with hurt and anger and loathing for everyone and he managed to look fairly all right and said oh cigarettes, left my cigarettes, won't be a minute, and he strode back into that massive room and slid open the drawer and took out the gun and stuffed it into his jacket and although there was a well of hate for everything in the world behind this action the trigger had been the photograph, for the last time he had seen that face was in his own bloody bed, with Susan's screams shredding his consciousness, and he could hear them now, he could hear them now, he could hear them now.

Chapter Five

MAYBE, THOUGHT ANNIE, building up the logs in the grate, maybe she had been too soft on Barry. Maybe if she'd taken a tougher line, he wouldn't be so hopelessly irresolute. Maybe . . . oh blow, it was done now anyway. But he was in an awful mess, poor soul, and these days he seemed to think she was nagging, or something, but it was only that she cared. Why couldn't he see that? Still. Tonight she'd take the pressure off a bit. Find out what was wrong. Comfort him. Help, if she could. But how could she get across to him without being, well, *heavy* about it, that he really had to stir himself and *do* something? Before it was too late. Sometimes he seemed *so* depressed, though. Sometimes there seemed to be so much pent-up violence in him that Annie was worried, and she wouldn't mind admitting it to anyone. Except that she never spoke to anyone. Not about Barry. She wondered from time to time – she did now – whether she was the only person who worried about Barry. What about his wife? Susan. Did she care? Did she go on at him? Annie didn't know. Barry never talked about Susan. He loved her, Annie thought. Which was strange. But Barry was a bit of a strange fellow. He loved, he was sincere all right, but he did take an awful lot for granted. Still. Annie did not love him for what she could get back. Which, she reflected wryly, was just as well. Anyway. Get the logs in the fire, that was what to do. Get a blaze going. Warm the place up. At least if she did what *she* could . . . then maybe

Barry would see. No. Anyway. Annie really *must* stop talking to herself. First signs. She was alone too much, that was the trouble. Apart from Barry, she really didn't see anyone at all. Except for people at work – but not to *talk* to. And mother, of course. But that was the same as no one, really. They didn't talk at all. They merely inhabited the same space, and irritated each other when they met on the stairs. Her mother would squeeze past and jostle and tut as if her daughter's presence on the staircase – her staircase – vexed her more than she could say. Sometimes, Annie would pointedly await the woman's descent, tapping a foot on the landing. She could be so *slow*. But Annie harboured no antagonism. Not really. She couldn't care one way or the other, if she was really honest. She did her best for her mother; saw she had everything she needed. If only the woman wouldn't behave as if she was ancient instead of merely old. She hardly went out at all now. Even to the shops. Her interest in Kensington declined when they closed the Derry and Toms roof garden, and now she thought the whole High Street a bazaar. And agoraphobically, she detested even drawing open the curtains in her room. Soon – a few years, less maybe – she will have decided that she is a helpless and spurned invalid, and what would become of Annie then? Sometimes she thought about it. More often, she chose not to.

There had been a time when Annie thought Barry might have lived with her. Married her, even. But not now. It didn't seem possible now. At first, they had been so deeply in love, and yet with all the silliness there had been no time to discuss the serious side. It seemed, looking back, that they *had* been together for every hour of the twenty-four, but Annie supposed that this was impossible. For she remembered that the time without Barry had been intolerable. She found it hard. Just knowing he was coming *still* gave everything a point. But Annie had been a bit of an innocent in those days, a bit of an idealist. She had not liked the thought of being seen to be a marriage-breaker. She had never even met Susan: could be quite nice, for all she knew. And then again – just say Barry *had* left his wife and lived with Annie and it hadn't worked out – Annie would have felt so *guilty.* Then there had been a period when Annie had not wanted to live with Barry. She saw how bored he might become. He always came to see her when he could, and because he *wanted* to. It would be awful if he came because he had to, simply because there was nowhere else to go. Anyway, the whole thing of love was quite irrational. Of course what she was doing made no sense at all, but a *bit* of Barry was better – so very much better – than no Barry at all. Odd, really. Annie had never seen herself as a 'mistress'. Silly word. And yet, look at it how you like, put whatever word to it you choose, that was the reality. The girls at the office thought Annie a bit odd. She didn't talk about men friends the way they did. They *always* did, which rather sickened Annie. She did not know whether or not they knew about Barry. There had been a time when Annie had gone to very elaborate lengths to prevent anyone at work becoming even remotely aware, but she didn't trouble now. She did not flaunt it, of course. She still never mentioned his name. But she did not conceal. If Barry buzzed her on the intercom, Annie merely spoke to him, feeling no need to invent a reason why she was in communication with Editorial.

But she *would* like to live with Barry. She could help him, she was sure. And the thought of his always being there, to cook for, to care for – it was very warm, that thought. Secure. It would be lovely if, after dinner, he would not get up and leave. It was not that he was peremptory. More often than not, he did not *want* to leave, Annie could see, but he went off anyway. Which left Annie with a stack of dirty plates and glasses, which she did not mind at all, and a cold hole at her centre, which she did. She did not feel used, she did not feel cruelly treated, but she did experience what came close to a childlike sense of letdown when the party was over. Every single time. For even a few bits of something and a bottle of wine was a party with Barry. And yet he did nothing special. Didn't go out of his way to entertain her. Funny, really. After all these years. And what now? What did the future hold for Annie? Would Barry maybe eventually come to her? It didn't seem likely, somehow – but one never knew. Annie clung to that: one never knew. But even if he didn't she'd never let him down. Never go away. No disloyalty. Barry was very big on fidelity. He would have killed her – probably quite literally killed her – if she'd ever gone with another man. He told her so often, when he was drunk. And Annie said all the appropriate staunch and soothing things that one does to a scared and ruffled man, but she smiled inside because she knew she just *couldn't*. She loved Barry. She nearly adored him. Maybe she did even adore him. And the thought of anyone else was not so much repellent as just impossible. It just could not *be*. But men never understood things like that. How could they? They were different.

The fire was crackling bright by now, and Annie's face was warm on one side. She switched on the lamps and drew the curtains. There was a freshly roasted chicken on the sideboard, a couple of bottles of claret (quite good, nothing great) and loads of salad stuff. Lately, Barry enjoyed picking at things that were easy to eat rather than a proper sit-down meal. Which was what they used to do, once. Annie had enjoyed them. They were so romantic, so peaceful. But she did not miss them. Whatever Barry wanted.

The door opened, which made her jump. She had been miles away.

'What is it, mother?'

'It's dark in here.'

'It's not dark in here, mother. I've just drawn the curtains.'

153

Annie's mother walked in very slowly, each step calculated to display all the pain she was feeling.

'And there's a funny smell,' she said.

Annie sighed. 'Oh God, mother,' she said.

'There's no need to bring God into everything,' snapped back Annie's mother, which she usually did. The sour game of tennis was on.

'Why don't you go up to your room? Hmm? I'll bring you something nice to eat.'

'Getting rid of me again. I have just come *down* from my room. You *heard* me coming down. You don't suppose I came down from my room merely for the pleasure of going back up to it, do you? Have some sense, girl. I'll have something to eat down here.'

'You can't. There's nothing. I'll bring you something.'

'You must think I'm totally devoid of my senses. I can *see*, you know. I'm not totally ga-ga. Is that a chicken over there or is it a mirage? It's all right – you needn't worry. I shan't stay long. I won't be in your way. Oh – be a dear and get my rug, would you?'

'Mother, you're not staying down here, and that's that. You're doing this deliberately. You *know* I've got someone coming round. You always do this. Whenever you smell cooking. Whenever you see I've banked up the fire.'

'I like a nice fire.'

'Yes, well – I'll do a fire for you tomorrow. Promise. Now *please*, mother – just go up to your room and I'll bring up the portable, all right?'

Annie's mother sniffed.

'Doesn't get Channel Four. Not properly.'

'But mother – you never *watch* Channel Four. You *hate* Channel Four. You're always saying so.'

'All the same . . .'

'Look. There's a really good film on tonight. You go up and – '

'What film?'

'What?'

'You said there was a really good film on tonight. What is it? I suppose I've seen it. I've seen all those old films.'

'*Longest Day.*'

'Oh, I've seen *that*. I've seen that a thousand times. They're forever putting that thing on. Why can't they ever come up with any new films? Something one hasn't seen?'

'Whenever they put on a modern film you complain about the sex. Or the blood.'

'Well why can't they make *nice* films any more? Why does everything have to be – '

'Mother! Please! It's getting late. *Please!*'

Annie's mother sniffed. But she turned back, at least.

'That man of yours again, I suppose.'

'I'll be up soon with something nice.'

'He's no good. Not for you.'

'And I'll bring up the telly in a minute – OK?'

'You're out to ruin your life.'

'And mind yourself on the landing, mother.'

Annie carried up the portable, brought up all her mother's favourite tidbits, complied with some really quite outrageous requests, and finally got the door shut behind her. She put on a little Rochas in the bathroom, and checked the room again. It looked good. It looked homely. It looked just the way Barry liked it to look. Annie placed the bottle of Bell's by the chair, with a little carafe of Malvern. She checked her watch: just after seven. He should be along soon, poor old thing. Exhausted, she expected. She could probably dissuade him from going out with George, once he was here. Once he saw how nice everything was. He must be *so* tired. Annie would make him feel better.

155

'Annie!'

'Oh what *is* it, mother?'

'You forgot the thousand-island dressing!'

'It's on the tray!'

'Annie!'

'What?!'

'The thousand-island dressing! You've forgotten it!'

'It's on the – ! Oh God, mother. All right.'

And Annie stumped up the stairs thinking what's *wrong* with the woman? Why doesn't she just *look*? It's on the tray right in front of her, for God's sake. Was she doing it deliberately, or what? And then it occurred to Annie that she mustn't forget to light a couple of candles when she got back down. Barry liked candles. He said they made her look so beautiful.

There seemed to be no neck attaching Barry's head to the rest of him. His consciousness floated, it seemed, rather higher than his being. All the way to dinner with Tanya, all he could think of was the gun, and the unaccustomed weight of it dragging his clothes over to one side and what it could achieve and only incidentally how his holding it close to him through his pocket made Tanya even more tantalising – distant, yet now so much more within his grasp. Barry was lost, adrift, and yet he felt more in control than he could remember. He thought they called it power. It excited him beyond measure, and yet he did not feel cold fear as he had expected to. Going down in the whirring lift he had awaited the icy rush of it, and dwelt upon the pain to quell its coming. But nothing. He felt nothing approaching fear. He was in possession of a terrible and wonderful secret and he enfolded it and kept it warm and he wouldn't waste it, wouldn't even show it, not yet, and from now on the whole world had better look out because Barry was getting sick to death of kowtowing to everyone in sight and suffering merely because *they* decided to scare him, and arriving on the dot the minute he was summoned. His intelligence blanked out the truth that this was not wholly how it was, because from now on it would be as he, Barry, said it would be. He would rewrite his own history. No one could stop him now. And all this cowboy talk to himself thrilled and appalled him and he was even clenching his teeth – not, for once, to stem some new cruel agony, but as a demonstration of this big, potent adamance within him.

Tanya skittered through the gears, her elegant fingers only titillating the stumpy shift, and her legs sighed as they undulated over the brake and the accelerator. But Barry was humbled no more. He required no one to pinch him, for he knew he was not dreaming. His whole head had become a floodlight and he saw everything stark and alone and clear, each entity jutting back a harsh black shadow, shooting like a streamer and bonding with the darkness beyond. Nothing was a jumble any more. There could be no hiding from him; no ducking. Each facet was bolted down, and deathly still as in a negative. Nothing was going anywhere until Barry said so.

'Where shall we go, then?' said Tanya. 'Barry?'

'I haven't the slightest idea.'

'You must have *some* idea. I can't just drive nowhere.'

'I really don't know.'

'Well we'll go to a place I know, OK? OK? Barry?'

Barry just looked at her profile.

'Fine,' he said.

And then they were there, and then they were sitting at a table, were they? No, wait, other things had happened first. Barry was – yes, he *was* sitting at a table, this was true, and Tanya was opposite him, not looking at him but craning her neck around, the better to be seen. But other things had happened before, and Barry was finding it difficult to restore a cohesive order of events, his memory, recent memory, flickering like a respliced silent newsreel. The restaurant was known

– not known to Barry, but known – and the reception had been what? Warm? No, not warm. Mixed. Tanya was an old friend, clearly – and Barry? Barry was the thing with Tanya. Did the waiter say that? Did he? 'Ah, Miss Tanya. How nice it is to see you again. Always a pleasure. Would you and your thing care to follow me? Your usual table, Miss Tanya? Of course. And your thing. What of your thing? Will your thing be occupying a chair? Would your thing care for a bowl, maybe?' No, they couldn't have said that. But Barry hated that waiter who had looked too closely. Barry could see into men now, and he knew that this waiter was worthy of loathing. Veins had broken all over the thin long sides of his nose, this waiter, and it looked like ported Stilton and Barry felt that the decay was from within. And was not the place brassily busy when they had stepped down into it? Was there not the hot roar of mass indulgence and the clatter and crash of slicing, slicing, and the gurgle of wine and the steaming hiss of sudden flambée – were not Barry's eyes reddened and stung by the bluish canopy of Havana which was slung across them? But all was quiet now, it seemed. Everyone had gone away. And yet the tables were full. Tanya was looking at him. No concern. Too young and stupid to notice, too vain to care either way.

'Are you Jewish?' she said suddenly. 'Not that it matters.'

Barry was struck by this. Even in the grip of a distorted perception, he felt this brush with the bizarre.

'No, I don't think so,' he replied with suspicion. And then, buoying himself with confidence: 'No. No, I'm sure I'm not. Why?'

'No reason. I said it didn't matter. It's just that some people are, that's all. I don't think it's a *bad* thing or anything, do you?'

'What? Being Jewish? No, I don't think that's a bad thing.'

Tanya narrowed her eyes and nodded like a child who knows everything.

'Just not a very *good* thing,' she said.

'I didn't say that,' said Barry. I don't care, he thought.

'No,' agreed Tanya, 'but that's what you meant. There's a lot of prejudice. London is full of fascists.'

'I hadn't noticed,' sighed Barry.

'No, well, you wouldn't, would you? Not,' she tacked on, ducking out of sight behind a leather menu, 'that it matters one way or the other.'

The cloth was stiff and hard. It must have taken two men to bend it over the table. But there was still the faint peachy stain of soup gone by. Two carnations in a silver flute. The paintings on the wall were vulgar and for sale, and the notice called them artworks. Barry could hear a stifled ringing, but it must be part of the hubbub, he thought. There was so much silver: burners, buckets, bowls – all burnished black-and-white stripe bright. A man could go blind with all the silver in here.

'Barry, you're not listening to a single word!'

'I am.'

'Well what did I say, then?'

'How should I know? I haven't the faintest idea. Do they serve champagne cocktails, do you suppose?'

And that was all it took to wipe off Tanya's face whatever it was that had been there. She grinned with mischief.

'Oh great!' she enthused. 'Let's have one!'

'Let's have two,' Barry amended. 'Waiter! Four champagne cocktails, if you please.'

The waiter seemed surprised that Barry could speak. Barry for his part was conscious of an idle shock due to the fact that the waiter had seen fit to listen. They didn't, usually.

'Are you hungry?' asked Tanya.

'I could eat a whore,' replied Barry. He did not know why. He had never said it before. Tanya just nodded. She had heard what she had expected to hear.

'Me too,' she said. 'I'm starving.'

159

She went on to say other things, but Barry could not hear. Her mouth, lovely mouth, moved in time to the room. The white table receded askew into a rhombus and all before Barry curved up into the sides of a convex bowl. It was so peaceful. A stretched desert of tables, bobbling with quiet and happy people. The glow on the bottles seemed kinder than silver, and the bit of noise now seeping back was gentle, whispered, churchlike in its reverence. And even as it grew louder Barry could take it in, and now the movements of the people no longer resembled those of starched marionettes, and with the increased volume the fluidity of motion returned and Barry was back in the restaurant and Tanya was saying wake up dopey and he had drunk his two cocktails already. He smiled. He felt full of kindness. They would have a nice meal – Barry and his two new friends: Tanya, the body, and this great hard rock of a gun, warm as a coal against his stomach.

Hilary breathed through a reflective Gitane and thought dear old George, he's just like Nicholas in many ways: just look at the way they hate each other. Natural, she supposed. Flattering, actually. Hilary rather enjoyed it – and she acknowledged this – but she dared say it was very Freudian and dreadfully wrong and all the rest of it, but who cared, actually? She couldn't see anyone suffering unduly. It all seemed to work out all right.

Of course George *had* come over, eventually. By about eight, Hilary had become sure he wouldn't ring again – surprised he hadn't before – and felt rather hurt about it, if she was frank. Not like George at all. The tactical withdrawal played no part in George's handling of affairs. And then he had rung, and of course gone about it in quite the wrong way, which put him right in the palm of Hilary's hand, which was where she found it most comfortable to have him. Not that you ever heard him complain – no, not George.

'Hilary, for God's sake!' he had spluttered. 'I'm in a bloody call-box in Soho and it's raining and I've only got one ten pee left now for God's sake, Hilary!'

'What are you doing in Soho?'

'What?'

Hilary grinned with malevolence. Sheer gloating.

'It must be a bad line,' she said. 'I said, what are you doing in Soho? Naughty boy.'

'Hilary, you are not talking to your bloody son!'

'Don't bring my "son", as you call him, into this. Don't talk about Nicholas like that. Don't you dare.'

'I wasn't talking about – I didn't say – look, Hilary, I've only got one ten pee left!'

'Well I expect your salary will be through soon, George. I can lend you a pound or two till then.'

'Look, don't be funny, will you? Look, there are three bloody great black blokes outside this box and I don't like the look of them at all and *please* don't start on about racism, Hilary, you know what I mean and – Christ! That's the bloody pips, hold on, don't go away, where's the bloody hole . . . right. There. Hello? Hello? Hilary? You there?'

'Hello, George.'

'Right. Now that's my last ten pee so stop playing around and *tell* me, for God's sake. Oh, please let me come over, Hilary. Please. I really want to see you. You know I care about you.'

'Why are you in Soho?' Relentless.

George exhaled heavily.

'Look, if you really *must* know I was due to meet someone from work down here and the bastard hasn't shown. I've been hanging around for nearly an hour and if I have to shrug off one more tout I'll go mad.'

'I see,' said Hilary slowly. 'So you only want to come round now because you've been stood up. Is that it?'

'Look, I didn't want to meet him in the first place but he pleaded with me. What could I do? You can't let a bloke down. He's got a few problems at the moment. Please, Hilary. I'm very near some terribly good wine places. Taittinger? Yes?'

'I don't know, George,' said Hilary. But she did, of course. 'What about *my* friend? I've got someone coming too, remember.'

'Please, Hilary. Please. Look, the pips are going to go and I haven't got any – '

'Oh Christ, George, if you tell me you haven't got any ten pees again I'll scream. All right, then. Come over, if you have to. And don't forget you said a magnum.'

'Oh thanks, Hilary. Thanks. We'll have a great time. I really care for you, you know that, Hilary.'

'Save it, George.'

'I'll be there soon.'

'I expect you will. 'Bye George.'

Hilary had put down the 'phone thinking yum, Taittinger, lovely. It was all just as well, really, because her girlfriend, old school friend, actually, had let her down at the very last minute. Said she thought the waters were breaking and the thing wasn't due for seven weeks and so she and her husband had gone flummoxing off to the hospital in a right middle-class flap. Good of her to 'phone, really. Under the circumstances. But what a fuss. Hilary favoured home births: natural, simple, and buckets of blood.

George had arrived, a bit wet, with two bottles of Taittinger because they didn't have magnums and would that do? Hilary had said it would have to, wouldn't it? They had eaten her Chinese meal and George had pretended to like it and Hilary had said you never told me you knew Susan and George had looked perplexed and said Susan? Susan who? I don't know any Susan and Hilary had expressed surprise because according to Susan she knows you, George – says you

162

bought her a necklace, and this time George's protestations had a bit more guts to them and he riposted she's lying, then, isn't she, this Susan person, whoever she is, and Hilary passed the opinion that it seemed an odd thing to lie about, didn't George think? To which George replied that he didn't frankly care and had he told Hilary how lovely she looked tonight. He meant – *especially* lovely. And Hilary had said take your hand away, George, we haven't had pudding yet, and George had started to say who needs pudding when he can have – but he didn't finish because the looks Hilary gave out sometimes could really put a chill on the heart and anyway there was another bottle of bubbly to go yet, plenty of time, no need to rush. Take your time, he thought. But Jesus, it was getting late. And there was always the consciousness of that child Nicholas in the house; George could never shake it off. Sometimes the little wretch just marched into the room at particularly vexing moments. Hilary had gone to get the other bottle now, and George felt a stirring of tension between his legs as he watched her move. Christ, what an awful meal, he was thinking. In George's view, the woman who suggested that the path to a man's heart lies through his stomach had set her sights too high. Where had he heard that one? Somewhere, he supposed. He'd kill bloody Barry, when he saw him. Still, at least he was back with Hilary again. And Susan could go to hell too, if she thought she could treat him like that. All women were the same – all mouth. Unreliable. He was better off out of it.

George got up off the floor (they had been sitting on the floor – Hilary's choice) and sank into a sort of divan thing in the corner. Day-bed. Last Sunday's papers were bunched behind cushions, and George moved them away and lay back with his head against the wall. Hilary came back into the room with the champagne and sighed. The sheer lumpish predictability of George often made her sigh. George caught the sigh and thought hell, she could *try* and be a bit more romantic; she didn't *have* to make it all so mechanical, all such a bore. Christ, there *was* champagne, after all – two bloody bottles of it. And Hilary poured some out. She had opened it in the kitchen because George always played it up and made as if he was a racing driver at New Year and Hilary considered the reluctant pop and whoosh vulgar and wasteful and it made everything sticky afterwards.

'Come and sit beside me,' said George.

Hilary winced as he patted the bed. What was *wrong* with him? He was so cackhanded.

'I like sitting on the floor,' she said.

'I know but – oh hell. Stay on the floor, then. My legs were breaking down there.'

'Champagne, George?' Peasant, she thought.

'Thanks,' said George. Thanks, he thought. It's *my* champagne!

They sipped and fell into silence. George flicked through an *Observer* supplement, and Hilary watched the bubbles rise in the flute in strong thin golden lines. Friday nights were usually like this. Saturday tomorrow. Hilary had promised to play chess with Nicholas, which she was quite looking forward to. And the Taittinger was beautiful: so clean.

'Hilary, are you huffing or what?'

'What *do* you mean, George? I was just thinking. That's all.'

George sniffed. 'Not about me, I bet.'

'No, not, actually.'

'Who, then?'

'Don't be childish, George.'

George beat the bed with the flat of his hand.

'Don't *say* that sort of thing to me. You're *always* saying that sort of thing to me. It's so dismissive. I am *not* childish. I am *not* a child. Now come over here, for God's sake.'

Hilary turned to look at him.

'Puerile,' she said.

'Hilary, I'm warning you – '

'Juvenile,' Hilary said. 'Adolescent, at best.'

'Shut up, Hilary. I'm not telling you again.'

Hilary turned back and smiled and drank more champagne. Why, she thought, doesn't he close his mouth, get up, come over and *take* me? Why doesn't he do that? Because, Hilary reflected with quasi-affectionate despair, because he was George, that was why.

'Oh *please* come over here, Hilary,' he whined. 'It's getting awfully late. I've got a pile of paperwork to get through at home. I've been doing sod-all at the office lately.'

Hilary reviewed all the things she could say.

'All right, George,' she said, and got up in stages as if it was all a great effort. Standing in front of him, she let fall away the black sash holding together her kimono – she always wore her kimono when using the wok – and spread wide the wings of it, raising her arms like the Spirit of Ecstasy, except for the smile which was mocking, almost. Hilary was naked beneath, and the softness of the surrounding silk and the shadows it cast were kind to her body, she knew. George tried to be exasperated by the jeering in Hilary's flaunting attitude, but he was terribly excited and now, just now, the champagne hit him between the eyes like a stone.

'Which bit of me this time, George?' offered Hilary. 'It was a breast last week, wasn't it? The right one, I think. Or was it the other? I really can't remember.'

'Shut up, Hilary,' said George. His face felt so red, and a lot of it was embarrassment because she knew really, Hilary – she understood, but why did she always behave as if not only *she* was a thing, but that he was as well? He stood up anyway, because all his half-chewed resentment was overcome by this bloody lust thing, he had long since recognised, and anyway, it would be over soon, and then it wouldn't bother him, and then he could go. George dragged back the coverlet on the bed, and then just put his hands on her. Hilary was swaying in a slow, solitary dance which she once said made her feel so deliciously *common* and George had his hands all over her and he felt his fingers swelling fat like they always did, a hank of purple sausages, full-blooded and clammy, and he could not bear her undulations any longer and his own control was already slipping and he bundled Hilary half onto the bed and she *would* have to let out that winded sound – there wasn't an ounce of feeling in her, he was sure of it. He arranged her like a toy in just the position he wanted and he scrabbled at his trousers – they had a button inside the waistband as well as a catch, these ones – and *that* was always the moment she *moved*, curse her, and put herself completely differently and with one hand he tried to push her back where she was and he was half out of his trousers now and she did it just to render him absurd, he was sure of it, but he was beside her now and he had her thigh between his two hands and he yanked off his pants and pressed himself against her and he was as soft and warm and throbbing as that fine woman's leg, and he started moving himself against her skin and Hilary stroked his hair and said all right my baby? Hmm, he said, hmm, lovely. And Hilary said that he was a good boy, really, and was he warm enough and he buried his face between her breasts and rubbed harder and harder against her leg and threw an arm around her neck and looked up imploringly into her generous eyes and she put one engorged nipple into his open wet mouth and held him and he went stock-still and then he jack-knifed as the seed spilled out of him, glazing her leg and hip, coursing a little down into the folds, and his face was held in a rictus of something approaching pain and she said feeling better? Feeling better now, baby? And he whimpered and she kissed the end of his nose and ruffled his hair and he wiped dry his slackened mouth with the back of his hand and said thank you, Hilary, thank you. I really care for you. You are so good to me. Are there any tissues?

Hilary wrapped the kimono around her and lolled back with a cigarette while George put his clothes back together.

'I suppose you're going?' she said.

'Christ, Hilary. You could be a bit understanding. I said I had a hell of a lot to do. It's not early, you know.'

'Yes, George,' said Hilary. 'You did say.'

Actually, she didn't give a damn. Actually, she was rather pleased. It would be nice to have the place to herself again. George stooped to the table and took a pull at his glass of champagne.

'You don't *have* to drink it all before you go,' said Hilary.

'What do you mean? There's over half a bottle left.'

Hilary leaned forward to verify this.

'Good,' she said.

And then it just petered out. George said a few more things – it all sounded rather tedious and banal, Hilary didn't know, she wasn't really listening.

'Well, 'bye then,' said George at the door.

''Bye George.'

'You might be a bit – '

'What? A bit what?'

'Nothing. Doesn't matter. Well, 'bye then.'

'Oh go if your're going for Christ's sake, George.'

'Oh Hilary!' George pleaded.

'Oh, George!' she mimicked. 'Go on. Off with you. Work to do – remember?'

'Well I have, as it happens. 'Bye, Hilary.'

Hilary breathed out heavily.

'Good*bye*, George.'

And he went, thinking that's that, then, didn't go too badly, all things considered. Bloody Nicholas didn't barge in, anyway. Whether or not it was worth all the stress was another matter. To say nothing of the champagne.

Hilary sat on the floor when he was gone thinking God, I thought he'd never go. She savoured the rest of the Taittinger, and that was the moment she thought yes, George and Nicholas were not that dissimilar – except that Nicholas, of course, you could really *talk* to. When the doorbell went, Hilary actually said out loud:

'Oh no! What now? What has he left behind *this* time?'

She was really annoyed. And as she swished along to the front door, her annoyance grew until she was smouldering. Hilary had a little treat in store for herself tonight, and she wanted to be left in peace to enjoy it. He was such a bumbler, George. He fumbled everything. Hilary didn't know why she put up with him.

It was Susan at the door, but Hilary's tone was quite as flat and unwelcoming as she had intended it to be anyway.

'Oh,' she said. 'It's you.'

'Hello, Hilary. I know it's rather late but – '

'Yes, all right,' snapped Hilary. 'Come in if you're coming. I haven't got any food or anything. There's no booze.'

'I've brought a bottle, actually.'

'Yes, well, before you start asking whether I'm *sure* you're not intruding why don't you come *in*, for God's sake! You didn't bring any cheese as well, did you? We could spear little cubes of it on cocktail sticks.'

'I'm sorry, Hilary – if I've come at a bad time . . .'

'Oh come *in*, Susan, and do shut up for heaven's sake.'

Hilary just stalked back down the hall beseeching the gods to tell her – just to *tell* her – why people would never just go *out* and why they would never just come *in*. And why couldn't they leave her alone in the first place? She should charge by the hour.

'Oh,' said Susan, when she saw the plates and glasses. 'You've had company.'

Hilary hissed through her teeth with real seething venom.

'Christ, Susan, you could drive me insane tonight! What on earth is *wrong* with you lately? You used to be a thinking person! A real woman! You used to have a mind! All you do these days is come out with these ridiculous Mills and Boon clichés, or else you're breaking out into floods of tears!'

Susan's eyes began to swim and she bit her lip.

'Oh no Jesus Christ you're not going to cry *again*, are you!' exclaimed Hilary, nearly shrieking. 'God save us, Susan – what's wrong with you *now*?'

'Please, Hilary. Don't.'

Hilary threw up her arms and chopped the air once with stiff, splayed fingers. She was done with all this. Susan – everyone – could just do what they liked. People were so . . . how could they *be* so *stupid*! She cast herself onto the divan and turned over the pages of the *Observer* supplement fast, with deliberation, and a drumbeat precision.

'Can I sit down?' queried Susan.

Hilary's eyes flicked up, and then back again. The question was beneath contempt. Certainly it didn't bear answering.

'I want,' Susan went on doggedly, 'to talk to you.'

'And I want,' countered Hilary, 'some peace.'

Susan dropped her eyes.

'I'll go, then.'

'Go.'

'I really want to stay, Hilary!'

'Stay! Stay! Go! Do whatever the hell you want just leave me alone God Almighty!'

Susan slipped off her coat and took a bottle of Stolichnaya out of a Louis Vuitton barrel bag. She snapped open the capsule and sniffed a flute that was on the table, just managing to stop herself from asking if it was clean – God, what would

Hilary have said to that! It was odd that Hilary seemed to bring out the prissy in Susan: none of this mattered in her own flat. Odd. And she supposed she didn't dare ask if there was any tonic either. Susan really didn't know what was wrong with Hilary, flying off the handle like that. Problems of her own, she expected. After all, Susan *had* rather barged in, she supposed – but there were times when no one but Hilary would do. Even when she was like this. Anyway, she'd calm down soon. She usually did.

'Would you like a vodka?' asked Susan, and then quickly anticipating Hilary, she added: 'I know – just *pour* it!'

And Hilary *did* smile, Susan was sure. It was fleeting, but it was there. Just for an instant.

'I'm so sorry I don't have any doilies,' said Hilary, to cover it.

'Oh, come on, Hilary! Don't keep it up all evening, please! Here – have some vodka. It's supposed to be good, this stuff. I don't know.'

'Of course it's good. Supposed to be the best, isn't it?' said Hilary, taking the glass. 'Why – didn't you buy it?'

'No, it was – I was given it. He's got lots of. You should see what else he's given me – this bag, for a start. And I've only known him a couple of days.'

'Oh yes – this is lover boy, isn't it? Sounds like my kind of man. I hate those bags. They're common, and overtly expensive.'

'You're very cynical.'

'I don't quite see the connection, but I am, yes,' agreed Hilary. 'Anyway, you were the one to bring up money.'

'Not money. I didn't say money. He hasn't given me any money.'

'Money – things. It's all the same.'

'It isn't. They were presents.'

Hilary put on a lazy grin, full of indulgence.

170

'If you say so, Susan,' she said.

Susan drank vodka. 'It's a completely different thing altogether.'

'There's tonic in the fridge.'

'Oh great. I was rather wanting some tonic.'

'Why didn't you ask?'

'Didn't think. Didn't think till you mentioned it. But I would like a little tonic, actually.'

'Be my guest,' said Hilary. 'I won't, myself. Good as it is, this stuff.'

Susan toyed with saying I shan't bother either, then, but to her palate the 'stuff', as Hilary called it, tasted perfectly foul on its own – unlike gin – and so she went off to the kitchen for tonic, cursing herself inside. Why did even a *little* thing make her feel so clumsy and inferior and gauche? Why had she come here at all? It was so childish. It was just that Wiseman was so very sure of himself, so awe-inspiringly worldly and so downright *rich* that all evening Susan had felt her applied sophistication evaporating under her skin. She felt like a painted-up infant, at risk, out of her class, and wanting to see Hilary. He had a very strange effect on her, this Wiseman character. He was not suave, exactly, but his clothes were expensive and his cuffs showed crisp and blue. He was offhand – even rude – in restaurants, but he was treated very well because, Susan surmised, he only went to places where he was known, and the privilege of displaying moneyed ill-manners was included in the overall charge. He was a most conspicuous spender. It was in one of those little shops under the colonnades of the Ritz that he insisted on buying the Vuitton bag; to carry the vodka in, he said. The vodka he had bought a little earlier because Susan had said she liked vodka. She had been about to say that it was gin she liked, but changed her mind when the opinion was half out of her mouth. Maybe because Mark had been drinking vodkas throughout the evening. In two days, he had given her a job (a *responsible* job), taken her for very lavish meals, bought her presents, and made her feel female without actually appearing to flatter like a playboy. And she had slept with him twice. Well, three times if you counted the last. It was obvious to Susan that he was very taken with her indeed – that he had perceived her potential. She had been cramped and stifled for so very long, and he – a professional, a *businessman*, after all – had immediately spotted that here was no ordinary bored and stupid housewife, but a woman worthy of managerial authority. 'One of nature's bosses,' he had said. But she felt a little bit afraid. He said 'Have a drink', and it wasn't an offer. And if the drink put into her hand was not of her choosing, she drank it at the same speed as he did. If he had said 'Meet me at twelve, and wear something red', she felt she would be there ten minutes early, to be on the safe side, drenched in red from top to toe. Which was sort of what she had always wanted – although that was looking after in a *different* way, but nice all the same. So why did she feel so – it was hard to put a word to it – chilled, maybe? And a bit embarrassed. And scared. Once during the evening, he had forgotten her name, and covered it by calling her 'babe'.

'What the hell are you doing in there!' hailed Hilary.

And Susan remembered where she was; she hadn't even opened the fridge yet, but she did it now, and then she carried through a litre bottle of Canada Dry.

'That's soda,' said Hilary.

'It said tonic – oh Christ it *is* soda. Oh well.'

Susan poured the soda into the Stolichnaya and drank it. It tasted like sparkling turps. She didn't know why people made such a fuss of it. But before this evening, she had not known that people did. Even now she was not sure whether they did or not; after all, she only had his word. And she was a bit

172

drunk, and what had Hilary just said to her? Susan felt sure she had spoken.

'I *said*,' drawled Hilary, in response to Susan's blank and startled stare, 'if you're going to talk, talk! I'm getting tired. There's something I have to do later on.'

Susan crossed her arms on the table, and brought down her chin to rest on her wrists.

'Life is funny,' she said.

Hilary rolled up her eyes and mock-swooned backwards. She felt killed by feebleness, tonight.

'I don't mean,' Susan went on, oblivious, '*funny*. I just mean – you know – *odd*.'

'It's barely credible,' muttered Hilary, the tone beckoning an absent sympathiser to give her strength.

'What's wrong? What are you being sarcastic about now?'

'Oh God, Susan, I can't bear you any more. Look there's something I *have* to do tonight, and seeing as you're just *never* going to talk, and you're just *never* going to go, you might as well join in. Or watch. Or go. I don't mind.'

'Join in?' queried Susan, pouring more vodka. What a strange day it is, she thought.

Hilary was sitting at a little knee-hole desk in an alcove, fiddling around with something in the middle drawer.

'Whatever are you doing, Hilary?'

'Oh *do* be quiet. You're worse than a child. Here – do you want one or not? Yes or no? Don't preach, don't say anything – and *please* don't go through the business of being shocked.'

Susan examined the twisted-up rolls of paper in Hilary's hand.

'Good Lord, Hilary – you don't *still* smoke this stuff, do you?'

'Not always,' returned Hilary, with nonchalance. 'Sometimes I sprinkle it on salads.'

And you never knew with Hilary. She probably did.

'But *hash*,' went on Susan. 'I don't know – it seems so, well – *Sixties*.'

'I'll run out and get you some cocaine, if you think it's more in line with the times.'

'Don't be silly, Hilary. You know what I mean.'

'I don't frankly *care* what you mean, Susan. Yes or no?'

Susan looked again at the fat, yellow cigarettes. They always did look so unappetising, she thought. Dirty, somehow.

'I've been drinking,' she said, with caution.

'Oh well sod you then.'

Hilary just sat on the floor and placed the joint between her lips, just at the tip in the centre. The Vesta flared up the twisted end, and then it died down into grey. Susan received the sweet charcoal whiff of it, and then the coriander. She smiled. It was so nostalgic.

'Smells nice,' she said. 'Always goes for my eyes, though.'

Susan poured more vodka into her glass, and couldn't face the soda this time. Without a word, and without even trying to think about it, she picked up the second joint, and lit it. Tightly packed, she thought, but puffier than a cigarette. Then the smoke suffused her mouth and fled down her throat, an airy kick straightaway spiking to the top of her head. Susan only ever needed a swallow or two. They used to pass them around in the old days.

'Do you do this often?' she said of a sudden. 'Oh God I'm sorry, Hilary – I didn't mean to sound so, you know, awful.'

Hilary's mouth was agape, and the smoke drifted up into a lazy veil masking her eyes, the lids just touching.

'It's quite nice,' Susan said, putting the joint into an ashtray. Was it an ashtray? Or was it a plate? Anyway, so long as it didn't burn the table – Hilary would kill her. She drank more neat vodka, and thought she would smoke again soon. It was just that she had never known quite what she was supposed to expect – when, in fact, high was high – and so she never knew how much to smoke; too much made her sick. Certainly she had never experienced all the floating and the unreal dreams and the colours that everyone talked about. Or had that been the other – LSD? God, it was so long ago now, she could hardly remember. But it did include a feeling of peace, which was rather nice. Actually, already she felt unable to sense the chair beneath her, although she knew she was sitting – but this, she thought, was more down to the booze than anything.

'Are you there, Hilary?' she said. Of course, she knew that she was – had to be – but where? Susan couldn't locate her just at the moment. But there was a hiss, she heard a hiss. Hilary shushing her, probably. Or sucking in. Or breathing it out. Anyway, it proved that Hilary was there, somewhere about. Susan picked up the cigarette and it hadn't gone out, which they usually did ... yes, they usually went out ... and there was still a good half of it left. Very well made. How clever Hilary was. How very adept.

Below the knee, Susan's legs were very swollen. Where they ended she was not at all sure, but she kept them pressed very tightly together, or else the ballooning would know no bounds. Her feet, her two feet, were clad in padded lead, and seemed further away than the ends of her legs. Her glass was slid out of her hand and she told Hilary that hers was over there, that Hilary's glass was over there, and Hilary said something and Susan said what and Hilary said that it didn't matter and Susan thought she was right: it didn't, of course. Susan lifted up her head, taut and erect, and snapped open her eyes. She felt very alert, and all around her shone with an individual clarity. She laughed, and a fizzing echo of it spiralled with a twang around the inside of her head and spilled out beyond to prick and tickle her ears and she nearly fell over, then, but she was all right now. Yes. She thought she would not do that again. No.

When the flood of warmth from Hilary's hand swamped and filled the side of her leg, Susan sighed with the softness and the pleasure. As she stood, urged by hands, her neck could hold her head no longer, and it fell down and around like a dandelion on a sappy, flattened stem. Hilary lifted it up and told Susan that she was all right, all right, and Susan knew this to be true. And on the bed, Susan could not believe how simple and white the ceiling was above her and her arms wrapped with languor around a body. Clothes, cloth, fell away like petals and she was lapped with warmth from all around. As Hilary's eyes swam up to and into her, the gentleness of her power made Susan cry and she bit knuckles and washed her face with tingling hands. A feeling of bliss and of gratitude filled her now, and then the clarity came again as she looked and touched Hilary's beautiful body, hovering above the length of her, and then coming down on her to rest, before arching away again like a cat. Oh Hilary, was in her mind, oh Hilary this is so so good. And Hilary answered that it was, which didn't seem strange, and she said that it was better than men and Susan thought this so right, so *obviously* true, that she just cried out and then clung to Hilary and pulled at Hilary and if only Hilary and Susan could wash into each other they could blot out men altogether and as Hilary's hair whipped over her face, a truly astonishing knowledge razored into Susan's consciousness and as she saw the truth her stomach convulsed with the pleasure she was feeling and causing because the horror of men was now stark and cold and clear: they either just *take* you, or else they just *don't*.

'Who paid the bill?' said Barry. 'Who paid the bill who paid the bill who paid the bill?'

'Oh shut up, Barry,' exclaimed Tanya. 'We're having a nice

176

time aren't we? What does it matter who paid the bill? Why are you going on and on?'

'Who paid the bill?'

'Barry!'

Barry coughed. 'Who paid the bill?' he asked.

'Look, you're getting to be a real downer about this, Barry – now leave it alone, for Christ's sake. Where shall we go? Want to go to a club? I know a great club near here.'

Barry shifted in the bucket seat of the Porsche, lifted himself over the gear shift and half on to Tanya, which made her giggle and push him away and hold him against her. He kissed her mouth.

'Who paid the bill?' he said.

'Kiss me again.'

'Who paid the bill?'

'Jesus – I paid the bill! Now shut up about it, can't you?'

Barry widened his eyes like a comedian, and then narrowed them down into pantomine suspicion.

'Whooo paid the bill?'

And Tanya laughed and said: 'You're nuts.'

Barry kissed her again. He held on to her breasts, which felt very young. He could not remember the last time he had held on to such very young breasts. Tanya had just put on more scent and the whole car was alive with it. She ran her hands over his chest and under his jacket and then she stopped them dead.

'What the hell have you got in your pocket?'

Barry kissed her hard, fingering the baby softness of the nape of her neck.

'A gun,' he said, nuzzling her throat, and drivelling with amusement.

'Very funny,' said Tanya. 'Well come on – where are we going to go? D'you feel like a club? You can't come back to me,

I'm afraid – my dad'll be there. He's funny about things like that. We could go to a hotel?'

'A hotel?'

What an absurdly wonderful idea. Good Lord, yes.

'Mm. Somewhere full of reps and anonymous. I do that a lot – well, not that much. Post House, Holiday Inn – that sort of place.'

Barry sat back with a schoolboy grin, which he slid her way.

'Who'll pay the bill?' he said.

Tanya laughed, and kicked the Porsche into action.

'Shush!' she said, and the rain-glistened car swung out and gunned off into black, thrilling London.

'You know what?' chattered Tanya, skipping a light.

Barry didn't know what.

'I heard of a guy, once, and he was in love with two women. Well, I don't know if he was in *love* with two women, but he was married, and he was seeing someone else, see?'

Barry saw.

'Well, after a while – *Jesus*, why don't those cyclists look what they're doing! – after a while, things started going wrong for him, this guy – I don't know, money, pressures, usual stuff. And one evening, when his wife was downstairs, he killed himself. Just did it. I don't know how. Forget. Anyway. We're nearly there – you're not bored, are you? Anyway. The woman – the other woman – mistress, if you like, she got to hear about this and was dreadfully upset and all the rest of it because she cared for him, apparently, and all her friends said well that's over anyway, and she said oh no it's not because I'm burning with jealousy and they said *jealousy* – what do you mean *jealousy*? And she said why the hell couldn't he have killed himself when he was with *me*? Incredible, that. And her friends said – look, he was clearly round the bend. What if instead of killing himself he had killed his *wife*? And she said Christ, that would be worse. I'd rather he'd killed me than *that*

178

bloody woman. The place is just on the right. Ghastly, isn't it?
Barry? You still awake?'

'I'm awake.'

'OK. Let's go. Mr and Mrs Smith, shall we be?'

'You seem very . . . versed.'

Tanya was out and slamming doors.

'Don't be stuffy,' she said.

Barry walked into the blaze of the foyer, his eyes struck
open by hundreds of little golf-ball bulbs studding the canti-
levered portico, like a starlet's mirror. There were long, blue
velour sofas running the length of a pillared marble hall, and
Barry sat in one thinking this doesn't look reppy, this looks
swish. But his judgement, he knew, was unreliable, tonight.
Maybe it wasn't swish; maybe it was just flash. For up-market
reps – the ones with waistcoats and a smattering of German,
who knew? Along with a lot else, it all seemed rather beyond
Barry's comprehension. But one fact did percolate through his
sodden mind: if they were to check in – register, it used to be
called – as Mr and Mrs Smith, God save us, then the licensing
laws of this land were no longer applicable – at least, not to Mr
and Mrs Smith – and it was borne in upon Barry too that
above all else, he sorely needed a reviver. Or else young Tanya
would accuse him of being uptight or downbeat or some other
example of her lazy nonsenses, and although he felt well up to
countering such 'laid-back' jargon with eloquence from a
pulpit, he was fast tiring of the role of counsellor, of older
bloody man, of know-all sage. He didn't want to be that *wise*.
Christ, if Tanya had the life and the will (and the money) to
behave like a fresh-faced wanton, then Barry was damned if
he wanted to judge, or condescend, or even *play* at it. Barry
wanted to join in, right from the heart. He looked at the back
of her now. The reception desk was high and padded (same
blue velour as the sofas) and to get her elbows on a par
with the haughty-looking woman behind, Tanya's body was

stretched up on tiptoe, lithe and ready. Quite amazing. So young, and taking care of business. This was surprising. She looked used to the good things, as pretty and as vain as hell, but he had not been ready for the sheer *capability* that she displayed tonight. Money, he thought, breeds guts.

'All done,' she said, actually twirling this great brass key fob around her middle finger. And she was slinking, Barry would swear it. Yes, that was a slink, all right. No mistake about it.

'Well, I'm ready,' announced Barry, trying to catch her to-hell-with-it tone, but thinking this sofa is so bloody low, and I feel so bloody boozed, that if I stand up, I'm done for.

'Can I help you?' offered Tanya, which made him think.

'I'm fine,' said Barry. And he got up. And he was fine. Funny, that. Or was it? Not really.

She click-clacked over to the lift, but Barry couldn't hear his shoes, and he felt as dead as a shadow for a moment. The satin steel doors wheezed open and pinged and it was close and close-carpeted inside and the mêlée of the foyer was squeezed out of his head as the doors clunked to, and a silly tinny melody took its place as the lift streamed upwards and Tanya told him that they were right on top, which did not surprise Barry in the least for the lift was moving so swiftly, with such noisy silence, that it seemed they were standing still, and yet he felt sure that this polished little cubicle had left behind the roof of the hotel long ago. So if he was *that* drunk, why wouldn't his body stop screaming for more? And it was then, in that bloody little lift, that Barry thought he might have a problem. But what was a body to do?

If the entrance to this hotel had been brassy then the corridor had all the anonymity that Tanya had wanted. If it was true what she said, Barry didn't know. Thick blue carpet – *Christ*, they liked blue in this bloody place – flew away like a runway for a mile. The warm length of space was as enclosed and boomingly tranquil as the bowels of a ship, the ceiling stuck with globular lighting. A door slammed softly, somewhere, and a jailer's keys threatened Barry's complacency.

'We've got a suite,' Tanya said.

'Sweet,' said Barry. What? he thought. Whatever. Didn't matter. Whatever the hell.

'Didn't want a porter,' she went on. 'Did we? No luggage. They don't care any more. Used to, though.'

When they were inside – Tanya managed the lock like a professional – Barry just laughed. It was so outrageous. It was just like a set for a film. A Rock Hudson of a room, when he'd stumped off to the Plaza after a row with Doris Day. Sky blue and powder blue and off-white and charcoal and an Easter basket of flowers and Hokusai reproductions and bloody blue carpet and an exquisitely expensive blandness. If it reminded Barry of anything, it was the flat off Baker Street where he'd started this merry little evening. Strange.

'There's no bed,' he said.

'The bedroom's through there,' said Tanya. She seemed so at home.

Barry wandered off in the direction, and a hollow door gave way to a dusty pink chamber, quilted and upholstered, so filled was it with bed. A shingle of satin cushions covered the counterpane, and a clean, lush bathroom winked at him beyond, lit like a stage, and smelling of towels and lilac. It was just like Barry had thought it would be, this sort of place, and all he could feel was grubby. He splayed stiff his five fingers and probed the bed like a physician. It felt like a bed. Why did one *do* that?

Back in the main room, Tanya was whispering and shutting the door, and Barry would have asked what was going on, but when she stepped aside there was a chromium trolley, glittering with delight and bottles, two bottles, he thought –

yes, there were two – of Moët & Chandon, poking out of buckets.

'I asked for the posh one,' piped up Tanya. 'You know – the *great* Moët, but I couldn't think of the name, and I don't think they understood. What have we got here? '76. Oh, that's OK. My dad has '76. *Pérignon* – that's it! Damn! I couldn't remember the name. Still, this'll be OK, yes? Are you any good at opening it?'

Barry was unsure as to whether he was good at it or not, but the sight of those green, glistening bottles had long ago set his gullet aflame and those corks were coming out fast, *that* was for sure.

He made a hash of tearing off the foil, so eager was he for the cool prick of that golden stuff inside his throat, and Tanya was behind him, impudently pushing her groin into his rump and playing her fingers over his face and sharply down to the flat of his stomach.

'Christ – what the hell *is* it that you've got stuck in your trousers? And you know what I mean!'

'I told you,' said Barry. 'Oh hell, the little round bit's snapped off the wire. Ah – that's OK. It's a gun.'

'Yeah, sure it is,' she drawled, like a hostess in a saloon.

'It is. The trick is to twist the bottle and not the cork. You twist the cork – it breaks. And you have to *ease* it. Otherwise you get that Godawful explosion and you lose most of it on the floor.'

Tanya lay into a chair, and undid buttons.

'Is it *really* a gun?' she said.

'It's . . . coming,' grunted Barry. 'Yes, I told you.'

'A *real* gun?' she urged.

The bubbles were thudding up the neck of the bottle now, and it was all Barry could do to hold back the cork. If he could just prise it sideways and let off a bit of the pressure. Yes, the hiss began.

'Yes, a real one. Not a toy. A real, loaded gun.'

The bottle kicked and spluttered, but hardly any was lost. Barry quickly righted the angle to conserve the power of the wine. It wouldn't do to have it coursing down the sides.

'Jesus,' whispered Tanya.

This, thought Barry, was great. God he felt so *good*.

'Why?' he tossed over his shoulder. 'Don't you know people who carry guns? Have you never met anyone who carried a gun before?'

'Well,' said Tanya, 'I didn't think *you* would.'

Barry selected glasses from the trolley that were far too big for champagne, and hurtled the wine into two of them. It foamed up white and spitting as if tantalised by such unaccustomed treatment, and then fizzed down with female resentment. Or was Barry just seeing things in this peculiar way? Hard to tell. Every action, though, felt so bloody *good*. He thrust half a pint of Moët at Tanya's face, and both her hands clasped the glass.

'Are you a hard man, then?' she asked. 'Are you a big, hard man, Barry?'

Barry was smiling quietly, because this was such a lovely drunken game and he felt titillated by everything he touched and everything he heard, but he was thumped and astonished when he met Tanya's eyes and saw there a dark, gemlike glitter of absolute transfixion.

'It depends,' he said, rattled, and scrabbling for a word that would suit, 'it depends on the softness of the woman.'

And that seemed to do it. Tanya drank, gurgled, gave out a sigh as long as a song, and squirmed down into the chair. Her free hand meandered over her, and crept up her own black skirt.

'Barry,' she let loose, and longing was there, Barry knew it. Tanya's eyes were closed and her head lolled sideways, framed in hair gone wild. Her fingers worked on her, but she was hamming it up without mercy. She had seen this somewhere surely – woman trapped in ecstasy, dying from hunger for a man. An invention of pornographers, Barry knew, and now women were trying to do it for real. Anyway, he felt as tired as hell, and this champagne fulfilled him.

'Barry!' she softly screamed. 'Please!'

'Not just now,' Barry grinned. 'I've got a headache.'

It had been a device, true – part humour, part cowardice – but it worked like a bolt. Tanya stopped stock-still, but she had the goodness to grin.

'Bastard!' she hissed.

'Champagne?' offered Barry.

Tanya slithered to the floor, and made like a foetus.

'Bugger off, Barry. I hate you.'

He even contemplated saying charmed, I'm sure, but if he was frank – if he had understood any of this to date – he was getting a little lost, and although he was acutely conscious of the mood having shifted, he was buggered – her word – if he knew where to. Or from what. Or, indeed, what he himself wanted. At this moment – go on, then, finish it – in time. Meanwhile, the Moët was good, and Barry drank it down like lager. A bottle didn't go far, actually, once you got a taste for the stuff. He'd open the other one soon. And they – she – could always ring down for more. In fact, now he came to think of it, what with the lack of sleep and what seemed like an endless ocean of drink – and good stuff too, these days – it was amazing to Barry that he was vertical at all. He really felt quite fresh. A new wave of unsteadiness then rippled through him, and he thought he had better lie down. It was a long, quiet walk to the bedroom, but with careful navigation, Barry thought it might be managed. It was Tanya suddenly grabbing at his ankles that totally threw him, but even then he might have been able to save himself had not the room tipped up into such unaccustomed perspectives that his arms flailed in a despair of their own, unaware of what to grab hold of. He fell awkwardly, in several stages: his hip thudded down onto doubled-up legs, the rest of him caving in like a thick, sliced snake. Tanya received the weight of most of him, and the gun ground down into his pelvic bone. Tanya lifted more of him onto her, and this seemed to please her; she appeared to Barry all but winded, but she pressed him down into her and said crush me crush me crush me.

'I am,' Barry said. And laughed, because it struck him as not exciting now, but silly. He heard the laugh and thought no matter how I feel I must be very drunk because that did not sound like my laugh at all. More it seemed like a grizzled salivation over which his mouth had no control.

Not until the floor rushed up to strike him in the chin did Barry realise that Tanya was up from under him. Where the hell was she off to now? What the hell now? Barry nuzzled his face into the carpet and his limbs were numb and spent. This seemed a good and suitable place to die.

'Barry!'

Oh Christ.

'Barry! Come! Quick!'

Oh sod the woman, Barry thought with misery. What on earth could be so urgent? And why couldn't she come *here*? Oh my God: she has.

'Let go,' Barry slurred. 'Stop pulling at me. Look – *Christ*! You'll have my bloody jacket over my head in a minute! Get off, can't you?!'

But either Barry was imagining the burning velocity with which he was being dragged cheek-down across the carpet, or else Tanya was a very strong girl indeed. And yes, when he dared look up, the walls were pink, and the cool of the quilting flopped down over his reddened face. Barry thought he then quipped that it was the only way to travel, but there was no reaction forthcoming, so possibly the idea had never reached his mouth. Or he had been incoherent. Or gagged in the middle. Barry had no idea whatever what was true. But then, it hadn't been that funny in the first place. Now it seemed that Tanya was lifting, actually lifting him up on to the bed, where he bobbed heavily for a while, consciously subduing the rebellion in his stomach.

'Christ,' he said. 'It's the only way to travel.'

'You've just said that. Now just relax. I'm going to get the hampers.'

And she was back before Barry had seen her go. He really was very tired, and the bed was big and deep. He would be happy to let the evening go, but it was borne in upon him that Tanya had other plans. She was so damned hyperactive. Barry put it down to youth. And now she was tugging at him again, and none too gently.

'Take off all my clothes!' she panted, the excitement of the thought catching in her throat. 'Force me to take off all my clothes!'

Barry rolled away from her.

'You take them off,' he said. 'You do it.'

'No! You! It's got to be you!'

'Why?'

'Then you can beat me.'

Barry cocked an eye.

'Beat you? Why should I beat you?'

'Because you want to!'

'Ah,' said Barry. What an aggressive young girl, he thought.

'Then . . .' Tanya went on.

'Oh God. There's more.'

'Then you must tame me!'

'Impossible.'

'You must try!'

'Why?'

'Because I'm telling you! Co-operate, can't you?'

'But why should I tame you? *How* should I tame you, for God's sake?'

'You must subject me to your will. You *must* show me who is master.'

Barry lay flat on his back and focused hard on this face dancing over him. It was taut and full of energy, the eyes black and wet, the mouth urging him onwards. She was kneeling on the bed, her knuckles on her knees, lithe and catlike.

'Oh well,' said Barry. 'If I *must*.'

He raised a couple of his arms, and latched on to a button; but it was a very small button, and Barry was damned if he could get it to go through the bloody hole.

'Bloody thing,' he said.

'What the hell do you think you're doing?' asked Tanya.

'I'm doing what you told me to do. I'm taking off all your clothes. I'm mastering you. I can't help it if you wear such fiddly buttons.'

'Not like that! You can't do it like that! You have to *tear* them off'

'Tear?'

'Like this,' said Tanya. And she grasped the two sides of her blouse at the neck and dragged it apart and the silk split into shards and those little covered buttons spattered everywhere. She was wearing a very pretty lacy bra, and this too was rent into expensive tatters. Her small brown nipples pointed scorn at him.

'Now go on!' she near screamed. 'Go on!'

'Well Christ – you've done most of it. You do it. You do it.'

Tanya got him by the tie, and screwed it round into his throat.

'Look you bastard!' she hissed. 'I've never had this trouble before! Now subdue me, will you?! *Master* me or I'll break your neck I'm getting so frustrated. And it wouldn't take much breaking – look at you. Christ, you look pathetic just lying there. Are you a man or what? Christ, you really *are* pathetic! Are you a man or what? Be a *man*, can't you?!'

Barry was hurt and amazed. What had possessed the girl? He sat up, and tried to overcome a spasm of fear as he looked again at her face. All arousal had hardened into venom and a kind of mad anger. He passed her a glass of champagne.

'Here,' he said. 'Calm down.'

And he should have seen it coming, but he didn't. He should have covered his face, but it happened all in the same movement, and just as the glass was dashed away from his fingers, so it cracked across his cheekbone and splintered and Barry thought oh my Christ my eyes my eyes and he screwed them tight and thought is that right is that right is that the right thing to do and his mouth had opened in surprise and there was glass in it now he was sure and he didn't dare close it and already his face was tight and sticky with the champagne, and gobbets of drink and splinters were dropping onto the bed. He got to the bathroom, and he got there fast, hanging his whole head under the tap, and the water would do it, the water would wash it away, and it was a long time – hours, no, not hours – before Barry dared let his teeth meet and he opened his eyes with the care of a surgeon. He felt so cold, and his hair hung in limp coils. A gash swelled up from a washed pink to scarlet across his left cheek, but stopped just short of the pouch beneath the eye, thank God. Barry held a velvet towel against his face and let it seep in what it could. The anger rising in him was demonic.

Back in the room, it seemed that Tanya had barely moved. A veritable monument to unconcern, she sipped Moët & Chandon, and studied the ends of her hair. Something ugly slid into Barry, and he walked right up and rammed his tight-balled fist into her naked back, just above the lung. He connected with a bellowing thud, and Tanya was jarred off the edge of the bed and her face creased with pain as she went over, her arm arching back to her spine. Barry was on her before she hit the floor.

'Right, you little sow!' he spat. 'Now you'll get what you asked for!'

'No, Barry – I'm sorry!'

Barry held down her thighs with a bruising strength, and Tanya's head rocked with fear, the eyes black and blue with ruined make-up. He fought with his clothes – bloody clothes – but he wouldn't let up and she was fighting now and she clawed at his gash with her nails, the little bitch, and God if he wasn't so drunk it would help and the air was being knocked out of him with the effort, but he'd get her, he'd get her. And then Susan filled his mind. Why Susan? Why now? And then he saw again the photograph of this bloody girl's father and the anger teetered together with the pain and he was working for control of his face. Barry collapsed panting on top of Tanya and his chest ached badly. He could do nothing. He could do nothing and she was gaining strength. She was smelling his failure and he just had to destroy her. He calmed a little, then, and it seemed natural to draw out the thick, stubby weight of his gorgeous new gun, and the barrel caught the light as he turned it around, and he felt the waves of force as he ripped it into her and her eyes were impaled with disbelief and he did it again and he did it again and he did it again . . .

Later, some time later, Barry lay against the wall, and he stroked the gun gently with caring fingers. It was warm and the smell was of sweetness. He looked up once at Tanya crouched into a heaving ball and whimpering. What was she saying? Hard to make it out.

'Not *really*,' he thought she said. 'I didn't mean . . . oh God . . . I didn't mean *really* . . .'

She tailed off and her eyes swept the room for help, as she clamped her wrists tightly between her legs. She caught his face, and the contact sparked loathing within her.

189

'I'll get you . . . bastard! You just wait . . . get you! We'll get you . . . get you . . .'

Barry stopped listening. He didn't much care. He was getting sick of this life thing anyway, and while he had been sitting there, while he and the gun had just been sitting there, they had made a secret pact. And Barry was not going to let anyone know, not yet, nobody at all. But it was all right for his gun to know, because the gun would help him; the gun was his friend. Yes. It was clear now. After all this time, a decision about life: Barry was going to *kill* his way out. Yes. But shh. Don't tell a soul. Secret.

There were some crumbs, Hovis crumbs, speckling the maple worktop in Moira's kitchen. She garnered them in with the cupped side of a hand, tipping them over the edge into a square of cling-film. There. Even eating a sandwich seemed to make such an unholy mess, but now everything was spotless again. She had already washed the knife, and as it had just been for her, she hadn't considered it worth a plate, and therefore there were crumbs. Devil and the deep blue sea, really. But it was all neat and tidy again now. The kitchen looked just like an advert in *Homes & Gardens*, and Moira felt so at peace. The living-room too was just the way she liked it – sparkling ashtrays, cushions as pigeon-chested as a regiment on parade, rug in line with the fender: lovely. It seemed so easy to keep the whole house nice with Gavin out of the way. Confining his mess to just one room made all the difference in the world. And he was not going to burst in and spoil it all. No. Moira doubted if he could manage the stairs. Her eyes flicked up to the wall clock. Goodness. It was nearly half-past one in the morning. She'd go up and fetch his tray in a minute. Not yet. Make sure he'd finished everything. Poor love; he wasn't getting any better.

Moira was totally free to do what she wanted. It seemed

such a shame to go to bed and waste it. Anyway, she did not feel in the least bit tired. She'd see Gavin in a minute – see he was all right for the night – and then she'd come down again and have an illicit little party, all on her own. How perfectly lovely. Except that parties did seem to create *such* a mess, even if they were only for one. What could she do in the meantime, then? She could sit on one of the peacock sofas, cross her legs, and idly flip backwards through *Harper's & Queen*. Except that she had just rearranged all the magazines and smoothed the cushions, and if she was frank, she would have to admit that she never found anything to engage her in *Harper's & Queen*: all advertisements, and a bit too snobby. Gavin bought it. He brought it home every month. Said he deplored all her housewifey magazines, and why couldn't she ever get wise? We are what we are, Gavin, she usually replied, to which he said well *you* are anyway, that's for bloody sure. Gavin could get very silly at times, over quite the silliest things. Ah well. At least now he was all tucked up in bed, so that was a blessing anyway. She'd go up in a minute and check.

In the cupboard in the living-room, there were still quite a few bottles of sweet white wine. Not so many as recently, because Moira tended to drink them. Indeed, she intended to open another one right this minute. She did not know a lot about wine – thought that all this château and vintage business was so much nonsense – but it seemed to give Gavin a lot of pleasure, and there was no real harm in it that she could see. He hadn't wanted a drink, lately. What with his stomach and everything.

She pulled out a bottle and the name struck a memory. Château d'Yquem, however you pronounced it. *That* was the one that Gavin always mentioned while serving something else. It's not d'Yquem, he'd say, but I think you'll approve. Or somesuch. So presumably, then, this was the yardstick. The best. Moira had it open in a couple of minutes. She felt rather gay, tonight.

Was that a noise upstairs? A sort of whimpering? Couldn't be sure. She'd go up in a minute.

Moira sipped the wine. Very nice. Nothing special, so far as she was a judge, but very nice all the same. She'd have to bring up the bottle when she went to tuck him in. Yes. Now. Just throw away the capsule and the cork, brush up the crumbs – *more* beastly crumbs – and put away the brimming glass. What could be neater than that? Moira would have liked to sit, but it seemed such a shame. Everything looked so nice.

Yes, that *was* a noise. Funny noise. Sort of gurgling. Poor lamb. Moira smiled. What a to-do it is. A woman's work. Who'd be a mother? She'd bring him a little whisky.

As she mounted the stairs, Moira heard the noises more clearly. Like an old man gargling. What a funny sound for a fellow to make.

'Hello, Gavin dear,' she said. 'Everything all right? Was the soup all right? Not too hot was it dear?'

Gavin was lying flat and stiff in the bed, his head jammed at right-angles and bolstered forward by too many pillows. He looked intent upon seeing his feet. A bed-tray on legs straddled his chest, his chin just touching the gallery. His face was colourless, and his lips white and dry. A terrible clotted rasping issued from his throat and his breathing came thick and short. His wide eyes were beseeching Moira, his tongue too lost for talking.

'Oh you *are* a good boy!' trilled Moira. 'You've finished it all. You must have been a very, very, hungry little boy indeed!'

Gavin's mouth champed on air and the throaty rumble deepened as his head slipped further down into the bed. He batted his arms under the duvet, but it had been covered with a sheet and tucked under tight.

192

'Look, darling,' went on Moira, holding up the bottle. 'Moira's being very naughty. It's that lovely wine you're always talking about. I was *so* thirsty.'

Gavin's eyes shot bulbous, and his mouth was fighting for conrol. Only the thick, fat crease in his neck had any colour now, livid and swelling.

'But Moira hasn't forgotten little Gavin. Moira's brought up a little whisky because you've been such a good boy and let mummy get on with her work. Here you are!'

As she approached him with the glass, Gavin's face flickered with fear, his cheeks empurpled before flattening again into deadly white. His head thrashed sideways and hit the tray, and the glass inexorably followed. This time, when he snapped back his head, Moira caught it, and now she had him by the mouth.

'What a fuss!' she exclaimed. 'What a big fuss over such a little, little whisky! Now come on, Gavin dear – you *know* you like whisky. Open. Open wide for mummy!'

Gavin's chest heaved up in a spasm and a spoon clattered off the tray. The breath thumped in his heart and his eyes rolled upwards. Sweat dripped from his night-matted hair down onto his eyelids and hung there.

'Now don't make Moira cross,' warned Moira. 'You know how Moira can be when Moira gets cross.'

Gavin gasped for breath, and Moira darted out a hand to his jaw and held it. She poured the whisky straight into his gullet and shut his open mouth like a door. A tremor of agony passed over Gavin's whole face as it bloated like a toad, and a little whisky ran down his chin and into his jowls. Moira released the pressure, and Gavin fell away, pumping breath heavy and slow, his white eyes staring away in terror from out of a blanched and fleshy face.

Moira took away the tray and smoothed the sheet.

'There!' she said, like a nanny. 'That wasn't so bad now, was it? What a fuss! Moira's never *seen* such a fuss.'

She felt the duvet before she turned to leave.

'Oh!' she accused with revulsion. 'You've been *dirty*! You've been a dirty, dirty boy! Well, dirty boys can *stay* dirty boys – all night long. And let that be a lesson to them.'

And then she turned dreamy.

'Now then, have I got everything? Ah – my wine, my lovely sweet wine. Mustn't forget that, must I? That *would* be a waste. All right, then – nighty-nighty, Gavin. Moira will be down-stairs, so you mustn't fret. Be a good boy. Sleep well. Good-night, little Gavin.'

Moira looked down at his shocked, big chalky face, and paused for an instant, with a finger on the dimmer.

'Oh Gavin,' she tittered, before snapping the room into dark. 'You do look like a mammal, just *lying* there.'

There was a fly on the chicken. It was fixed on the golden breastbone, whittling its forelegs. The gloating blue eyes stared blank and sullen, and Annie just studied the filthy thing. The legs were twinkling like cutlasses. God, it must be so late. She must have been asleep. Her shoulders shuddered from the cold, but now the fire was only ashes. Hours ago, Annie had been angry: she had felt cheated and stupid and alone. Now she just hoped that Barry was all right. Where could he be? Where on earth could he be at – what time was it? – my God, it was nearly four in the morning. Not at home, surely? He couldn't have forgotten? Well yes, Annie acknow-ledged. Given Barry's behaviour over the last couple of days, he could easily have forgotten. So what should she do? She had Barry's number – had had it for years – but she had never rung it before. Had never wanted to. She would have hated hearing his voice booming hollow from somewhere else. From that place. And even now – how *could* she? What would she say if he answered? What would she say if he didn't?

Annie got up from the chair and flexed her hands. They were white. The room looked garish, now that it was so very, very late. Annie turned off a lamp, and turned down another. Now there was a grey and neglected air, and it made her sad to think how long she had sat there, all alone. Should she go to bed? No. She would never sleep. And yet what was there to wait up for? He would never come now. Oh well. She would wait a bit. A bit longer. He might come. You never knew. So long as he was all right. That was the main thing.

Annie should have collected her mother's pension today. She did not know why she thought of it now. She'd get it in the morning. A sense of desolation swept over her at the thought of tomorrow. And then there would be Sunday. Weekends were such a hopeless time. She never saw Barry at weekends – not really – so there was no point in having them. But they had to be got through. That was life.

The pounding on the door could have come a long time later. Annie might have slept. Certainly the noise startled her, and she was again sitting in the chair by the fire, except that there was no fire, and she couldn't remember sitting, and she surely couldn't remember sleep. But the bang, and then the bang-bang on the door shot through her like a shock, and even before she was aware she was thinking Barry, that must be Barry, oh God I hope it's Barry, what time is it? Doesn't matter, doesn't matter – so long as it's Barry. God, she hoped he was all right.

Annie flew into the hall and then hesitated. Everything was again so still and quiet that she was halted and confused. Then the bang came again and this spurred her to run to the door and she was fighting with the lock and now the banging was coming like a demented drumbeat and she was twisting the lock any way it turned and she could feel the urgent pulsing of each thud on the panels shaking into her own arms and still she couldn't get that lock to open and of course she was sure now it was Barry and God knew what was wrong with him, beating at the door like a madman at this time of night, and tears of frustration sprang out of Annie's eyes and God what was the *matter* with this door? And then she saw the bolt, of course, the bolt, Annie's mother must have shot the bolt, of course she would, that was just like her, just the sort of thing she *would* do, and Annie was easing it out now but it seemed as if there was a terrible pressure on the other side of the door and it wouldn't come easily and the battering on the panels was a hysterical tattoo inside her head and now the door flew in and caught Annie on the side of her face and Barry fell into her and on top of her and the whole dead weight of him sent her over and she was thrown onto her back and was near stunned senseless by the appalling weight lying right across her body and a little yelp was sent out of her and now lights were snapping on and Annie's mother came down the stairs and her chin shivered on the verge of dropping down into a scream and Annie shouted go back mother it's all right and Annie's mother came down faster with eyes as wild as a nightmare and she was yammering and her arms were shaking and soon she'd scream and Annie wrenched herself from under Barry who rolled over like a sandbag and Annie had the door shut and she caught her mother now rooted and trembling at the foot of the stairs and swift and silent she propelled her into the room and dropped her into a chair and Annie refused the fear and desperate enquiry in her mother's eyes and slammed the door shut on all of that and got back to Barry and she had him on his back now and his head was in her lap and he was breathing, it was all right, he was breathing, and his mouth gave out baby-noises and his dear, dear cheek was cut and blue veins jerked at the puffed-out lids of his eyes; now he was quieter and then he was peaceful, and

Annie pressed back the hair from his forehead and stroked his head and his whole body loosened and she would stay like that, just like that, for a while, for as long as it took, because it would be all right now, he would be fine now that Annie had got him, and then she'd move him gently, and he'd help her then, and then she could look after him for the rest of the night. The soothing motions of her hands were calming them both and a feeling of peace flooded into Annie and all the anxiety of the evening was over.

It was then that the racked and throaty scream ripped out of her mother still locked in the room, and it hung ragged in the air before fading back into the sounds of night. Something had fallen inside the room, but Annie really couldn't attend to it now. Barry needed her help, and she only had one pair of hands, and her mother would be fine, just as soon as she was calm. Annie would stay in the hall with Barry, and soon, very soon, everything would be quiet again. Barry's body jerked and tightened, and quicker than Annie saw, he was on all fours staring like a hunted animal, again on guard.

'Barry,' said Annie. He was showing life, that was something but the strangeness of his behaviour was becoming just a little sinister. Annie had seen him drunk before, but this was very different. He must, she thought, be ill.

'Barry,' she said again. It was just a form of contact. Annie stretched out an arm. It was like calming a frightened pet. She was even sliding her index finger against the side of her thumb in order to inspire a docile trust, and insanely, she was reminded of the fly.

'It's all right, Barry,' she said.

It was time, she thought, to move him. Upstairs would be best, but looking at Barry now, hunched up against the skirting, upstairs seemed unlikely. But she had to get him out of the hall. A barely controlled whine from her mother, stifled but regular, was throbbing through the house, and it was anyway ridiculous to be in the hall. Barry – Annie – needed seclusion, and the hall was a brutal and exposed place to be; at least that was how it appeared to Annie now, and *she* was in control, after all. It was up to her. No one else was going to do anything.

'Let's go up,' she said, as soft as was audible. 'Barry. We're going upstairs now.'

Barry's body seemed to give in at the very words. He fell again, and Annie knew that she could only hope to get him in to the back room. The room where her mother lay whimpering, damn the woman. Why couldn't she have stayed in bed? Why did she always have to make everything so difficult?

'Can you just get up, Barry?' Annie pleaded. 'Can you stand? Let's just get you into the room and I'll get a nice blaze going again and then you'll be all right. Barry? Did you hear me, love? Come on.'

Annie hitched her shoulder under Barry's arm, and with knees bent and the strain near breaking her, she dragged him the length of the hall, his own weight hitting open the door which swung back into him, but they were in now, they were in, and Annie had him over by the chair and Barry fell into it and Annie's mother whinnied in fear, tight in the opposite corner. Annie looked over at her; she had forgotten that her mother was in the room, or even on earth, and she could never remember seeing before the childlike expression on her mother's face. The chin was varnished with saliva and her wet eyes were beseeching. And something else was strange. The table had capsized and the roast chicken was being tugged at and gnawed by a speckled cat intent upon its feast, and neither Annie nor Annie's mother possessed a cat and the window was open and Annie did not remember leaving the window open – indeed she felt sure she had closed them all because the evening was a cold one. The cat was wary but gluttonous as it ripped into the chicken, and Annie's attention was caught by Barry slumping sideways and something fell out of his jacket and clunked to the floor and Annie instinctively picked it up and held it and it was a gun and the barrel was streaked with blood.

Annie just stared, and a steady staccato moan started up from her mother's mouth. It rose in tone and threatened more. Then Annie just wheeled round on Barry and her lips drew back from her teeth in terror and fury and she screamed at Barry Christ Jesus Barry what have you *done* what have you *done* what have you *done* oh Jesus what have you *done*?! And Annie's mother's face gashed open into a shriek and then a wailing, and her eyes rolled upwards before she fell.

Annie trembled and continued to stare at Barry, her mouth ugly and ajar, the gun hanging down from her paralysed fingers. Barry looked at her for the very first time. He looked at her, and his face gave nothing. His eyes cruised away, and took in the huddled form of Annie's mother, and then came to rest in the watching eyes of the cat. A sliver of chicken hung down from its mouth, and its back was drawn up into a stealthy unease. Barry stared into the black-green eyes, and impassivity was slid off his face and his mouth twisted up thin and could have split into a cackle. One rose in his throat, but he stifled it. He sucked in his lips and his eyes were gleaming. He really wanted to savour this single moment of insane delight.

Chapter Six

GEORGE WOKE UP bright and early on Saturday morning
and he thought oh shit. There was something about last evening that had not been altogether satisfactory. He had said as
much on one occasion to Hilary, and she – insensitive cow –
had said yes, quite, I know exactly what you mean, and he had
said no I didn't mean that and she said well no, you wouldn't,
would you. Hopeless. You couldn't get through to women.
What George meant was – well, more *subtle*. Yes, yes, he knew
it was easy to laugh, but it was difficult to verbalise one's
innermost feelings – to find the words – and it didn't help
matters if some superior bitch was forever sneering. But he
supposed he saw her point. No he *didn't*, damn and blast her.
She was just out for herself. Cow. Well he was done with
her. He didn't need that. Why should he? Why should he
abase himself? Why should he plead and crawl? It wasn't
dignified. *And* she played it up for all it was worth, bloody
woman. It always seemed so *clear* on Saturday mornings. So
why was he always reduced to penitent rubble each and every
Friday night? Because a man was a man, he supposed. *Really?*
– Hilary would have drawled, you could have fooled me. That
was what really *got* to George. She let him do it, do what he
could, even encouraged him – and then she threw it all back in
his face. But he wasn't taken in. That was why the arrange-
ment had lasted so long. That was the only level she could

take a man. No threat. He knew that. But it killed him on Saturday mornings. He *wanted* to be a threat. Damn her.

And Susan. He didn't understand Susan at all. She was another one. Following their brief performance the other day, she had said to him is that it, then? And George had said well, you know – I didn't know if you were *using* anything (he always got away with that the first time) and she had said oh, but she wasn't that convinced, he could tell. He supposed women sensed these things. It was all a great mystery. He would have thought that women would be *pleased* – grateful that some great brute didn't just pounce on them and, well *endanger* them. But no. They never seemed happy. Mutual pleasure didn't seem enough. *Mutual*? Hilary had said, ladling it on like she did. Shut up, said George. And then if Barry was to be believed Susan had spent the same night with someone else. No. Incredible. Not Susan. He had always thought she was such a nice girl. Obviously not. Slut. But they always made sure they got lunch first, didn't they? Oh yes. Or dinner. Or two bloody bottles of fucking Taittinger, didn't they? Oh yes. You never got their clever bloody comments *before*hand, did you? No chance. So why did he go on *doing* this, for Christ's sake? Because a man was a man. And shut up, Hilary. Leave me alone.

Well, at least it was Saturday. Didn't have to go in, that was something. George had just about *had* work. Arranging publicity for authors so that they got the fame, and the house got the credit. Still, it was a living. But by Friday, George had had his fill, and this had been a very weird week. Now then – to business. What to wear? What was George going to stun them with today?

George had found, over the years, that with a little care – a bit of discretion – you could get a Jermyn Street look, at Oxford Street prices. Actually in Oxford Street, as a matter of fact. Incredible, wasn't it? But if you were clever, it could be done. And George had the knack – he had it down to a fine art, how to look slick at a fraction of the price you'd expect to pay. Just take the blazer: 70 per cent wool, embossed anchor buttons, double vents, the lot. Was it smart or was it smart? Thirty-nine quid, Debenhams sale. George knew the value of a blazer: you could dress it up or dress it down, while always remaining neat and tidy. Not dressy – just smart. And shirts. Everyone was doing those white-collar jobs now – you didn't have to lay out a fortune. He had noticed years ago on those Hooray Henry types that it didn't matter how bloody garish the actual shirt, just so long as the collar was white. But George wasn't talking Turnbull & Asser. You could get them at Selfridges, Man at C & A – even M & S, but those looked a bit accountanty, he had to admit. As to the rest, well – trousers look after themselves, fake Guccis (Lilley & Skinner, twenty-five quid, give or take) and plenty of Aramis Bronzing Gel. Only in the summer, though: it didn't do to go overboard. And George was very aware of the value of little touches: Dunhill-type lighter (Taiwan, via Berwick Street market), a big steel diver's watch with a face like a porthole, and a chunky signet ring on his little finger, same as the Prince of Wales. The car – those all-important wheels – was a slightly different matter, and deserved a little thought. The Capri had been done to death, and although the Sierra had the right sort of look about it, it smelled of the fleet car, and that was no good. So George had gone for a BMW – red, secondhand, and sheer bloody class. He was still paying for it, but he didn't resent a single penny. That car was money in the bank. Pound for pound, he really couldn't see a better-value alternative to the BMW, at the end of the day. What else matched it for comfort, performance and out-and-out style?

George was nearly ready for today's new challenge. He knotted a spotted cravat and fanned it out beneath his chin.

He had slapped his face with Victor of Milan, and now he felt good enough to pick up the 'phone.

'Hallo, Christine, love. It's George – Georgy.'

'Low Georgy. How you?'

'Fine, love, fine. Look, Chris, love – I know I've kept you pretty hard at it just lately – that pile of letters and what-have-you – and I was just wondering whether we couldn't have a bite together. Make up for being a taskmaster.'

'Oo, yeh, lovely, George. Be nice.'

'Super. I thought the Charlotte Street Wheeler's one o'clock. Use it quite a lot. Oh of course – I don't have to tell *you* that, do I?'

'Booked it often enough,' giggled Christine. 'Yeh. Triffic. Be nice.'

'Great. See you then, then.'

'Yeh, thanks, great. 'Bye, George. Triffic.'

Dozy bloody moron, thought George. She was also a pretty lousy secretary, but she covered for him well, and was too bloody thick to query his grosser buck-passing. And she did have an absolutely gorgeous body. George didn't know why he hadn't thought of it before, to be frank. She was just right, right there, and George hadn't seen it. Lovely to look at, and dense as bone. What more could a man ask? *And* she was impressed by George's evident sophistication (he just *knew* she'd put off something to be with him today) and she already thought him great at his job – which was more than could be said for bloody clever-clever types such as Hilary. And as for Susan – well, Susan, it seemed clear to him now, had just been *using* him for her own selfish ends. Yes. Well to hell with that. This Christine thing, though, had only occurred to him on the way home the night before. Inspired. Yes, she'd co-operate. Bloody flattering for her, really – being asked out by her boss. Something to squawk about with her Christ-awful friends.

Still – why not? She was a good girl, she deserved it. Did her job and kept her mouth shut.

But to George's mind, there could be no doubt about it: he'd been a sucker for far too long. Caring – *that* was the trouble. As soon as you began to *care* about someone, then you were in line to get trampled. Look at Barry. What more could George have done for him? Lent him money, everything. (And he'd be bloody sure he'd get it back as well.) Who the hell did Barry think he was, standing him up in the middle of Soho? OK, Barry had problems, granted. But that was no reason to go round behaving like a madman. OK, so George had felt a little bit guilty about Susan – but he sure as hell didn't any more. They were as bad as each other, those two. First Susan more or less tells him to get lost, and then Barry doesn't turn up to his own bloody binge! Well they could stick with one another, for all George cared. George was done with the both of them.

And then there was Hilary. She was *so* condescending. Treated George like an inferior, like a child. Sometimes he didn't mind – quite liked it, as a matter of fact – but at other times it really drove him wild. He had told her that too, but she had just said she didn't associate him with *wildness*, and George told her to shut up because she knew perfectly well what he meant and sometimes she *would* shut up, but always with that damn knowing, clever, superior smile of hers which drove him to distraction. And did George *really* need to plead with a woman for permission to come and see her once a bloody week? And was the price to go up every single time? What would she expect next week – a *case* of the bloody stuff?! It wasn't that he resented the money. No, come to think of it, that was *exactly* it: he resented the money. Why did women have to be so bloody mercenary? Well – no more. This time, he would *not* go crawling back. Finished. Hilary could find some other licensed victualler to fulfil her needs, and George wished him the very best of British. He wasn't worried. By the

end of the day, he'd have sexy thicko Christine doing whatever he wanted, and he doubted whether it would take more
than a Pina Colada and a bag of nuts. All in all, Christine was
the sort of girl that George *understood*.

He slapped his pockets as he made to leave, checking that
he had all his bits and pieces – keys, lighter, chequebook, fine.
But when he came to think of it, George supposed that finally
being without Hilary after all this time would upset him. But
the fact that he had at last made a definite decision would go
some way in helping him over the pain. And anyway, he had
until Friday to change his mind.

No, he *would* be upset, but not today. Today he was going to
invest in a rather natty yellow slipover that he'd spotted last
week – the sort that the horsy set favoured, and which would
pull together quite a few of his outfits, as well as adding a
rather piquant touch of class. So not today. And then he was
meeting Christine for luncheon and if all went well (and
George saw no reason in the world why all should not) one or
two other diversions as well. No – no upset today. But tomorrow was Sunday, which was usually a fairly lazy day for
George. So maybe tomorrow. Yes. He'd be upset tomorrow, if
he could find a moment. But life was so fraught, you never
could tell.

'You see,' explained Susan to Hilary over a mug of Blue
Mountain, 'in a small concern, one of the great difficulties in
getting garments that are just that little bit different is that
most cut, make and trim factories are reluctant to consider any
order less then, say, a thousand pieces a week.'

'Really,' said Hilary. 'Fascinating.'

'Well it is rather interesting, actually. I think so, anyway.
And even with the cloth itself, you know – *fabric*, I mean – you
can't get less than about two hundred metres at a time.

They're all geared to producing the stuff to a – what was it? Price-point.'

'A price-point. What the hell is a price-point?'

Susan gulped her coffee. 'I'm not absolutely sure, as a matter of fact. Anyway, the point I'm making is that none of this bothers a firm like Mr Wiseman's – Mark's – because he's got so many shops he can spread the stuff all around. Order hugely, and the mark-up is viable. Which is what it's all about, after all.'

'You sound quite the little tycoon. More coffee?'

'Oh I wouldn't say that. But it is rather absorbing. Yes, I shall, actually. It's rather good without milk, you were right. Wasn't it nice of Nicholas to bring it up to us?'

'He always does on Saturdays.'

'He's a lovely little boy.'

'I know.'

For most of the night, Susan and Hilary had slept entwined in each other's arms. Hilary had turned away towards dawn, and Susan had barely stirred, aware of an atmosphere, but very deeply asleep. In the morning, she was rested, and Nicholas was smiling down at her.

'Hello,' he said.

'Hello,' Susan replied. Oh dear, she thought.

But it seemed all right. Both Hilary and Nicholas behaved completely as usual and Susan fell with relief into the easy friendliness. Just like the sixties. Susan remembered how she had glided into becoming a weekend hippy, and how very pleasant it had been.

'I'll just go up and set up the board,' said Nicholas to Hilary. 'Don't forget we're playing this morning.'

'I hadn't forgotten,' said Hilary. 'And it's my turn to be black.'

'You've really done wonders with Nicholas,' said Susan, when he had left the room. 'I think he's far more, well –

advanced than if a father had been around. I don't know –
think men tend to mess things up.'

'I know what you mean,' said Hilary. 'I'm messed up again
myself.'

Susan didn't get that.

'Sorry, don't get,' she said. 'What do you mean?'

'I mean,' said Hilary, 'that in a few months – six, I think –
I'm going to be doing wonders with a brand-new brat.'

The first thing Susan felt was hurt, which was ridiculous.

'Are you *sure*?' she said.

Hilary nodded. 'I was sick as a dog at aerobics. Test's come
up positive. Oh well.'

'But how – '

'Good question. I'm not quite sure. There it is.'

There was a lot Susan wanted to know, but she thought she
had better not ask. Hilary really was a remarkable woman. So
calm. In her place, Susan would have been wild, one way or
the other.

'Does Nicholas know?' she asked.

Hilary poured herself some more coffee.

'It's gone cold. Oh yes, he knows,' Hilary smiled. 'He has
expressed a desire to be present at the birth.'

Susan was shocked. 'Oh but Hilary you can't possibly – '

'I don't see why not,' Hilary returned. 'I'd rather have him
there than anyone else I can think of. And anyway, he'll be the
man of the house, don't forget.'

'So you wouldn't consider, you know – marrying or
anything?'

Hilary blew out Gitanes smoke and fixed Susan with one of
her looks.

'Don't be absurd,' she said.

Susan nodded hurriedly. It had been a stupid thing to say.

'So you feel – all right about it, then?'

Hilary shrugged. 'It could be worse. It's not as if it was

herpes or anything. Friend of mine's got that, apparently. Did I tell you about her?'

'No.'

'Yes.'

And Hilary narrowed her eyes and looked pensive through the smoke. Susan too fell silent. It was odd. When she had just woken up, things had seemed simpler. There was no real reason, she acknowledged, why things *should* have seemed any simpler, but now it was all clouded again. Susan wondered what it was she really wanted.

'Hilary,' she began. 'Hilary?'

'I can hear you.'

'I don't suppose – I mean, last night was, well, new for me. I'd never – well, you know what I mean. What I mean is, I don't suppose you'd sort of like me to, well, live here, or somewhere, with you, would you? You know – sort of together, I mean.'

Hilary let out a bark of a laugh, which threw Susan completely. She had thought she was getting through. Why did Hilary always have to do that? As soon as some sort of rapport, contact, was established, she started jeering. It must be something within her.

'I don't see that there's anything particularly funny about it,' said Susan, rather primly. 'I mean, if you don't think it's a very good idea, all you have to do is say so. You don't have to laugh in my face.'

'I'm sorry, Susan – I wasn't laughing at you. But you *must* see that anything like that would be absolutely hopeless. I mean – just look at us! We'd drive each other barmy within a week.'

Susan smiled. It was perfectly true.

'I suppose so,' she said.

'No,' Hilary went on. 'Homosexuality is just a hobby for me.'

And Susan felt embarrassed.

'I wouldn't exactly call it *that*, Hilary,' she said quietly.

'No, well, I dare say you've got some far more acceptable word for it – *sharing*, or something – but it comes to the same thing. Of course, it's far more palatable in women. It's all narcissism with us, you know. That's why we love to pore over all those luscious women in *Vogue* and all that. We're all in love with ourselves. But I must admit I do find it quite endearing in men when they're terribly *old*. Do you know what I mean? When their cheeks are soft and pink and their hair is like fluff – they look like everyone's favourite auntie. They must be so pleased and at peace, just holding baby hands and looking back on their days at Oxford. They always look so *contented*, when they've finally "gorn sorft". They're really rather lovable.'

Susan was laughing.

'You are weird, Hilary. God you come out with some funny things.'

'Are you staying?' asked Hilary.

Susan looked down. 'I'd like to,' she said.

'Open house,' said Hilary. 'For the weekend,' she added on.

Susan nodded. 'Thanks, Hilary.'

'I'm going to get dressed. You can come up later, if you like. I'll have the bathroom first, if you don't mind. You can borrow a shirt or something if you want.'

Susan lay back and had a think when Hilary was gone. Dear Hilary. She could be such a *good* friend when she wanted to be. But poor thing! Another kid to bring up. Still, she didn't seem very bothered about it. And of course Susan was wondering about the father. And hating him, for various complicated reasons of her own. But what Susan really *had* to get sorted out was her own little life. It was unbelievable, really. In just a few days, everything had changed so much. Susan had been so bored for so long that she had got out of the way of thinking, but she must, she really must. Step by step. But although everything was so dreadfully unsettled, Susan could not help feeling excited about the sheer grown-upness of everything that had been going on. In a novel, it would all seem rather too much. But it just went to show: life could be really amazing.

Hilary, Susan knew, had no time for types like Mark Wiseman. She thought them boorish and flash. 'For all their clothes and money,' she had said to Susan once, 'they always make me feel I want to *wash*.' But Mark was different. Or maybe he wasn't. Maybe Susan just responded to that sort of person. Certainly she liked the closeness of that warm wall of money, and she was flattered by so much of it being lavished on herself. A life of ease, with the spice of business, rather appealed, she had to admit. And apart from the job, and the presents, and the attention, he had already hinted at very much more. He owned, he said, one or two flats 'up-west'. West End, Susan supposed. That's all he said, but it had made Susan think. As, no doubt, was intended. And he had mentioned that he would soon be spending a week or so at a health hydro in Buckinghamshire, and Susan, he had offered, could come along, if she liked. But of course, Susan was not a fool. She saw very clearly where all of this was destined to lead her, and she tried to be like Hilary and coldly decide whether or not she wanted to be a rich man's mistress. Her mouth grinned with nerves just *thinking* the word, it seemed so very illicit – and yet apparently such women *did* exist. Susan wondered what sort of people they were. They couldn't all wear purple négligés and white mink coats and be thoroughly vampish *all* the time. Susan supposed that really they were very ordinary, just like everyone else – except that they looked better, lived better, and had a different set of problems.

But Susan didn't see this new job as just a token thing. She really wanted to make her mark on that shop, make it do really well. She wanted to show that she could *earn* her money, and not just be handed it on a plate. She'd go up and see it in the morning. She expected that Tanya would have dropped the keys through the box. It seemed odd, in a way, that Mark should have a grown-up daughter, but really there was nothing odd about it. Annoying that Susan had missed her. Still, no harm done.

And what about Barry? It was all most unfortunate, the way things had developed. If only he hadn't come back so early that evening. No, it was Susan who had been in the wrong, she had to be fair. They should have gone to a hotel. Still, spilt milk. It was, Susan had to remind herself, the future that was important. That was the thing. But poor old Barry! He really did seem to come out of this rather badly. Susan didn't even know where he was – hadn't seen him since, well – since. And of course she knew that Barry lacked the equipment to deal with a situation like this, because Barry could never deal with anything new, and Susan doubted very much whether he had ever come face to face with a crisis – yes, it was a crisis – in any way comparable. And of course Barry had thought terribly badly of her – probably still did – because the one-night stand was all his little male mind could get around, and therefore Susan became equated with those cheap little telephonists and waitresses that he used to pick up in provincial hotels. To whom, of course, Susan bore no resemblance whatever. With Mark, it was different. He *understood*. He took care of her, treated her like a lady. And for a woman, of course, it was more than, well, just *that* – but Barry would never understand, that was for sure. What man would? Susan doubted whether Barry had ever known true commitment. The trouble with Barry – and Susan had seen it for so long – was that you could read him like an open book. Nothing wrong with that, of course – simplicity, honesty – it was just that it became so dreadfully boring when you always knew *exactly* what was in someone's mind. There was no mystery about Barry. He was all on the surface.

Thank goodness Susan was managing to see things more clearly. This was definitely one area in which adults – true adults – held supremacy over more volatile youths: insight. It really helped when you needed to be rational. But there was a plus-side to Barry too – Susan wanted to be just. He worked hard, and quietly he had been putting all that money into a building society. And he was faithful. Oh dear. That hurt a bit. Poor old Barry. But was all that what Susan really *wanted*? Oh God. It wasn't easy, was it? Barry must be pining for her now. He couldn't still hate her, he just couldn't. But did she want him back? Did she *need* him back? She had a job now. And Mark. Or maybe that was a rather one-sided way of looking at things. Oh, it was all so *difficult*. Susan wished she could talk to Hilary – *really* talk – but it wouldn't work. Hilary refused to see problems anywhere. God, how Susan envied her detached and sensible attitude. Her coolness. Oh well. Everyone couldn't be all the same; what a dull world it would be. Susan would just have to work it out on her own. And that thought nearly made her cry for herself. But maybe Susan didn't *have* to choose. After all, Barry was her husband, and Mark was her employer. Susan would be *working* after all, and Barry need never know about the other side of it. He didn't even know that Susan *had* a job, let alone the identity of her boss. Yes. That was a thought. At least that way Susan wouldn't have to humiliate herself by buying her own tacky little necklace, just to give people a jolt. Yes.

No. She couldn't let Barry down. It wouldn't be fair. She'd keep him on as well. It would save a lot of trouble in the long run, when you considered all the mutual acrimony and pain, and all the bother involved in moving. Yes, Susan was inching closer to sorting things out.

Jacques Loussier was playing next door. Susan smiled. It

was all so fond. They'd have Segovia later, and Hilary would burn joss sticks and they'd drink some Barolo. Susan was so pleased that some of the peace, some of the *timelessness*, was back with her again.

Nicholas came in to fetch a clock.

'Hilary and I are going to have a game now,' he said. 'The bathroom's free. You can go up, if you like.'

'Thanks Nick, Nicholas, I mean. I like your pullover.'

'Yes, it is quite nice. More of a sweatshirt, actually.'

'How do you feel,' began Susan, thinking should I? Might as well. 'How do you feel about having a baby brother or a baby sister? Do you have a preference? Which would you like more?'

Nicholas scratched his nose.

'I really haven't given much thought to that side of things,' he admitted. 'Of course, it would only be a half-brother or a half-sister anyway. No, I'm rather more concerned about the mechanics of the thing, actually.'

Susan double-took.

'The *mechanics*?'

Nicholas nodded. 'The actual procedure,' he clarified. 'Hilary's not so young as she was, you know. One just hopes all goes well.'

Which hadn't occurred to Susan at all.

Annie thought she would not forget that weekend for as long as she lived. Before she rallied round, she felt aged and really at a loss. But of course she had to act. No one else was going to, were they? And everything seemed as urgent as everything else – it was difficult to know quite what to do and she was still so rattled by Barry and the gun and everything and then her mother had collapsed and he was just *staring*. Thinking back on it now, Annie was amazed that she coped. But it had to be done.

The first thing, she thought – how absurd, why did she think that, she wondered now – was to get rid of that cat. God knows where the creature had come from. Annie could not recall ever having *seen* it before. It smelt, rather; she had picked it up but it clawed and leered at the chicken carcass, and so Annie picked that up too and strode the length of the hall with them and threw them out of the door. She slapped and wiped her hands to be rid of them for good and cat's hair stuck to the grease on her fingers, and Annie was unnaturally revolted by the thought of it. She did hope – silly, she thought now – that when she returned to the room beautiful normality might have been restored, but it was just as horrible as before. Worse. Barry still looked at the spot where the cat had been and Annie's mother lay slumped in a heap like a trussed-up rug or so many rags. She looked dead, she was so bony and still. Could *be* dead, Annie supposed. The next thing was to get Barry to bed. She called to him, and although he said nothing, there was a movement at the back of his eyes that told her he had heard.

'Can you walk upstairs now, Barry?'

Barry put away his tongue and rolled his head round.

'Walk,' he said, and then that awful smile tugged at his face again.

'Oh God,' whispered Annie. And then she thought I mustn't look as if there's anything wrong, and I mustn't appear frightened, and Barry must believe that I am on his side. Annie did not know why she thought of any of this: instinctive.

'Let's go upstairs,' she urged. 'And then you'll be comfortable.'

Oh God, Annie thought. He's going to say 'comfortable' and then he's going to giggle and then I'll get scared because he'll seem so mad, but Barry did not open his mouth at all. He shifted his legs and sat upright and he was looking at that

214

square of carpet again and Annie followed his gaze this time and there was the gun where the cat had been and she walked across and picked it up and it was only then that Barry spoke.

'I'll take that,' he said.

'I'll look after it,' Annie offered.

'No, Annie, no. *I'll* look after it.'

And Annie handed it to him thinking it doesn't matter, it doesn't matter just so long as I get him upstairs, and as soon as Barry got his hands on the gun he appeared to relax and he stood up and he seemed a bit more recognisable now. Not *well* – not at *all* well, and obviously very drunk, but at least it was clearly *Barry* again. Annie had been getting worried.

She walked up behind him, but he seemed quite steady. This is mad, she thought. Barry has a gun hanging from his hand and we're going upstairs and it must be nearly dawn and my mother is lying on the floor downstairs. Unconscious. Yes – must be unconscious, or she would have moved by now.

'Which room?' said Barry, at the top.

'Don't be silly – any room. My room.'

Yes, it must have been nearly dawn. It was fresh in Annie's bedroom – cool, and so much more clean than downstairs. But it was that time when very late becomes rawly early, and the air was shot with fine ash. Barry lay down and he told Annie that that felt good and Annie said good and Barry said Annie. He put down the gun with care and he reached up and touched her cheek. Annie held his hand there, and his smile became kinder.

Annie had been surprised by how quickly he had fallen asleep. It was as if his whole body just fell over the edge of consciousness and he snorted like an engine with each deep breath. Back downstairs, Annie had other things to attend to. There was a spilt drink, grease marks on the carpet, and also Annie's mother. Annie touched her arm. It was warm, and the skin was softer than she ever remembered. Annie turned her over, gently. Poor mother. She looked so small and frail, just like a fledgling after a fall.

The ambulance men behaved very efficiently. They cooed solace and encouragement at Annie's mother, although they knew she couldn't hear. She's well out, one of them remarked. Howdit happen, love? A fall, Annie had said. She fell.

They wheeled her out, and they assured her that her mother would be right as rain in the morning, and Annie believed them. She wondered how much her mother would remember. Too much would not be good for Barry. One of the men looked a little surprised – did he look a little surprised? – when Annie declined to ride along to the hospital. She was, she said, rather shaken. She would, she said, be over in the morning. The man said he understood and also – she didn't mind him saying – that sometimes it wasn't good to be on your own and Annie had said no, really, I'll be fine, honestly.

In the bedroom, Barry was just as she had left him. He growled deeply in time with the steady rhythm of his chest. He looked as if he might never wake up again. Annie's mother had had that look about her, too. But the gun was gone. No. Yes. Not possible. But it was. It wasn't on the table where Barry had placed it. Where, then? And Annie was sure that Barry hadn't moved. Well she wouldn't disturb him hunting for it. She'd find it in the morning. And what on earth, Annie enquired of herself, would she do with it then? Where had it come from? And how did Barry come to have it, and why? And the – oh God – the blood? And why had Barry behaved so . . . ? So many questions. But Annie knew that she'd ask none of them. Not one. Barry would either tell her, or else he wouldn't. Just so long as he was all right. That was all. Everything else would fall into place, just so long as Barry was all right. Annie lay down beside him on the bed, willing her own weightlessness so as not to disturb the balance of the mattress. Over a period of nearly an hour, she inched nearer to him, ears erect for the slightest change in his deep, long breathing, and then they were touching and Annie laid an arm on his waist and she thought yes, it's all right now. This was so good. It was ages since she'd spent a whole night with Barry, in a bed. She would attend to all the mess tomorrow. Maybe they'd even do it together. That would be marvellous.

How odd that there should be blood on a gun.

Barry was thinking he must be going mad. I'm breaking up, he thought; I must be. What time was it? Doesn't matter. What do I remember? Everything, fuck it. Christ, I am, I am. I'm breaking up.

He turned over onto his back and his eyes hurt as they swivelled within him and the ceiling came down to meet him and he hid his head in the pillow. He had the gun underneath. When Annie had come in last time Barry had felt her missing it, but he hadn't moved, he hadn't blinked. He had concentrated on droning deeply and thought hee hee hee I've got it and she doesn't know where it is. Now that's mad behaviour, isn't it? Yes it is, yes it is, and I don't care.

Barry loved Annie. He really did love her. He just lay there thinking how much he loved her and how nice it was to be lying in her cool white bed and was that a crack, could that be a crack on the ceiling? No, it was just a shadow. Just a flicker, a passing shade. Gone now. Barry couldn't even remember where it had been; where he had seen it. But he loved Annie – really loved her. He felt it as deep as his bones. He'd been a fool. He smiled: cliché. A blind fool. Yes, cliché. Did it matter? No, didn't matter. Why had Barry never decided to spend his life with Annie, properly? He didn't know. Well, he did – sort of did – really. Susan and cowardice. That was it. Barry loved Susan. He really loved her. But she wasn't good to him; didn't look after him like Annie did. And Annie was loyal. Annie didn't behave like a common little tramp. No. Barry loved Annie. But Susan *wasn't* a common little tramp, was she? Hard to say. Barry would not have said so, but apparently she was. He hated her for that. But he did still love her. He loved leaving her and coming to Annie and he loved going away from Annie and returning home to Susan, except that it hurt him every time, and he hated the deception and now it was in his blood and he didn't love it, he didn't. He loathed it. He could live with Annie, really *live* with her, but he would hate to leave Susan. Why? Many reasons, really. Couldn't think of one at the moment. Bit tired. But having them both seemed better than having just the one. He sometimes thought he could be alone, but not have just the one. Why? Didn't know. Many reasons really. Example? Couldn't think of one at the moment. God, he was glad no one had heard him actually *say* that. It was nice, sometimes, being on one's own, thinking one's thoughts. One could be so indiscreet.

And now Barry couldn't think at all. Couldn't put two coherent ideas together. Funny. Things had begun to seem clear, and now he felt tired and drunk all over again. He would have rather liked a drink at that moment, as a matter of fact, but that would have meant calling Annie and he needed to be alone just now, until he had worked something out. No, the thoughts wouldn't come. Maybe a little sleep. No, too many flashing little pictures flicking in his head. What was that one? Gone. Too late. It was like a kaleidoscope of topical events: the brain hovered at recognition and the image was replaced by another, and *that* looked familiar and then it was gone and here was another and Barry *knew* that face but now another picture came and then it was gone again. Closing his eyes intensified the colours and the speed and it all became mad and painful and now he *really* would have liked a drink but he'd try and last out a little longer and then there was a face and he latched on to it, yes, it was that girl, that rather luscious girl, what was her name, who came around and then they went out and yes by Christ he had it now, the whole damn thing: girl – flat – pain – gun – restaurant – hotel – pain – yes. Oh God yes. How very lovely to be at Annie's. How the hell had he got there? Didn't know. Didn't matter. Annie would look after him. She always did. He would be lost without Annie.

'I would be lost without you, Annie,' he said, and his words sounded old and odd and the forming of them made his lips feel too large and numb. Barry hoped Annie had not heard him. Not because he did not wish her to know, but because he did not wish her to come, not yet. He hadn't worked it out yet and so he had nothing to tell her.

Was she in the room? *Some*thing was in the room. Maybe it was the cat. Barry had quite liked that cat, and he didn't normally. Or dogs. Animals, really.

'Did you call, Barry love? Are you OK? Can I get you something?'

It was Annie, then. She was in the room.

'Are you in the room, Annie?'

'I'm here. Can't you see me?'

'My eyes are closed. I think I'm breaking up, Annie.'

His brow felt cool and then warm when Annie touched it.

'Don't be silly,' she said. 'You're too strong. And I'm here to look after you. You're not the type to break down.'

Uncertainty flickered into Barry's eyes.

'I said up,' he said.

Annie smiled. 'Up – down. It makes no difference.'

Barry nodded and turned away contented. It seemed as sane as anything else.

And then he must have slept.

'I slept then, did I, Annie?'

'My God did you sleep! You were asleep for hours and hours.

I was pleased. You were so exhausted. Do you feel better now?'

'I do. I do feel better now. Yes I do.'

He really did. It was quite extraordinary how very fresh, how very different, how very much *better* he felt, just for having slept. He was sitting up now, and Annie was shaving him with a very curious little chromium-plated safety razor, and avoiding with care the gash on his cheek. She had lathered his face with Palmolive, and the blade was a new one, extracted gingerly from its blue paper sheath, and Mr Gillette stared out at her while she did it. And she was shaving him well. Barry said it felt like a wet caress and Annie just laughed; but she was pleased, he could tell.

'You're very good to me, Annie,' said Barry.

Annie smiled. 'I love you,' she said. 'Everything will be all right now.'

Barry was not quite sure what she meant, but he said:

'I hope so.'

So do I, thought Annie, and she smiled again.

'Now! What do you feel like? Are you hungry?'

'What's the time?' asked Barry.

'It's afternoon.'

'I think maybe a sandwich or something,' said Barry. 'And God, Annie, I'd love a drink.'

'I thought you would. I've got something special for you.'

Annie drew out a bottle of Glenmorangie as if from nowhere, and held it out for Barry's inspection.

'Lovely,' he said. 'You're very good. Glenmorangie,' he read. 'Single Highland Malt. Ten Years Old. You're very good to me. I don't deserve it.'

'Of course you do. You've been going through a bad time.'

'I have, yes,' agreed Barry. 'Worse than you know. But still.'

Annie poured him some whisky, thinking worse than I

220

know, what does *that* mean? Never mind, doesn't matter, leave it alone.

'You just don't worry about anything,' Annie urged. 'Not yet. There's plenty of time for talk. But a bit more rest is what you need. Tomorrow's Sunday. We've all the time in the world. And don't worry about mother, by the way. I 'phoned the hospital this morning and they say that she's sleeping.'

'Mother?' said Barry. He was a blank on this one.

'Don't you remember?'

'Of course I remember,' returned Barry, with some irritation. Mother?

'Well, she's OK.'

'I'm glad,' said Barry. 'I didn't know she was ill.'

Annie glanced up at him, and took away his empty glass.

'It's very good whisky,' he said.

'You sleep now,' said Annie.

'I don't feel tired.'

'Sleep anyway.'

'But I really don't feel tired, Annie. I'm wide awake.'

Annie slid her arm down under the counterpane and across his stomach.

'Shh,' she hissed, with gentleness. 'Go to sleep.'

Barry relaxed as she coaxed and stroked him.

'You're so good to me, Annie,' he said. 'So good. So good.'

'Shh,' Annie soothed.

Barry's muscles fell loose, and he sighed.

'I'll go to sleep soon,' he said. 'Thank you, Annie.'

It was not quite dark. It could be dawn or late afternoon. Barry felt at rest and drained of energy. He had been asleep on his back for what seemed like a long while, but of course it needn't have been. Wouldn't it be good, he thought, if I had been asleep for weeks, months? Then I wouldn't have to live through them. But it was probably only hours. Yes, certainly it was hours. Must be. And the first thing he really focused on was the bottle of Glenmorangie, and he smiled, and he went for it. Dear Annie, he thought. An angel.

Barry's head felt flat at the back, where the heavy gun had pressed into it through one of Annie's frothy pillows. It was not an ache that bothered Barry at all. In a way, he found it rather reassuring. Now was he slipping into that strange way of thinking again? No, he didn't think so. He felt quite rational, quite excited by how very ordinary he felt. No hidden anger. No dark secrets. Well, maybe one or two. And where was Annie? It would be nice to see her again. He was hungry.

Was it Sunday yet? Could be. Barry would go back to the flat tomorrow; get some clothes. And then work, he supposed. Yes. God, it seemed a very long time since he had been to work. Maybe, if he could raise a few quid, he and George could get a game going. How was old George, Barry wondered. It seemed as if he hadn't seen him for ages. Wasn't Barry supposed to have met him somewhere or something? He couldn't be sure. Still, George wouldn't mind. For Barry well knew that George was the sort of person you could depend on, and Christ knew there weren't many of those around these days. No. You only had to look about you. There was no – well, *faith* any more. Barry could count himself lucky, he knew. Look at Annie. Look at how good to him Annie was. And he hardly deserved it. Well, Barry modified, maybe he did. After all, he had been pretty good to her in the past. And he knew too that she needed – Annie *needed* – to look after Barry, so it was all very reciprocal. Barry dared say it was something psychological on her part, he didn't know. But he loved her, they loved each other; that was for sure. And where was she? Where was Annie? Christ, Barry could have eaten a horse, just then.

He called out for her, and it seemed that she had darted into the room even before the sound of his voice had died.

'I'm here, Barry,' she said. 'Did you have a good sleep?'

'I had a *won*derful sleep, Annie. *Wonderful!*'

Annie's eyes glittered with joy. It was so marvellous to see Barry looking like Barry again. Annie felt so relieved and so much love and the tears sprang straight out of her eyes and she whispered silly, sorry, and Barry said come here and she fell into his neck and they hung on to each other and Annie's tears were soaking their faces and it was just like it was in the old days, with bright eyes blinded by love: just Barry and Annie against the world.

It was Annie who drew away first, but only after a good long time. She just had to see his face.

'I must look such a mess,' she said.

'You look beautiful,' said Barry.

Delight tugged at Annie's cheeks as she looked down and pulled at the sheet.

'Don't be silly,' she playfully admonished. 'How can I?'

'You just do. You always do, Annie. I love you.'

And then the tears jetted out of her again and she snuffled with impatience and said that Barry must think her so silly and it was just that she loved him so much and Barry said he didn't think she was silly, not a bit, and he loved her, he loved her, he loved her.

'You must be starving,' sniffed Annie, after a while.

'You've read my mind,' grinned Barry.

'Steak?'

'Seductress.'

Annie giggled like a schoolgirl, and Barry just managed to slap her bottom as she skipped away like a coloured feather. He poured a Glenmorangie when she had gone. Good and warming in the mouth, and surprisingly gentle on the swallow. Mellow, Barry supposed was the word. Anyway: bloody good. And then on the crest of love, Barry decided to live with her. It would be stupid to do anything else. Susan? He would talk to her. She would understand. No she wouldn't. In which case, she just wouldn't. At that moment, it didn't matter. Annie had just left the room, and already Barry was missing her. Why should he ever leave her side? Why had there been so much pain? Whatever in the world had been *wrong* with him at all? Anyway, it wasn't too late. He'd put it right. But he wouldn't tell her yet, not yet. It would be a surprise. He'd tell her soon, at the right time, when he'd got one or two things sorted out. Money, for a start. And that gun. Oh Christ, that bloody gun. Suddenly, it did not seem to be his friend any more. That gun was an intruder. Had Barry *really* believed that this was the way out of his troubles? His mouth twisted when he thought of what might have happened, where he might have gone if he hadn't had Annie to turn to. Dear, dear Annie. His haven of rest. Yes, that gun would have to go. Of course, technically, Barry had stolen the bloody thing, and he really ought to give it back. But he never again wished to see the inside of that ghastly flat, and anyway, anyone who had a gun would probably have another. Might not miss it for ages. And as for the girl – what was her name? – well, they had both been very drunk. She'd probably forgotten the whole thing by now. Barry expected that she was pretty used to – well, things like that. It was just another evening for her. He hadn't liked her at all. No, he'd just have to dump the thing. Clean it, of course, like they did in the films, and then just dump it. Where? Anywhere. Yes but where? Wherever. Thames. Anywhere. Anywhere at all. Just get rid of it, that's all.

Annie came in with the steak and it was enormous and Barry said Jesus, Annie, that's absolutely enormous and Annie said you said you were hungry and Barry said I am, I am and Annie said well then. She poured more Glenmorangie, and she watched him eat the steak.

'Good?' she queried.

Barry indicated his full, champing mouth, and widened his eyes in appreciation. He swallowed, sipped whisky, nodded and said:

'*Very* good. Beautiful. Excellent.'

'I'm glad,' smiled Annie. 'It looked good. Cut well.'

'Annie,' began Barry, 'you're right. You're really right. Everything *is* going to be all right. I know what you mean now. I really am going to try. Sort everything out. Do a bit better at work – Christ, I could hardly do any worse, could I? Get a bit of money together. I'm going to try and be how I used to be. I swear it.'

Annie's whole face broadened with pleasure.

'Oh, Barry! I can't tell you how good it is to hear you talking like this. It's marvellous. I *knew* you wouldn't give up. I told you you're not that sort. And I'll help you! If you take on anything extra, I can always type it up, you know. Or a bit of copy-editing, or proof-reading. And I've still got some money till you get back on your feet.'

'Angel,' said Barry. 'But do you think they're still interested in me? I mean, Christ – I really have been behaving like a raving madman lately. And particularly with DJ. He must think I'm a lunatic.'

'No! They all *know* you're a good editor, Barry. *Every*one goes through a bad patch at one time or another. You just see – as soon as you start turning in the work, they'll back you every inch of the way – I just *know* they will.'

Barry put down his knife and fork.

'You really are a wonderful woman.'

'Don't be silly,' Annie said. 'I just love you.'

Barry touched her hand, and they looked at each other. He went on with his steak and said:

'I've remembered about your mother. I had forgotten, Annie. I'm sorry. Is she all right?'

225

'Oh God – mother!' said Annie. 'I forgot to 'phone again. Oh yes – I'm sure she's OK. They would've 'phoned, wouldn't they?'

Barry slid away his plate.

'That was great,' he said. 'Just right.'

He sipped whisky. Yes, it would be OK now. And he hadn't forgotten about Gavin. He *must* be better by now. Barry could call on him – maybe even tomorrow – and finally put forward his famous proposition. With cash up-front, credibility with DJ, Annie's love and backing – what could stop him? Nothing. Nothing nothing nothing.

And Barry stared at the bottle of ten-year-old Glenmorangie. All of a sudden, a wave of tiredness had overcome him. So many decisions, and so much to do. He stared at the label and he felt so weary.

'I wish,' he said.

'What, Barry?'

'Oh, nothing.'

'What is it?'

'It's silly. I was just going to say I wished *I* was ten years old. That's all. Silly. I don't really. It just occurred to me.'

Chapter Seven

IT WAS MONDAY morning, and Annie was telling Barry that she'd cook something really special for him when he came home in the evening. He could also, she said, do with a few new shirts. She had seen some last week; she would get them today. Don't worry, she kept on saying. I'm not worried, Barry replied.

'Have you got the – you know?' Annie queried.

'The what?'

'The – you know. That gun thing.'

'Yes. Yes, I've got it. Don't worry. It'll be all right. I'm all right now.'

'I'm not worried,' said Annie. 'I'm just a bit anxious, that's all.'

Barry kissed her forehead.

'Well don't be,' he assured. 'By this evening, everything will be fine. I promise you.'

He doesn't believe it, Annie thought.

'I know it will,' she said. 'Have you got everything?'

'Yes, I think so. Pity the car's not here. I'll get a cab to the flat and then I think I'll drive in. Thanks for the, you know – all the. I'll pay it back. I promise.'

'That's the least of our worries,' Annie said.

'We don't *have* worries any more,' said Barry. 'Everything's all right, I tell you.'

'I know, Barry. I know.'

227

She doesn't feel it, he thought.

'Well then,' he said.

The fresh air knifed his lungs. He felt cold and new right through. God, he hoped he was up to all this. He couldn't let Annie down again. He just couldn't.

Barry got a taxi easily and thought: at least – good start. He held on to the grip bar in the back and wished there wasn't such a smell of rubber and diesel. The cab rolled like a boat, and when it stopped outside the flat, Barry got out grateful and sick.

In the hall, it was as if he had been away a long, long time. Everything was the same, but far more distant. Barry was disoriented. He felt exposed. On the stairs, he reassured himself: one step at a time, and everything would be all right. He'd had a bath at Annie's, but a change of clothes would be a rather nice thing. The flat itself didn't bother Barry; just the future.

As he turned the key in the lock he knew that someone was inside and he thought oh God *now* what the hell and then no, it's OK, it must be Susan, why not, he had to face up to it some time and now was as good as ever, maybe better.

She was standing in the middle of the room with letters in her hand and her eyes were blazing.

'Hello, Susan,' said Barry.

'Where are the *keys*?' she screamed.

'What?'

'The keys! The keys! Where are the bloody keys?'

What on earth was this now, Barry thought.

'What keys?' he said.

Susan stared with wild disbelief.

'*What* keys?! Oh Jesus Christ – *what* keys?! The *keys*! The bloody keys to the *shop*! I'm supposed to *be* there by now.'

Obviously Barry did not yet possess total recall. He wanted to be of assistance – he could see that Susan was very distraught – but for the life of him he could not understand, could not remember. It made no sense at all.

'What shop?' he said.

Susan smashed the crumpled letters against her thigh, and drove a crazed hand back through her hair.

'Oh God no please don't let this happen! Oh Christ as if I wasn't scared enough about this! Barry for *God's* sake think! It's gone *nine*! I'm supposed to be starting a brand-new job today! I'm *late*! I don't have the keys – I don't even know where the bloody place *is*!' Now she was quieter, and dealing with a simpleton. 'Think, Barry – please! There should have been a set of keys, in an envelope, with a letter. *Think!*'

And then Barry had it. Tanya, of course. Keys.

'I remember,' he said.

Relief and impatience fought on Susan's face.

'Well?!' she insisted.

'I don't know, now. I haven't got them, I don't think. No, I'm sure not. I don't know where they are now.'

'You *had* them?'

'I had them at one point, yes. I really don't know where they could be now. A few places, I suppose. I don't know.'

Barry looked up at the helpless horror on Susan's face.

'Sorry,' he said.

Susan was chewing a fist, her eyes rolling with panic.

'He says he's sorry,' she whispered with near-hysterical incredulity. 'He says he's sorry. The first decent thing to come along in years and he's shattered it and he says he's sorry!'

Susan wheeled round and raising both arms she began shrieking like a demon in agony.

'You're sorry!!! You're sorry!!! You're sorry!!!'

'I *am* sorry,' Barry said, but he knew she wouldn't hear.

Susan quivered with her legs apart and her mouth was wet and pleading for help.

'What can I *do*!' she wailed.

Barry looked down.

'I don't know,' he said.

Susan just stared at him with hate. Her whole face was distorted with loathing. It was as if she could hardly believe that so great a wrong, so vile a wound, had been inflicted upon her. During those moments of venom, Susan approached adoration of herself.

Barry stayed quiet until she had gone. She had just scooped up her coat, and avoiding his eyes, banged out of the flat and down the stairs. The letters had fallen from her knuckled fingers, and Barry stooped down to them. He felt shocked, and he stayed on his haunches. Everything was all right, he told himself. It would have come better from Annie, but she wasn't here. The staircase thudded and throbbed again, and Susan threw wide the door and stood and seethed, her face blotched with pale and red, rigid lips well back from her teeth.

'*Christ* I hope to *Christ* I never see you again as long as I live you *bastard*!'

The door imploded, and the whole building trembled until she was gone.

Barry stayed still for quite some time. Then he looked down at the letters. They were addressed to him, and all of them had been opened.

One was from the bank. They pressed for an urgent meeting, and coldly requested the return of Barry's chequebook. In the meantime, they said, they would be returning all his cheques to the payees, that they might refer to drawer. There was a court summons from the Borough of Camden. Was it a summons? It seemed such a complicated thing. Yes, it was: a summons. And a letter had been delivered by hand from the landlord. He wanted the back rent for seven weeks (Jesus, was it *really* seven weeks?) and full vacant possession of the flat fourteen days from the date of the letter. The fourth piece of paper was highly coloured and offered Barry the opportunity of acquiring authentic scale models of great railway trains of the world, each finely cast in English pewter.

Was it cold in the room? No, Barry wasn't used to being up and about, that was all. His forehead was icy, but that was nothing. It was just a question of getting a grip. Everything would be all right, Barry knew it. Annie had said so. And Annie was right. She had to be.

'Morning, Mr Turville. Lovely day for it.'

'Morning, um, Len. Think I'll take the stairs, actually.'

'Keeping fit, ay? Watching the waistline!'

'Yes.' Fuck off, he thought.

'Morning, Barry. Bit later than usual.'

'Leave me alone, will you Selina?'

Today, Barry knew, was going to be tough. He had 'phoned Annie from the flat, just to hear her tell him again that everything would be all right, but it was engaged, and then he remembered that it was he who had been assuring her of this and not the other way around, and that had sent a blade of fear right into him. He sat in the Panda thinking I've got to get back to Annie: Annie is all I have left. And then he drove to work. Annie was all he had left and he could not lose her now. She was not coming in today. She had said that she had to see to mother, and get things ready for Barry in the evening – and anyway, she had added, it would be better if she weren't there today. Did he know what she meant? Yes, of course, he had replied; but he had thought no, no I don't.

'Morning,' said Jean the temp. 'You feel OK this morning? I wondered if you'd be in. You looked a bit not quite all right on Friday. You OK now?'

'I'm fine,' said Barry. 'Thank you.'

'I often feel like that,' breezed Jean. 'But there's nothing like a weekend for bucking you up, is there really?'

'No,' said Barry. 'Nothing.'

231

What *is* she talking about? he wondered. Why am I responding?

'I remembered the coffee!' trilled Jean, in triumph.

'Oh good,' said Barry.

'But I forgot what brand you said – but this'll do, won't it? Do you want milk? Only I didn't get any milk.'

'Black's fine.'

'You sure? I can always get some from Heather.'

Barry pressed in his eyeballs with the tips of his fingers.

'Jean – just make the coffee, there's a good girl.'

Jean grinned like an accomplice, and picking up the kettle she passed the opinion that they were both a bit Monday morning, if he were to ask her. She wouldn't, she said, be a tick.

This day was barely under way, and already Barry knew he was weakening. He swivelled away from his desk and looked out at the downpipes and the fire escape of another building. The gun in his pocket swung against his hip, and there was a sore spot there from the weight of it. What had happened with Susan didn't matter. He didn't *need* Susan any more. Susan was over. And from what he had seen, it would appear that she was pleased to be rid of him. And in spite of what she'd done to him, he didn't really blame her. No, not really. But what a fuss over a couple of keys.

The door of Barry's office was swung wide open, and he thought thank Christ: coffee. But it wasn't Jean, it was June.

'Ah, Barry,' she said. 'You *are* in.'

Barry turned to face her.

'It would appear so, June, yes.'

June acknowledged the predictable sarcasm.

'It's just that I called earlier, Barry, but you had not yet seen fit to grace us.'

'Yes,' sighed Barry, suddenly very tired. 'Well, I'm here now.'

'DJ would like to see you.'

'DJ?'

'At half-past eleven. Prompt, please, Barry.'

And June smiled at him before she left. It was the most cruel expression Barry had ever seen on her, and he straight away wanted to ingratiate himself with June, be nice, find out more – and he would have done so if she was there, but she had gone away now. Well, he wouldn't think about it. Couldn't – not intelligently. Anyway. He had just under an hour, then. He wondered how George was. Maybe they could get up a game for tonight, make himself a bit of money. Then he could buy something for Annie – something special. She deserved it. Dress, or something. But something really good. God Almighty why did DJ want to see him? Never mind. Don't think about it. Know soon enough. But how appalling just to hang around, waiting, while his head sang out with the urge to flee. Barry was suddenly put in mind of when he was very, very young, and out shopping with his mother. Come here, she had said once, following some aberration or another, come here – I'm going to smack you. He had darted into the road, and narrowly avoided being crushed by a van. His father had been furious with him for disobeying his mother, and nearly getting killed.

Jean came back with the kettle. Why did she always take so long to do everything? She had been ages just filling a kettle – but of course her face looked like it had received another coat, and her hair was newly brushed, and tousled to look natural. This time she said she wouldn't be a mo and Barry had just said oh plug the damn thing in for God's sake, Jean, and she had pouted and wagged a finger and said temper temper, and only then did she start clattering around at the tray on top of the filing cabinet. It was a dispiriting thing, that tray. The very sight of it often caused Barry unaccountable depression; there was always a puddle of something pale in it and the handle of the spoon got wet and one mug said Boss and the other said Arsenal – God alone knew why *Arsenal* – and the box of sugar lumps looked so very old. But it was when the carton of milk spluttered up and added to the puddle that the whole thing became so awful. In fact the very thought of it now made Barry get up and make for the door.

'Oy,' said Jean. 'Coffee.'

'I don't want it, Jean. It's the milk spluttering up that's so nauseating.' He did not wait for: Milk? Milk? We ain't got any milk. He was on his way to see George. Maybe he'd get a cup of something decent there.

Barry tried to *stroll* like he used to, but it didn't seem to work. He didn't know what it looked like, but it felt damn close to a bustle. Two young female things skittered by.

'That's him,' giggled one of them. And they looked at and away from him, squeaking through their noses.

No, thought Barry; she probably didn't say that at all: paranoia.

George's office door was shut, which was unusual, and it seemed to be held by a weight when Barry pushed inwards.

'Hang on!' shouted George, from inside.

Barry hung on, thinking: odd.

'OK!' hailed George, and when he saw it was Barry: 'Oh. It's you.'

Christine was smoothing down her skirt and adjusting a sort of Alice band thing with the other hand. George was fiddling with his tie and his hair was all over the place. If only they hadn't Barry wouldn't have known. He had not realised that George and Christine were like that. Well well. And so what? So nothing. What the hell did Barry care? And looking at George again – he was grinning like a cat – it seemed obvious that Barry was *meant* to be aware. Oh well. George always had been a little insecure in that sort of way. Oneupmanship of this nature was very big with George. Sexual politics, he called it, but Barry felt sure that he was misusing the phrase, while never being able to pinpoint exactly what he meant. And none of this mattered a devil damn anyway. Barry really was so uninterested in what other people did.

'Anything special, Barry? Bit busy this morning.'

That shook him, though. That was not like George at all.

'What's the matter with you?' asked Barry, uncertainly. Please, George, don't cut me, he was thinking. The atmosphere was cold.

'There's nothing the *matter* with me. I've just said I'm rather busy, that's all. One has to work *some*times, you know.'

And then Barry got angry. Who the hell did George think he was, talking to him like that?!

'Look, George – I've got just about enough on my plate at the moment without – '

'Barry, I'm sick to *death* of hearing about you and your plate! We're not all on this earth just to help *you*, you know. Does it ever occur to you that your problems just aren't very interesting? That people have their *own* lives to think about?'

Barry was amazed, and acutely aware of Christine, who was looking at him.

'Would you mind,' he asked Christine, 'leaving us for a couple of minutes?'

'Stay where you are, Christine,' snapped George.

'What the *hell*!' exclaimed Barry.

'Maybe,' suggested Christine to Barry, 'you ought to – you know – go.'

'Shut up, Christine,' ordered George.

'George – !' tried Barry.

'I'm sorry, Barry – I've just about had enough. If you can't even be bothered to turn up to an appointment when you *knew* the trouble I'd been to fixing it up, well – '

'Was I supposed to meet you? I *thought* there was something, I just – look, George, if that's all it is, I'm really sorry –

truly I am – but I forgot, I just . . . so much has happened,' he ended.

'I just don't want to hear it, Barry. I really don't want to hear a single word of it. And before you mention the possibility of a game tonight – just forget it. That's over. I've dropped a fortune on that bloody farce since you made it such a big-deal thing – and God *alone* knows how much you've lost. To say nothing of the money you owe me, which I expect I can kiss goodbye.'

'George – '

Barry just stopped. What the hell had got into George? All this was so hurtful.

'Look,' said bloody Christine. 'Why doan chew go? Carn you see Jaw jizz upset?'

'Shut up Christine,' said Barry.

'Don't talk to my secretary like that!' boomed George.

'Jubilee-vit!' exclaimed Christine.

Barry turned away, disgusted.

'Shut up, George,' he said, and slammed the door on all the rigmarole that followed. What a ridiculous scene. And how absurd that Barry should feel so betrayed. And soon he had to see DJ, and he was really scared about that now. He went back to his office. Jean was typing.

'I'll have that coffee,' Barry said.

'Cold now,' said Jean.

'I'll have it anyway.'

Barry drank into the Arsenal mug and although the coffee was vile, he had to get comfort from somewhere. Why wasn't he given the Boss mug? Oh God. Barry was getting into a state.

The intercom on his desk rasped at him, and Barry said:

'I'll take it. Hello?'

'Barry? June.'

'Oh God it's not eleven-thirty yet is it?'

'No, I'm just buzzing to say DJ can't make it at eleven-thirty after all. Has to go out. So it's half-past three now, OK Barry? Half-past three.'

'Oh God,' said Barry.

'Oh – and Barry?'

'Yes, June.'

'Don't be late, will you Barry.'

Barry let the air out of him.

'No, June,' he said. No sarcasm. No cleverness. No courage. How in God's name could he get through until half-past three?!

'I have to go out,' he said.

Bell's, he thought.

The skin on Susan's face felt pulled back tight by drying tears, and her eyes were stung and bloated. But she had done all her crying now and she was just staring straight ahead of her. She simply could not take it in. Again her eyes swung up to Hilary for help, or something.

'You'll get another job,' said Hilary. 'There are plenty of jobs.'

'Oh God it's not the job – it wasn't just a job anyway. It's not the job I feel so . . . oh . . .'

Susan put her fist against her mouth, which was still wet and trembling. She had not the courage to even think about it. There was so much, so much to get her mind around, and lately she seemed to have been so supremely elated or else whingeing over what was only, then, inconsequentiality. All this was too much, too suddenly.

'I've got nothing,' she said.

Hilary could not bring herself to say 'Of course you have.' She couldn't even tell her not to be so silly. If what Susan had told her was right, then 'nothing' seemed a fair summing-up. What was left of the marriage must surely now be over, Hilary

237

judged – though she wouldn't be at all surprised if Barry had another woman tucked away somewhere, despite Susan's protestations that this was impossible. And apparently all this building society stuff had been nonsense, and there was no money anywhere at all. This alone pointed to a woman. Money always went on women, drink and gambling, and from what Hilary knew of Barry, he didn't seem the type for the other two. Hilary understood, though, why Susan was frantically upset. Susan was essentially so weak and middle-class that the only things which possibly could have compensated her for all this injury were money and the flattery of someone else, and now it would appear that all that was gone, for when finally Susan had made contact with the Wiseman, he had been cool to the point of hostility. The job, he had made clear, was off. He had wasted no words – they didn't, that type. It was to be as if the last few days had never occurred. At which, of course (Hilary had been gratified to hear), Susan had become quite angry, for although it was true that the keys to the shop had been mislaid, it was hardly only *her* fault, surely! Wiseman's daughter – Tanya, was it? – had delivered them late, and she could just have left them in the hall instead of giving them to bloody Barry, and the only reason Susan had had to rush off in the first place was to meet bloody Wiseman himself and she wouldn't have dared be late and now she couldn't understand why he was behaving in so cold-blooded a way after everything that had passed between them, and why he was being so *brutal*? All he had said to her, according to Susan, was never to utter the name of his daughter – who was worth ten of her any day – and then warned her that if ever he encountered this filthy Barry person, he'd do for him, final. Which so amazed Susan that she had just stood there transfixed, and then he had told her to get out, and she still just stood there, thinking he's joking, he must be, and then he bawled go on! Get out! And Susan had never seen his face ugly like that and he wasn't joking and she turned and ran, and it seemed to her that she didn't stop running until she had got to Hilary. How, she kept asking, could he have behaved with such *violence*? Surely there were *other* keys to the bloody shop?! Was he *mad*, then? Was Susan, did Hilary think, *cursed*? Don't be paranoid, Hilary had said. Why not? retorted Susan, and Hilary shrugged.

'I was happy yesterday,' mumbled Susan, the pain of her own words making her feel so tender and hurt.

Once again, Hilary felt boxed in and mute. She just could not stutter out garbage about looking forward, and a new tomorrow, and futures, and sleeping on the bloody thing. Although she suspected that this was just what Susan wanted. Yes, Susan would be prepared to settle for that. It would make her feel so much better.

'Yes, well,' Hilary had said. And she smiled a bit. It was almost funny that Susan had forgotten that Hilary *had* got a job, and at this very moment was taking time off just to listen to all of this. It really did appear sometimes that Susan expected lives to stop whenever her own was faltering.

'Do you want some tea?' offered Hilary.

Susan nodded dumbly, and Hilary walked into the kitchen thinking well why don't you fucking get up and make it, then?

'Oh my shit,' said Barry, miserably.

He was back at the office, it was gone three, Jean was off God knows where, and Barry had just caught himself in the act of what could only be called the clearing-out of his desk. Well what else was it, Barry demanded angrily of himself, when a man started rummaging around in the filthy recesses of drawers he never opened? And this just minutes before he was going in to see DJ, with a bellyfull of Bell's? Bloody Freud. And it almost made him cry, excavating all this dog-eared rubbish that had once seemed so immediate. Even his scrawl had changed beyond recognition. He had written down everything so purposefully, once: there was dynamism in every stroke. And what was this? Barry's eyebrows rose in real surprise, and a sort of unease, only barely tinged with pleasure. He blew pencil shavings off a few sheets of foolscap stapled together. 'Radio Revues' was written in bold capitals along the top, and Barry remembered it all, and shivered. In the days of 'The Big One', he had decided that as he was soon to become a publisher of note, then this was the time to consolidate his success by breaking into the field of writing. He knew someone around that time who was something to do with the BBC (he had known someone who was something to do with *everything*, but never, it transpired, much) and Barry had thought he might begin small: one or two sketches, a pilot script, perhaps. Eventually, of course, he had visualised his name high on the lists of the firm's bestsellers, while he remained in-house, maintaining a discreetly low profile. Yes, thought Barry now; that was the plan. And it had not seemed wild at the time, whereas now it was all Barry could do to go over it in his mind, and still he winced away from the hot humiliation. And what had he written for God's sake, all those years ago? Barry flipped the page, and read:

'Good . . . ?'
'Evening.'
'To open, what would you not care to do to your ordeal as long as you live?'
'Repeat it.'
'Had you no idea?'
'I had none.'
'Should I have seen the place with my own eyes, and would I have believed the state it was in?'
'Yes you should. No you wouldn't.'
'And what was it thick with?'

'Dust, basically. It was thick with dust.'

'What could you have scraped off with a knife?'

'The grease in the kitchen.'

'How long would you say it was since the place had seen a lick of paint?'

'Yonks. I should say yonks.'

'And what was the place only fit for?'

'Pigs.'

'All in all, would you describe the state of the place as indescribable?'

'In a word, yes, I would.'

'And do you find yourself incapable of understanding how people could actually *live* like that?'

'I honestly do.'

'To recap, what would you be the first to admit?'

'That cleaning a house is no joke.'

'And you could put up with . . . ?'

'A bit of dust here and there.'

'But you would, I presume, draw the line at out-and-out filth?'

'I would draw it most firmly.'

'And tell me, what were you to your stomach?'

'Sickened. Quite sickened.'

'And what would you rather have died than done?'

'Sat down in that place.'

'And you couldn't wait to . . .'

'Get out.'

'And in your candid opinion, what do you think people who allow a place to get into such a state should be?'

'Thoroughly ashamed of themselves.'

'What did they have?'

'Not one iota.'

'In your entire life, have you frankly ever seen anything like it?'

'Never. I never have.'

'To this day, have you *quite* got over it?'

'To be honest, no, I have not.'

'To what, then, were you shocked?'

241

'My very core.'

'To round off – what *is* it?'

'It's disgusting – *that's* what it is.'

'And there we must leave it. Tell me – what would you like to do to me?'

'Thank you for both your time and understanding.'

'And say . . . ?'

'Goodnight.'

Barry read it over again. Had he *really* written that? Yes. And it had been no effort, either. Barry remembered that he had even earmarked actors with the right voices, to bring the dialogue to life, and not for a second had it occurred to Barry that the sketch might be turned down. As it was, after 'The Big One' fiasco, he had never even submitted it. Which was possibly, Barry thought now, rather a shame. Was it a shame? No, not really. It wasn't that good. Was it good? Christ, Barry didn't *know*, he didn't *know*, he didn't *know*. It seemed as good as some of the things you heard, but were the things you heard any good themselves? Were they a yardstick, in fact? And if they were no good, *why* were they heard – or seen – in the first place? Maybe not very good was good enough. Barry didn't know, anyway. But he'd keep it; he'd keep the sketch, and have a look through it again later. Who knew? It might even inspire him to write another, and if he got together a few things, it might even be not too late to . . . Christ Al-bloody-mighty! What the *hell* was Barry thinking about?! Surely he hadn't *totally* taken leave of his senses! His whole life was on the line and he was musing over radio scripts! He roughly folded the sheaf of paper and crammed it into his jacket pocket and his knuckle grazed against the chamber of the gun, and he thought Christ oh Christ life is different now.

Barry stayed at his desk and allowed his eyes to alight upon this and that around the office. He was not amazed to find himself gazing with sentiment at objects previously unnoticed, and some even loathed. He felt cast in the role of victim, taking a fond farewell. Not that he cared much for the job either way, now – he knew there was no future for him in the firm – but it was the money. Yes, the money. That, he supposed, was why people attached such grave importance to their nine-to-five existence, why unemployment, redundancy, were so emotive a subject. The money. A job was only the commonly accepted method of obtaining money, and acquired status solely by implication, it seemed to Barry. No one wanted a job; just the money.

He stared at the filing cabinet, and honestly wondered what was in it. He had never opened it. Jean – or whatever temps preceded her (Barry had never been accorded a permanent secretary, a proper secretary) – had occasionally been seen to go to it, but Barry didn't know why. Nor was he moved to find out. Along with so much else, it just didn't matter. He felt it was half-past three, and checking his watch, he saw he was very nearly right. Make your mind a blank, he told himself; difficult. It *felt* blank, but it was crowded with stuff. The main consciousness was tugging him now to the half-bottle of Bell's in the bottom drawer, but he had had so much in the pub that he knew most of it had not had time to work, yet, so what was the point of topping it up? And if he went in to DJ freshly reeking like a wino, that would be the certain end of him before he had the door shut. And he must be on time, dead on time. Not two minutes early – as he would have been if he set off now – and not a second late, God no. Barry would just sit quiet for a minute and a half – no, say a minute and three-quarters, well a minute and a half, now – and then he would go along to DJ and listen to what the man had to say.

It was then that the spasm of loneliness and cold shuddered through his frame, and he planted his elbows firmly on the desk and thoroughly washed his face with his damp, soft hands. It will be all right, he said out loud, and his voice

243

sounded so reedy and far away, and only now was he beginning to feel a bit drunk. It will, he said again (with emphasis), be all right – and yes, the voice was firmer, a bit more human. He tried it again. It *will*, he intoned, be all *right*. Yes, good enough. He sounded passably like an executive.

The buzz of the intercom made him flinch like a child, and his eyes were open wide and his fingers were scrabbling with the buttons, and he had hold of the receiver now.

'Hallo, yes?'

'Barry – June. It's gone half-past.'

'On my way, June. I hadn't forgotten, honestly, June!' he babbled with fright. 'It's just that – no, never mind. I'm on my way'

Barry stood up and ran to the door and stopped and thought no, this won't do, and he walked back to the desk and got the bottle out of the bottom drawer and opened his mouth to it. Twisting a bulging mouthful of the liquor down into his throat, he slowly screwed back the cap and thought, right, this is it.

June was beating an electric typewriter when Barry walked nto the ante-room. She was not looking at the copy or the keys, and she was certainly not looking at Barry.

'Go straight through,' she said.

'June – ' began Barry.

June typed on, and stared into the space before her.

'DJ is waiting,' she said.

Oh God, thought Barry, it's just like school. It was amazing that with all the horrors of adult life, the worst bits were just like school. But by the time he was inside DJ's office, Barry felt quite cool, quite ominously cool.

'Ah, Barry!' said DJ, as if he hadn't been expecting him. 'Do sit down. Sorry about the mess-up this morning. Couldn't be helped. Have a seat.'

'No problem, DJ. Thank you, DJ.'

Barry sat down in the chair that had been placed quite close to the desk, and as usual felt uncomfortable on the chicken-wire, and too low down. DJ wheeled back on his swivel chair at Barry's approach.

'I thought,' he said, 'that it was about time we had a little chat.'

'Fine, DJ,' said Barry, and in the split second that followed he thought no, this is no good, responding in monosyllables – he had better seem eager, he had better seem keen. His next word cut across DJ's resumption, and they both stopped and apologised and Barry said:

'Go on, DJ, sorry. I interrupted you.'

DJ smiled at the courtesy.

'I was merely about to remind you, Barry, of this re-organis-ation business that I touched on during our last little talk. Internal – ah – realignment. You remember?'

'Yes, DJ, of course. I'm still – I should just like to say that I am still very enthusiastic about this imprint idea of mine – I mean, I know that it would be quite a, well, gamble, I sup-pose, for the firm, but I'm sure that once the list is established – '

'But Barry,' interjected DJ with mildness, 'I thought I explained quite clearly to you the last time we spoke that such a venture was quite out of the question?'

Barry was thrown for a minute. In fact he had forgotten that, but he remembered now. Things were getting confusing.

'In fact,' went on DJ, 'this makes it all rather difficult for me.'

And DJ shifted in his chair. Had it been anyone else, Barry would have sworn that he saw embarrassment in the man, and before he could quell the panic, DJ was talking again.

'No,' he said heavily. 'What I have to say, Barry, is not, I feel, what you would like to hear.'

His eyes flicked up to Barry's face, but Barry was unaware

of this, as he was intent upon DJ's crossed feet beneath the desk. That awful sense of being not quite present had a hold of Barry now, and he hung on to it tightly, for then maybe he would be only half hurt, when it came.

'Are you all right, Barry?'

Barry sighed, and he idled heavy, defeated eyes over to DJ.

'Why are you always asking me that, DJ?' he said, wearily, the question shocking them both. DJ seized on it, and sat forward with urgency.

'The reason, Barry, that I forever seem to be asking that question is that your behaviour, your manner, your general *attitude*, constantly provoke it. You do not seem to me, Barry, to be quite well. Possibly you are rather over-tired?'

Barry was looking down again. He nodded.

'Possibly,' he said.

DJ nodded too.

'I thought so,' he said, the accuracy of the diagnosis affording him great satisfaction. 'I thought so. Now, under – ah – normal circumstances, I should insist that an editor takes a break, a few days away from it all – complete rest, sort of thing. But really, Barry – this situation, this *state* of yours, seems to have become endemic to your personality. It seems to have taken over.'

Barry noticed that the ceiling was not quite white. It couldn't, he adjudged, be said to be *cream*, exactly, but it certainly wasn't white.

'You're not listening, are you Barry?' tested DJ.

Barry let a couple of seconds pass before looking at the man.

'Not really, DJ,' he said. 'Not really, no.'

DJ narrowed his eyes. He seemed perplexed by this specimen before him.

'You're not happy here, are you Barry?'

Barry considered with pursed lips.

'Do you mean here, here and now, DJ, in this office? Or more generally, DJ?'

'Are you being facetious, Barry?'

Barry let out a snorting smirk that could in context, he supposed, be deemed facetious.

'Good Lord, no,' he said.

DJ blew out air. He was, his spread hands made it clear, at his wits' end with this particular problem.

'You leave me very little alternative,' he said quietly.

Barry inclined his head in what could have been acquiescence.

'I expect not,' he said, his voice growing deader with every sound. And then suddenly his jaw thrust outwards and his eyes faced DJ, alert and belligerent.

'Oh this is ridiculous, DJ!' he exclaimed. 'Have you got a drink around here?' And then more softly: 'It doesn't matter if you haven't.'

'Drink would appear to be one of the problems,' answered DJ. He spoke quite tenderly, now. There were no more points to be made. 'Help yourself. The cabinet is behind you.'

Barry stood up. He was now so hopelessly outside understanding that he was unsure as to what he should say.

'You don't have to say anything, Barry,' said DJ, which Barry thought weird. 'Have your drink.'

The cabinet was a bulbous affair in walnut, atop cabriole legs. This much Barry assimilated, but he had to glance around for help, for he could see no way of getting into the thing.

'Just push the doors,' DJ said.

Barry did as he was told, the doors pushing back and then springing open. Inside was a mosaic of mirror, and Barry stood mesmerised by the fragmented reflections of his own tired face. He reached out for the whisky, and was so caught by the hangdog pallor of himself, winking out from unfamiliar angles, that he became distracted and his sleeve hooked on to something and a bottle of, what – Bristol Cream, was it? – cracked over and the glass split just above the label, and now it was oozing around the bases of little porcelain dishes full of olives and bits of lemon and what seemed like bright green cherries. I really can't be bothered to apologise for this, he thought. I can't even be bothered to pick up the bottle.

'It doesn't matter,' said DJ, who was beside him now.

Barry nodded. It was true. It really didn't.

'I'll go soon,' said Barry, looking in at the glistening little glasses ranked on shelves. If I reach in there again, he thought, I'll destroy the lot. He decided to apologise to DJ for the very last time.

'I'm sorry, DJ,' he said, and he tilted up the bottle to his lips. His throat worked like a piston, but he didn't feel it going down. No heat – nothing.

DJ laid a hand on Barry's shoulder.

'You go home now,' he suggested. 'Keep the bottle. My parting gift, if you like. I'll have a word with Accounts, have everything brought up to date. Shall we say, what – two months' pay in lieu of notice?'

Barry wiped the whisky off his mouth.

'Very kind,' he said, and he made for the door. He considered putting back the bottle, but then he thought what for? The man's given it to me, after all.

'Oh – and Barry?' ventured DJ. 'A doctor might not be such a bad idea.'

Barry nodded. He hadn't quite caught that. Something about a doctor, was it? Anyway – just nod. Can't go wrong if you just keep nodding.

June looked stunned when Barry came out. It crossed his mind that she might have been listening. It further crossed his mind that it couldn't matter less. He indicated the whisky bottle hanging loose from his arm.

'He gave it to me,' he said.

June batted her eyes once and looked blank and frightened, which Barry could only enjoy.

'Dear June,' he said, which was not what he felt at all.

When he got back to his own office, Jean the temp was there, ramming bits of flimsy into a manila folder. Barry laughed out loud when he saw the very same expression grafted onto her face: shock, horror. Ridiculous. Barry sat at his desk, and with the bottle half raised to his lips, he checked the action and glanced back at Jean, who was still staring at him, her mouth ajar.

'It's all right,' he smiled. 'It's quite all right. He *gave* it to me, you see. It's mine now.'

And more stupidly pleased with himself than he could ever remember being, he concluded with an almost paternal indulgence:

'So you really mustn't worry any more.'

Moira had discovered quite recently that those aerosol wax polishes which she had always reserved for the living-room veneers could also be applied with great effect to laminates, and with a good deal of elbow grease such surfaces could be worked up into a glowing shine not unakin to that of glass, or even marble. And a silky film remained, very pleasant to the touch. Of course, it marked easily. All one had to do was put down a glass, and the sheen clouded dull; this was particularly noticeable if you crouched down low and placed your eye on a level with the surface, at which times it became really quite offensive. Now, whenever a plate or a glass was absolutely necessary, Moira would place them upon the raffia seat of one of her kitchen chairs – which, of course, did not mark at all, although one had to be careful of anything sticky.

She would spread a special tea-cloth over the rush seating if she thought there was the slightest possibility of anything clinging within the interstices, but normally, if one was careful, mess could be avoided. A beautiful home, Moira knew, required hard work and dedication, but really all one needed to make it run smoothly was a *system*. Moira put down her recent success to her system. Most people were so *untidy*. Why lately, Moira could get out of her bed in the morning and defy anyone to say whether or not it had been slept in, so virgin did it appear. Moira was so tranquil in sleep. This came from all the order around her; even in the night, she could sense the peace.

Moira had been pleased when Barry had 'phoned. However, it was irritating – it irritated her – that his enquiries centred around Gavin. It seemed ridiculous that Gavin should matter to anyone any more, but Moira saw that she would have to say what was expected. Not too much, though. Just enough. And Barry had sounded so desperate. Poor Barry.

'So he's OK again, then, Gavin, is he?'

'I've *told* you, Barry. It was just a bit of a gastric thing. He's as right as rain.'

'When – um – will he be in tonight? It's quite urgent, actually.'

'Oh – he's in *now*,' responded Moira, thinking got you, Barry, *got* you. 'I thought he ought to take a couple of days off, just to be on the safe side. He'd love the company.'

Barry's tone lightened a little as hope flew up to his throat.

'Well, if I could just pop over for a couple of minutes . . . there are one or two things . . . I shan't, you know, well – *keep* him. Tire him, or anything.'

'I'm sure he'd love to see you, Barry. We both would.'

Oh Christ, thought Barry, as he clanged back the 'phone, please let this work. Please. It's my only chance left. It's all I've got in the world, if I want to save Annie. Please, God, let it work.

Barry's mind had been madly ahead. He had left the office, quickly and drunk. He wanted to avoid faces, and he felt he would never return. This made him neither happy nor sad, but now there was a deepening pit of fright in him because he needed to keep Annie and he had lost everything else and that made her impossibly fragile and vulnerable and he had to have something else as well or he'd reach for her, grab at her, and he'd mess it, and she'd break. He just had to get to Gavin before the news of his job was everywhere. His crazy old scheme just *had* to work, but now it was no more than a blatant con. Now he just had to get some money – it didn't matter how – and then he and Annie could vanish somewhere, just go off.

He drove fast, and he thought be normal, act normally, don't rush it, don't appear too desperate. Certainly he'd aroused no suspicions in Moira on the 'phone. If he could keep that up, he'd be in the clear. It was a pain that Moira had to be there as well, but it couldn't be helped – it *had* to be done today. And thank Christ that Gavin was well again – that had been Barry's biggest worry.

'Barry,' said Moira. 'How lovely.'

'Hello, Moira,' said Barry, and he just stopped himself rushing Where's Gavin?

'I'm sure,' cooed Moira, 'that you'd like a drink. Whisky, isn't it? I think I'll join you.'

The house seemed different. Quieter, more antiseptic. Yes, that was it. Even Barry noticed how phenomenally *clean* everything was. There were essences of lemon, and lavender and polish, and yet the whole place seemed heavy and guarded, protected against the air.

'The Macallan,' said Moira in the drawing-room. 'All right?'

251

'Lovely,' approved Barry. 'Good God, Moira – *you're* not drinking the stuff, are you?'

Moira smiled like an imp, nodded and sipped.

'It's really very good. I got tired of all the wine. It bloats you up. And the corks make such a mess. This is – I don't know – altogether *cleaner*. And vodka I find is rather nice too, don't you think? Barry?' Moira folded back the hair that had fallen down over her forehead. 'I'm really becoming quite a spirit-person.'

Barry was surprised, but so much was surprising, lately, and as usual, it didn't matter at all. It was all quite outside Barry; it just didn't touch him. He registered mild surprise, and threw the whole business away. It didn't really matter if Moira became a creosote-person. Not really. Not to Barry.

'Where's Gavin?' he asked. Damn, he thought: too early, too eager. Should have left it a bit longer.

'Do you have water with yours?'

'What?'

'Your whisky. Do you water it at all? Or do you just drink it as it is?'

Barry bit his lower lip, and his eyes raked the room. He was beginning to sweat.

'I . . . I, um, sometimes water it a bit. Not usually. I don't know. It doesn't really matter to me much. Where's Gavin, Moira?'

Moira sat down, plump and proud. She hadn't stopped smiling since Barry had walked through the door.

'I *never* water it,' she announced. 'Not ever. It's so lovely just the way it is. It's so – '

'Moira, for God's sake. Where's Gavin?'

' – strong.'

'What? What?'

'The whisky, Barry. I was just saying how beautifully *strong* it is.'

And now Barry was losing it. Why was no one behaving in character any more? Why, just when his own identity was crazed into fragments, was everyone behaving so strangely?

'Moira,' he said, measuring out each word, 'Moira, please just let me talk to Gavin. It's terribly important – honestly. I won't keep him long, I won't stay or anything. Please, Moira.'

Barry looked across at her and his eyes were gelled with tears. First time, he thought; first time for a long time.

'Please,' he said again.

Moira looked at him. She just looked at him, and Barry thought oh my God she's just going to go on looking at me and then I'll start crying and then I'm finished.

"He's upstairs,' she said suddenly. And then half-hiding a sliding smile: 'You can talk to him.'

Barry nodded with relief and bounded up the stairs, calling back:

'It's the door on the left, isn't it?' not hearing or waiting for a reply, for it was, he knew, the door on the left. He just had to say something, and that's what he said. Barry puffed out his chest, put on a smile and pushed open the door.

It was the smell that knocked him back. All traces of cloying hygiene were annihilated by that first, shocking lungful of filth. The room was in total darkness, and the fetid air hung like a tarpaulin. Barry glanced back in alarm, and then he found himself walking on in, his arms out in front, cutting swathes through a black, rotting jungle. He tugged the curtains and a bit of late light sent a shaft of grey across the floor.

During those seconds – it can only have been seconds – Barry had not known what he was expecting. Even time and reason, though, could not have prepared him for what was now thrust into his consciousness. The stench rose up from the very floor. The bed was a pyre of sullied rags and fat flies clustered on hardened plates. Revulsion gave way to terror when the mound of the bed gently shifted, just shifted, sending up a fresh wave of nausea into Barry's skull, even so slight a movement seeming impossible among so much waste and deadness. Barry approached the bed, but something as hard as a fist rose into his gorge, and his fingers stayed hovering at the edge of what had once been a sheet. He swallowed down, and before his guts could reassert themselves, he plucked back the sheet and fell back with a whimpered squeal when he saw, when he glimpsed, what lay there. His shoulder had collided with something high – a shelf, a wardrobe – and a mad orchestra of metal hangers dully clanked against a hollow door.

When Moira's voice came, it was as fond as a nun.

'I see you've found my *dirty* room.'

Barry gaped across the landing. He couldn't see her. Now he could see her – she was coming in.

'I tried to tell him,' she explained. 'I told him quite firmly that I wasn't here just to clear up after *him*. But he didn't respond. Got worse,' said Moira. 'As you can see.'

Barry's mouth was as hard and as dry as a matchbox.

'Moira – ' he started, and it was just a croak, when it came.

Barry licked his lips and tried again.

'Moira – the filth – how could you? He's *dying* for Christ's sake. He's nearly dead.'

Barry had his face stuffed into his sleeve now, the vile smell was so overpowering, and he just watched her as she nodded and said:

'Yes. He is. Very nearly. It took ages.'

'But the mess – a doctor – ?'

'No, no doctor. Gavin wouldn't have doctors. That was part of the plan. But you needn't worry, Barry. I've got what you came for.'

Barry moved towards her. He had to get out of this room. But what had she said? Plan?

'What *plan*? What *is* this, Moira?'

Moira looked up like a schoolgirl.

254

'Oh, didn't you know? I've been killing him. Slowly. It did take ages. Gavin was always so *stubborn*. But it's very nearly over now. Yes. And then sometimes he was faddy over his food and he didn't want *this* and he didn't like *that*, and so I had to keep putting the stuff in something else. Terribly wasteful. Anyway. Nearly over now. Then I can give this room a really good turn-out.'

Barry was gliding into a state of mesmery.

'You – *you* have done this?'

'Oh I know what you're thinking – Moira can't do anything. Well Moira *can*. Moira did *this*. Anyway, it was his own silly fault. He was just *never* in. Always going here, there, and everywhere. Never staying in.'

Moira smiled down at the heap on the bed.

'But he's been in quite a lot, just lately. Poor lamb.' And then very earnestly, full into Barry's face: 'He's been *very* ill, you know.' It was as if she was seeking to excuse him.

Barry held his head, and then tried to barge past Moira and out into the light.

'Where do you think you're going?' she demanded.

Barry held her shoulders, and stared. Everything else was gone from him now.

'Moira,' he insisted, 'you're mad. You're *mad*! You have become a . . . murderer.'

Barry's own voice was causing him a deep and electric terror and he was trembling badly and as he held onto Moira they both shook together but she just smiled and then said:

'No no no no no. It's not like that at all. It's just that lately – don't laugh – Gavin's become a bit of a poison-person.'

Barry pulled away and got out onto the landing, but one hand held onto him with shocking firmness.

'Wait!' urged Moira. 'I've got something for you.'

'Got? *Got?*'

Barry's face was contorted with perplexity and a personal

255

agony, and he could no longer articulate, he could no longer think.

'Look,' she said, and she opened her housecoat and she was plump and naked underneath, save a sash stuck fatly with a vast wad of money.

'Take it,' she said. 'Take all of it.'

She need not have held onto Barry any longer, for he stood transfixed. She pulled his hand all over her, and brought it to rest on the money.

'I 'phoned Susan when you said you were coming. I rather thought I'd like *her* to watch as well, but she was out. She's always out, these days. Just like my Gavin was. Anyway, Gavin can watch – or sort of. He knows all about it. I've been telling him for days.'

Moira lay down on the putrid floor, and spread wide her legs and arms.

'Take it,' she said.

Barry sank to his knees as if demolished at the roots. His mouth was wet through lack of control and his eyes were glittering like blades. He rammed both palms into Moira's stomach, and as the air was knocked out of her he clawed at the raw lump of money rammed deep into the sash. He nearly got away, but now she had him by the hair, and so desperate was he to be gone, that he could feel it tearing. When he knew he could make his escape, Moira shrieked out:

'Thief! You're a thief! You can't just *take* it! Thief!'

Barry fled down the stairs taking the smell of the room in his head and Moira was making a noise like no human ever could and suddenly the whole house was so full of *crime* that Barry, devious as a villain, slipped out of the garden door, climbed the wall, and walked around to his car. The street was silent. Everything was perfectly normal.

Barry started up the engine, threw a heap of money onto the seat, dipped the headlights, and headed for home.

Nicholas crept down the stairs, came into the room and shut the door softly.

'Susan seems to be sleeping now,' he said. 'She had some pills.'

Hilary nodded. Yes, Susan would have had some pills.

'She seemed upset before,' said Nicholas, quietly.

'Yes, well,' sighed Hilary, thinking why do I suddenly feel so terribly sad? I could cry right now, if it wasn't for Nicholas.

'Are you all right?' he asked.

Hilary smiled with bravery, and beckoned him.

'I'm fine,' she said, and she held him tight. 'Poor Susan. She's got a lot to be upset about, really. Life can be so – oh. I hope you never get old enough to find out – but you must, really. You have to. Everyone does.'

'Earlier,' remembered Nicholas, 'Susan asked me whether I wanted it – you know, the baby – to be a boy or a girl.'

'And what did you say?'

'I said I don't know. I don't know. I haven't thought about it.'

Hilary nodded, and sucked the smoke from a fresh cigarette deep down into her. If only she didn't feel so *sad*.

'Hilary?'

'Mm?'

'Do you want it to be a boy or a girl?'

Hilary revolved wet eyes away from him.

'No,' she replied. 'Not really. No.'

It was strange, Barry thought, that his mind was so clear. All the way back, he drove like a champion. Quite simply, nothing had happened. Like the cold sweat of a nightmare, it just had to be rinsed away.

He stopped at an off-licence and requested a bottle of Bell's. The man said he had no Bell's and would Dewar's do? Dewar's would do, said Barry, and paid with one of Moira's twenty-pound notes. Actually – make it two, he added as an afterthought. He parked right outside his house – there was no space, usually – and went straight upstairs to the flat to pack. He took up one of the bottles of Dewar's: it would help him think; about the future – only about the future. As he unlocked the door, he smiled at what Annie would say. Just *look* at all that money! Where *did* you get it? *How* did you get it? And Barry would say – what would he say? Sh, probably. With a finger to his lips. They did that in films – seemed to work. Yes. Say sh, and hope to Christ she leaves it.

'The room' smelt of soiled linen and old cigarettes. Barry hoiked a suitcase down from the wardrobe and started opening drawers. He didn't mind that most of his clothes were crumpled and dirty, or crumpled through washing. Easier to stuff into the bag. He swigged Dewar's as he rammed things in. Think of the future. Think of the future. Think of the future.

What about his books? Should he take his books? Sod the books. Who was that outside on the landing? Was that a noise on the landing? Never mind, doesn't matter. No, he would not take the books – or the records. No trinkets, no stuff. Just get the clothes in the bag, get over to Annie's, and tomorrow they would go. Anywhere. But it had to be tomorrow. Or – who knows? – maybe even tonight. That *was* somebody on the landing. Oh God – not Susan. Barry really didn't want to see Susan. Not now. Right – shirts, ties, that bloody awful suit, couple of pairs of shoes – that's about it. Not much. Never mind – he'd get some new things. First thing tomorrow, Annie could choose him some brand-new things.

Barry pulled again at the Dewar's, threw a scarf into the case, and snapped it shut. He felt a childish thrill as he strode across 'the room' for the very last time. Thank God he'd be out of here for good.

The man outside was standing so close to the door that Barry walked right into him.

'Sorry,' said Barry, and he made to squeeze past. Another man was standing behind him.

'Barry,' said the first, with no enquiry.

Barry glanced round, screwing up his face. Do I know you, the eyes were asking.

The second man moved away to the top of the staircase, as the other one went on talking.

'Barry, Barry, Barry,' he smiled. 'It is Barry, isn't it?'

Barry nodded, thinking what's this now? Police?

'You are a very difficult boy to find. Not easy to track down. My friend and I have spent quite a long time on you.'

And then to his friend:

'She coming in?'

The other man scratched a thick, black beard and nodded.

'She'll be here.'

'Let's go into the flat, then, Barry.'

Barry's chest fluttered with fear.

'Who *are* you?' he demanded.

And the man laughed out loud.

'I *told* you,' he said to his friend. 'I told you that's the first thing he'd say. Who *are* you? And now he's going to say – what do you *want*? – right, Barry? You don't mind me calling you Barry, do you, Barry?'

Barry was subdued and terrified.

'I *would* like to know what you want,' he said.

'Course you would,' said the man. 'Only natural. Shall we go in, then, Barry? Not very nice, is it? Talking on the landing.'

' I don't want to go in. I want to go. I was on my way out.'

'Well it's very lucky we happened to catch you, then, isn't it Barry?'

And the front door downstairs clanged shut, and the man's wheedling and menacing politeness cracked into harsh command.

'In!' he rasped, and pushed Barry back through the door.

259

Barry fell over in amazement and the man got hold of him by his lapels and dragged him upright. As soon as Barry could focus, he saw there was a girl in the room.

'This him, Miss Wiseman?' said the man.

'That's him,' answered Tanya, and her eyes burned filth into Barry's face. 'The *bas*tard!'

Barry was shaking and felt choked by fright and the scent of her. He dropped his suitcase which still, absurdly, he was clutching, and made a dash for the door. The second man flicked him back as if he was made of paper.

'Please . . .' he said.

The man turned to Tanya.

'You want to go back to the car?'

'No bloody way,' said Tanya.

Barry opened his mouth at her, and the vision of her blue-steel eyes was shut out from him as his stomach was thudded to the back of his spine. He was sick over his hands and he fell like a dead man. His ribs were splintered as feet cracked into him and again his stomach was beaten and his lungs were too crushed to take in any air. His stiff, shuddering fingers were prised away from his face and the first blow split the skin beneath his eye, and his brain was jolted back into his skull. Barry shrieked out as a fist came down again and his back was being kicked and he knew that he could die. The weight of his chest and the smell of horror were sending his mind away. Only when the gun was in his hands did he know he'd reached it. He saw white faces and one with a bellow came in closer and just before the explosion rang plangent in his ears so the world stopped dead as the man was hurled up and back against the wall, the front of his shirt gaping wide in scarlet tatters. There was a scream, yes, a scream, and a hissing fountain of blood sprayed into the air. As the man slid crookedly down, a jamlike plastering squirmed over the wall, the big dead man dragging off the red until the floor. Pounding on the stairs, then, and doors, and more screaming, and then it was quiet save for the gurgle of blood oozing from the dead man's chest, and splattering in gobbets onto his spread, white hands.

Barry leant against the opposite wall in a silent, hovering fever. Some brilliant error had just been committed, and his head was still booming with the din of it all. He would, he thought, just wait, like a character now used up. For the moment, he was insensate, so he would just lie there and wait. It wouldn't be long. And anyway, it seemed that there was nothing else he could reasonably do. A figment of someone else's delirious imagination, he simply lay there, gutted and empty, over and done.

Annie replaced the receiver gently, thinking poor mother, poor soul. No one had expected her to die. The people at the hospital had been very nice, and Annie had said she would be along later. For her things, and everything.

Maybe, thought Annie, walking back to the kitchen, there was a meaning here, somewhere. Could a death (oh God, cliché) signal a new beginning? And then she felt remorse for thinking only of her own future, instead of dwelling upon the end of her mother's life. She had, they said, weakened in the night. By morning, all they could do was to keep her comfortable. Annie had been out the first time they called. When they got through, they said it was just a matter of hours, now. Annie had been expecting Barry back, so she thought she would leave it a bit, and now there was nothing to hurry about.

And he still wasn't home. Annie smiled. How like Barry – to be late tonight of all nights. She hoped everything had gone well at work. She hoped he had had a good day.

Annie put the Bell's and water next to his chair, drew the curtains, and lit a white candle. The smells of dinner wafted into the room, and the fire was crackling bright. Annie knelt on the rug and held on to the arm of Barry's chair as thoughts clambered into her. She would wait for him.